VIRTUAL DESTRUCTION

KEVIN J. ANDERSON
DOUG BEASON

ACE BOOKS, NEW YORK

This book is an Ace original edition,
and has never been previously published.

VIRTUAL DESTRUCTION

An Ace Book / published by arrangement with
the authors

PRINTING HISTORY
Ace edition / March 1996

The Putnam Berkley World Wide Web site address is
http://www.berkley.com

ISBN: 0-441-00308-7

ACE®
Ace Books are published by The Berkley Publishing Group,
200 Madison Avenue, New York, NY 10016.
ACE and the "A" design are trademarks
belonging to Charter Communications, Inc.

PRINTED IN THE UNITED STATES OF AMERICA

10 9 8 7 6 5 4 3 2 1

To GORGIANA ALONZO,
who helped me make sense of the
Lawrence Livermore National Laboratory
and its intricacies (KJA)

To MARV ALME and CLIFF RHOADES
for steering me to LLNL (DB)

ACKNOWLEDGMENTS

We relied on the help and advice of many people for the writing of *Virtual Destruction*. Some of those who contributed greatly (and in no particular order): our editor Ginjer Buchanan, our agent Richard Curtis, the crew in B Division (Bob, Jim, Chris, TT), A Division (Marv and Len), and LASNEX (Dave, George, Menoj, Judy, and Alex), Walter Scott, Rod Hyde, Warren White, James S. Johnson, Walter Jon Williams for his marvelous book *Days of Atonement*, John Stith, Lil Mitchell, Avis Minger, Dan'l Danehy-Oakes, Lori Ann White, Michael C. Berch, Claire Bell, M. Coleman Easton, Dan Marcus, Michael Meltzer, and—of course—Rebecca Moesta Anderson and Cindy Beason.

AUTHORS' NOTE

Although the majority of this novel occurs at the Lawrence Livermore National Laboratory, we have taken certain liberties in describing the people, events, and circumstances of that facility. The Virtual Reality lab, T Program, Building 433, and the Laser Implosion Fusion Facility do not exist, and the characters live only in the authors' imaginations. While we have attempted to depict the Plutonium Facility accurately, we have altered certain details and aspects as the story required. The toxicology and hazards of HF are similar to how we have described them here, with some minor modifications.

The views expressed herein are totally those of the authors and are not to be construed as those of the U.S. government, the Department of Energy, the University of California, the Department of Defense, the FBI, or the Lawrence Livermore National Laboratory.

Monday

**Building 433—T Program
Lawrence Livermore National
Laboratory
Livermore, California**

Gold, purple, and red streamers flowed across the airplane as it soared in total silence toward infinity, parting as the jet plowed through the multicolored atmosphere.

Without a sound, the contour-enhanced streamers sluiced over the swept-winged aircraft, skimming smoothly down the fuselage, skating unaffected over well-burnished seams and rippling over precisely calculated angles.

"Can't you get the speakers on, Gary?" Hal Michaelson demanded, standing amidst the clouds.

At the rear of the craft, the streamers lifted off the metal skin, curling up like psychedelic wood shavings, then tumbled together in a growing turbulent vortex wake behind the plane.

Suddenly a screeching, whistling howl roared past Michaelson's ears, rattling his teeth. "Too damn loud!" he yelled to his deputy.

Outside the chamber, Gary Lesserec adjusted the volume. Michaelson could just picture him grinning with his stupid "gee whiz" expression. "Yeah, but it's impressive,

Hal. The Air Force weenies will love it." Lesserec's voice came over a loudspeaker implanted in the wall.

Michaelson stepped into the imaginary airflow, resembling a looming titan intruding on the image. A canary-yellow strand of fluid whipped around his steel-gray hair without disturbing it, enveloping the bearlike researcher in the simulated airstream. At six feet six, his massive frame took up a large part of the wind-tunnel simulation. But the computers worked around him, as if he were a foreign object in the path of the aircraft.

"You're sure we're at max q?" Michaelson shouted out of the chamber. "This the best we can do?"

"We've calculated all the other possibilities—"

As usual, Michaelson paid no attention to the answer, battering ahead to see for himself, a jungle guide hacking away at the underbrush with his machete, unconcerned that someone might have already built a road.

Bluntly, he reached into the image and tugged on the nearest wing of the plane, sweeping back the airframe even farther than before. He watched with interest, like a toy maker adjusting one of his creations.

Within seconds the holographic airflow of streamers evolved, tangling like an angry storm. Supercomputers galloped through billions of calculations by the time Michaelson could blink. With motions dictated by a massive three-dimensional matrix of discretized Navier-Stokes equations, the streamers exploded in an unsteady burst, jumbling together and peeling away from the skin of the aircraft.

"So much for that," Michaelson muttered.

"Hal," Lesserec said with a sigh, "why can't you ever just listen when—?"

Michaelson chose not to respond to his deputy's carping and nudged the wing back to its original position. The aircraft felt flimsy, as if he could punch a hole through the illusion by moving too fast—but the fact that he could feel it *at all* made the project far superior to anything else he had ever worked on. As he watched, the colored vortex streamers once again became stable, relaxed to flow smoothly over the airframe.

He grunted in annoyance. "I spotted the delay. It was just a simple modification. I shouldn't have noticed."

"Give us a break, Hal. This is a full-up simulation, with over a billion equations solved every second to bring you that flow!"

Michaelson chewed on his reply, but did not spit it out. He knew damned well how much supercomputer time he was gobbling, since he had masterminded the project from its inception. He had railroaded the work, been a slave driver, insisted on perfect performance— but he had to be even more skeptical than the Pentagon and On-Site Verification boobs would be. He wanted no warts to detract from his show. All Lesserec needed to know, though, was that it was slow.

"Okay, then, enough kindergarten stuff. Switch away from the wind-tunnel simulation and give me the Nellis sequence."

Lesserec's voice came over a babble of other technicians scurrying to call up the new program. "Better strap in, Hal. Use one of the observation seats. We hooked this one up to the accelerometer."

"I'll be fine," Michaelson said, scowling. His pencil-thin moustache, which was supposed to make him look suave, tickled his lips.

"No, you won't, Hal," Lesserec's voice was insistent, vaguely paternal. The thought of red-haired and freckle-faced Gary Lesserec, who looked like a chubby Jimmy Olsen with a hangover, being paternal to *him* made Michaelson want to laugh. "You're forgetting these Air Force pilots love to make people puke."

Michaelson grumbled, but he glanced behind him in the Virtual Reality chamber and found a row of seats padded with the currently chic teal fabric. Clicking his safety belt and feeling like a paranoid fool, he wiggled down in the seat, which barely held his large frame.

"Please remain seated at all times," the voice deadpanned over the intercom.

"Just hurry the hell up," Michaelson growled. "I've got a flight to Washington this afternoon."

The holographic image of the airplane and the simulated flowlines disappeared like pixels going down the drain into the Twilight Zone, leaving him disoriented in a strange void as the new simulation booted up.

Michaelson felt as if he were lost and falling for a second as the swirled white cumulus clouds vanished beneath him—a powerfully odd sensation, he noted—when just as suddenly he was transported into the cockpit of an Air Force fighter jet.

The repainted sky was blue and cloudless all around him, like a piece of crockery. An instrument panel magically appeared, complete with throttle, avionics package, and control stick. He reached forward for the controls.

The sky began to spin crazily around him. His stomach lurched as he "felt" a surge from the jet engines kick him in the small of the back. Just like a ride at Disneyland, but this was so much more, even if the audience wouldn't grasp the difference. Wrapping his right hand around the control stick, Michaelson tried to steady the aircraft. The primitive part of his brain screamed that he was going to crash!

But his reason took over, as it always did. *Doesn't feel flimsy at all*, he thought. Was it the adrenaline pumping through his body, or was the tactile response that much better in this simulation? He squeezed on the control stick, not too hard, but he definitely felt something solid there. No tactile-response gloves, no fake hardware—he was touching a matrix of electrostatically suspended microspheres, patterned according to the desired shape. It looked the same as some of the other expensive VR simulations, but the suspended microspheres could make you feel *anything* the computers could draw. It wasn't real—but his instincts "knew" he was holding a control stick.

Michaelson didn't have a chance to think any longer on the wonder of the upgraded chamber as a pair of jets roared overhead, just inches above the cockpit. Twin tailpipes, burning white with raw power, disappeared in the blue distance with a sound of fading thrust, like echoes going down a funnel. He flinched in his accelerometer seat as the sound reverberated over him, shaking the cockpit, stereo-adapted and appropriately projected from all directions. The illusion was perfect. He felt the cold, hard rubber of an oxygen mask snug against his face. He felt the jet throb with the power of imaginary engines, and the aircraft went into a roll along the programmed flight path.

His muscles responded to violent curves, slamming him against the seat in tight top-gun maneuvers and screaming descents. Michaelson felt as if his teeth were jarring loose; but he was only sixty, and he intended to keep his own teeth for some time to come.

He raised his voice and shouted, "All right, Gary. Disengage the accelerometer part. I feel like I'm on the Star Tours ride at Disneyland."

"Oh, come on, Hal—we're much better than that!" Lesserec chided over the loudspeaker.

Michaelson's seat ceased its convulsions, and once again he sat back as an observer inside the fabric of the tactile scenario that completely engulfed him. When he was certain he wouldn't be thrown off balance by his own misguided equilibrium, Michaelson unbuckled and stood up through the image, plowing through the aircraft's illusory control panel. All around him in the inverted bowl of sky, the dogfight continued to play out—the visual cues were enough to disorient him, but at least he experienced no physical motion to trip him up.

Walking to the center of the chamber, Michaelson raised his voice to be heard over the screaming jets in their air battle. "Okay, Gary, now put me ten kilometers over the flight range, large scale so I can get a view from a distance."

The scene in the chamber flickered and bounced, like faulty reception on a television set.

Michaelson stood miles above the ground, his feet invisible through the clouds below. He had a sudden fairy-tale vision, like Jack and the Beanstalk with his own legs rising from the ground in a towering trunk.

Just above the clouds tiny fighter craft chased each other about the sky, around his ankles. Contrails spewed from their engines. Through torn openings in the blanket of clouds, Michaelson saw splotches of brown desert, barren mountains, and in the distance toward the blurred horizon a glint of silver civilization where Las Vegas should be.

The spectacle made him reel. Michaelson felt as if he were a god on Olympus, standing above his sprawling kingdom of Nellis Air Force Base. With a few giant steps he could stroll into Las Vegas, or over to the Hoover Dam, like the Amazing Colossal Man.

He drew in a deep breath inside the sealed chamber and he thought he smelled faint traces of the pungent JP-8 jet fuel, no doubt sprayed into the air by the new odor synthesizer package Lesserec had been working on; artificially generated wind blew past him, ruffling his thinning hair. He felt giddy.

He *was* a god, in a certain sense. He had supervised the construction of this chamber; it had been his idea. His political arm-wrestling with the good-old-boy network had broken the impasse between the boobs who had no vision for the national laboratory system and the enthusiastic hydrocode designers who had no worthwhile work left to do.

Without Michaelson's controversial and unorthodox strongarm tactics, this VR project would have gone the way of his former baby, the Laser Implosion Fusion Facility—an unrealized promise for cheap and clean fusion power, borne on the shoulders of incompetents, a victim of too much talk and too little planning.

The buzzing jets miles below him looked like flies darting among his legs. They continued to twist and roll, executing perfect maneuvers real pilots only dreamed of.

One more test, thought Michaelson. He purposely hadn't drawn attention to the next phase, working on his own and hoping not to arouse suspicions from Lesserec or the technicians. They didn't need to know his real plans for the Virtual Reality technology.

He cleared his throat. "Hey, Gary, do you still have access to those outside test sensors you installed at the Lab pool?"

Gary Lesserec's voice rang over the wind and faint droning of the jets below. "Piece of cake. We've got the feed if you're ready. It'll be a letdown after this sexy stuff, though."

"Indulge me."

"Always do, don't we?" Lesserec quipped back, just this side of sarcasm.

Again, the universe around Michaelson flickered and bounced, a TV changing channels. This time his vantage placed him standing just above an expanse of too-blue water with black depth lines painted down and coming up the other side of the Olympic-sized swimming pool. He hovered there, invisible to the crowds below, as the sensors piped in a three-dimensional, tactile, real-time simulation. *Like Jesus walking on the water*, Michaelson thought. *It must be my day for delusions of grandeur.*

From behind and below him he heard the sound of children squealing, playing a riotous game of Marco Polo. Turning, he watched a slender young woman bounce off the diving board, arc gracefully into the air, and slice directly through him on her way to the pool. Sparkling droplets splattered in the air around him, falling back into the water. The children continued to shout, their voices flattened by the water.

The outdoor swimming pool was crowded with employees of the Livermore Lab and their families enjoying a lunchtime swim. Unnoticed and hanging in midair, Michaelson stared at where the walls of the Virtual Reality chamber should have been, but saw no break in the image.

"I give up," said Michaelson. "Where did you hide the sensors? Is this a live feed?"

"We put up six of them." Lesserec's voice came to him strangely disembodied in the air around the Lab's pool. "One at each corner of the pool area mounted on the fence above, one anchored to the bottom of the pool, and the last on a wire strung out twenty meters over the water. They're so small nobody notices them. The six sensors give more than enough overlap, and we're getting near real-time smoothing from the computers."

"Okay, this is perfect. Shut down."

Before the images sparkled into nothingness, Michaelson groped his way to the door of the chamber, reaching his hand through two sunbathers to find the right spot. The heavy vault door split from the wall, disrupting the entire illusion as Michaelson left the chamber.

Sterile white fluorescent lights gave the boring cubicles and computer workstations of the T Program trailer complex a washed-out, unreal quality. Michaelson allowed himself a smile, wondering how the catchphrase would go over in Washington. "More real than reality." Some might be disappointed because they had seen so much flashier stuff done with special effects in science fiction movies. But this was real, done with real technology, the most perfect remote-sensing surveillance system ever developed.

Sunlight from a clear California day splashed through the miniblinds on the trailer windows. The VR chamber's control room was no more than a large common area of large-screened computer workstations walled off by low, fabric-covered partitions that a man of Michaelson's height could peer over easily. He always thought of the movable fabric partitions as "illegitimate walls," but they were inexpensive and changeable as programmatic needs shifted, and they fostered a closer teamwork atmosphere among the programmers.

A half-dozen men and women stood at various workstations in the common area, dressed in blue jeans, unusual T-shirts, and garish Hawaiian shirts, as if in an effort to prove they were all oddballs, which ironically made them all look the same. Everyone wore a bright-green Lawrence Livermore laminated badge, complete with identifying photo and a yellow stripe bearing his or her name. Clipped beside each green badge was a homegrown blue badge, also with a photo, made by Tansy Beaumont, the administrative assistant down the hall in Michaelson's main office.

The green badge indicated the employee had a security clearance and allowed access through the guard gate into the Livermore Lab itself; but one needed the special blue badge for access to T Program behind its additional security fences. Not many people had blue badges, and even though it wasn't immediately obvious why the additional security was needed for a mere image-processing project, Michaelson had convinced the right people. The additional access security allowed him greater freedom for handling classified material and software in the programmatic trailers. Hal Michaelson could be very persuasive when he needed to be.

Gary Lesserec looked up, stepping away from a high-resolution monitor and smiling like a real butt-kisser. Michaelson held a hand to his eyes in the bright fluorescent light, which seemed much harsher than the outside sunlight he had just seen around the employee swimming pool.

Dressed in shorts and a Spiderman T-shirt, Lesserec contrasted with Michaelson's more formal attire of dress pants and long-sleeve shirt. Lesserec's chubby body looked soft and white from not being out in the sun; his skin had toothbrush-paint spatters of freckles. His dark, brownish-red hair framed a face with muddy green eyes and an insincere grin, even when he meant it.

"So, are you a believer now, Hal?" Lesserec looked smug.

"It certainly works," Michaelson admitted.

"And damn fine, too," chuckled one of the programmers. Katie something-or-other, Michaelson thought her name was. He could never remember the names of all the underlings and simply read their badges when he had to. Katie turned and gave a high-five slap to the person next to her. "That swimming pool is so real, it's refreshing just to look at it."

Though the pool scene seemed lighthearted and ordinary, Michaelson knew it was the most indicative, the most realistic use of the VR surveillance technology that had so interested the President and the defense community.

But the scene he remembered most was the vision of himself standing up in the clouds, like a titan looming over the world. He actually longed to be back in the chamber, controlling everything that happened, tweaking reality with a twitch of his fingertips.

With the deep importance of the moment, it disappointed Michaelson that he couldn't switch off Lesserec's catty grin. Things had been much better in the old days when he had been surrounded with other hard-driving physicists, rather than Yuppie computer whiz-kids who were smart far beyond their social abilities. Of course, some people might have said the same about physicists, but Michaelson worked with the best raw material his budget would allow, and he wrung out results far beyond anyone's expectations.

Michaelson pulled himself up to his full height so that he loomed over everyone there. He stepped around the cubicle partitions into the control room. Every station seemed to have at least one can of Diet Coke resting unsteadily in an open spot among the papers and software manuals, as if it were some sort of official team drink.

"Congratulations—but we've celebrated enough. The Pentagon will be slobbering to buy these chambers to replace their current inventory of airplane simulators. That's an easy sell, so we'll dismiss it for now." He waved his hand. "That's not where I want this project to be heading."

Lesserec rocked forward in his chair, looking wary. His grin flickered once, then died. "You're not going to change our milestones again, are you, Hal? The Department of Defense sponsored the research behind the VR chamber. I thought they were *expecting* new simulator technologies."

Michaelson frowned disapprovingly at Lesserec's Spiderman T-shirt, but the kid never seemed to catch subtleties. "Don't worry, the Pentagon will earn their investment back tenfold, but not the way they imagined."

Lesserec leaned back in his burnt-orange swivel chair. He rubbed his freckled hands together. "So we'll still have a job even after we're through with this project?" He picked up one of the pens the Livermore supply mavens had deemed to be the popular pen of the month, a Pentel ballpoint with rubberized grip, and flipped it end over end, clacking it on the table. "Give us a hint about this mysterious new direction?"

Michaelson watched his young assistant for a moment before answering. Lesserec should have known to ask that question behind a closed office door, not in this zoo with every member of the project watching. Michaelson didn't like to burden his technical team with too many details, but lately Lesserec had been pressing him for information he should not have had to worry about.

Michaelson had kept his upcoming announcement on a "close hold" basis for long enough. It was part of his automatic habit of secrecy, carried over from the way business had been conducted at the Livermore Lab throughout Michaelson's career. He had spent his career establishing the Laser Implosion Fusion Facility, then moved to a stint as an on-site disarmament inspector in the former Soviet Union, to the formation of T Program for virtual reality surveillance.

Even now, more than a half-century since the first atomic blast in the New Mexico desert, the detailed knowledge of the design and manufacture of nuclear weapons was highly classified. The entire Livermore Lab infrastructure, and its overlord, the Department of Energy, had been predicated upon producing nuclear weapons and keeping that knowledge away from upstart nations. The political bosses were still warming up from the Cold War, not sure what to do with their mittens.

"You'll need to move your sensors to a new location. That's the only hint you get, Gary."

Gary's eyes widened. "Didn't like the swimming pool? I could move the sensors to the women's locker room if you want."

Michaelson ignored Lesserec's statement. "Our plutonium processing facility will give a more realistic test of how the VR chamber is ultimately going to be used. The Pentagon will want statistics on VR surveillance, reliability, and resolution. Just plan to have another demo up and running within the next few weeks.

"I'm leaving for Washington this afternoon, but I've already worked it out for you to have access to install the test sensors in Building 332. Our Associate Director promises his 'fullest cooperation.' " With a change in the tone of his voice he emphasized the last two words.

Even Lesserec snorted, and Michaelson resisted a smile at his deputy's reaction. Everyone in T program knew how much Michaelson despised his de facto boss, José Aragon, Associate Director for Tech-Transfer/Defense Conversion.

Lesserec caught the rubber-grip pen he had been flipping and looked up with his muddy eyes. "I still think those Pentagon dudes would rather fly the jet simulator any day. What's the rush?"

Michaelson crossed his arms over his broad chest, feeling like a schoolteacher in front of the group. Why couldn't Lesserec just shut up and do what he was told?

"If you haven't noticed, we are no longer in the bomb business. Defense conversion. Technology transfer." He lowered his voice. "Scrambling like panicked chickens to find something important to do before the budget goes away entirely. Somebody's got to look ahead. We've got to respond to market conditions now." He focused on Lesserec, ignoring the others in the common area and knowing that was the best way to get them all to pay the most attention.

"Look, I've got the President's ear on this. I'm not at liberty to say exactly what we're going to be involved with, but it'll make your little airplane simulator look like a piddly Nintendo game."

Lesserec tossed the pen across his desk where it clattered against an empty Diet Coke can. He flashed his insincere smile again. "Don't sell the videogame business short, Hal. The entertainment market is growing bigger than the weapons business. Maybe it's already bigger."

Michaelson sighed. "Just watch my news conference tomorrow afternoon. I don't think the networks will broadcast it, but CNN carries everything. I'll be back from Washington the day after tomorrow, and by then I want you to have a plan for installing an entire suite of sensors in the plutonium building."

The telephone in Lesserec's private cubicle rang, giving Michaelson a chance to depart as the young deputy went to grab it. He slipped around the fabric dividers as Lesserec waved for him to wait. *Got to have a reason for everything*, Michaelson mumbled to himself. What ever happened to the concept of group leader?

"Hal—hey, Hal?" Lesserec called, the slim black telephone pressed against his ear. "Aragon's on line two. Tansy transferred him down here."

Michaelson felt a sour sensation in his stomach. "Tell him I've just left."

"He says it's urgent." Lesserec held out the phone, blinking his eyes innocently. He looked like a Cheshire cat. "I told him you'd be right on."

Michaelson set his mouth. Aragon thought his hangnails were urgent. Not saying a word, he looked around for a phone on one of the computer tables, knocked a few manuals and Coke cans aside, and picked up the phone, punching the flashing button pad. "Michaelson here."

"Hal, how are you? How is—"

"I'm in a hurry, José. I've got to catch a flight to Washington."

"Ah, yes. Important business, I suppose. Well, this will just take a moment, my friend. You know, I think your health would be much better if you slowed down a little, took the time to enjoy—"

Your own damn health is going to suffer if you don't hurry the hell up. But it was no use arguing with the boob. "What *is* it, José?"

"Ah! Your Virtual Reality chamber—I hear that you've met your milestone with the tactile response?"

"Been there, done that. I briefed the director last week, José. That's why I'm heading out to D.C."

"Hmmm, I wasn't at the director's staff meeting, and—"

"José, can I call you later? I've *really* got to head out to the Oakland airport."

Aragon sounded patronizing. "No problem, Hal. I'll catch up on the details some other time. But since you've obviously already met the milestones, I need a big favor. Really means a lot to me. I'm going to bring a high-visibility tour group through the VR lab tomorrow. The Northern California Coalition for Family Values—Fred Unteling's old group?—bringing a bunch of physically challenged kids to see the simulations. Show them something exciting. Great PR. *Newsline* will even run a story on it. You'll love it."

"Tomorrow?" Michaelson shouted into the phone. "Thanks for the warning! We're making the IVI announcement tomorrow, José. For God's sake—"

"Well, I'm sorry I didn't let you know ahead of time, Hal. I did tell you we were planning to open up more of the site to visits from community groups, and this is our olive branch. Your chamber would be the highlight of their tour. Let these poor children see things and go places they could never manage on their own. And remember, Livermore Lab is community sensitive now."

Michaelson started to retort, but he decided against it. Unteling's name closed the discussion. "Tell you what, I'll turn it over to my deputy—but make sure the kids don't touch anything."

"I knew you'd understand, Hal. Say, by the way—"

Michaelson slammed down the phone with an unsatisfyingly hollow *clack* and turned back to Lesserec. He saw the technicians watching him, their own eyes wide but seeming to mask their amusement at his bluster. "Did you hear what I said about getting the sensors ready?"

Two of the programmers mumbled and turned away. Lesserec grinned at him, rocking back in his chair and folding his hands behind his head. "So, what's Aragon got to say?"

"Every time Aragon opens his mouth, something stupid falls out. Call him and get the details yourself." Michaelson felt his heart race; he'd have to watch his temper. He was on his way to an appointment with the President, and José Aragon wanted to play tour guide. What fucked-up priorities. No wonder the Laser Implosion Fusion Facility went down the toilet once Aragon got in charge.

Michaelson whirled for the door. The last thing he heard was Lesserec's chirping voice. "Hey, have a nice trip, Hal. See you on TV."

Tuesday

NanoWare Corporation
Cupertino, California

Dressed in casual but no-nonsense uniforms—dark suit, deep-red tie—Craig Kreident and the four field agents stepped through the mirrored doors of NanoWare Corporation. They wore brittle smiles on their faces.

As soon as he was out of the bright California sun, Craig snapped off his dark sunglasses and blinked to adjust his eyes to the indoor lighting of the lobby. He pushed the sunglasses into his suit breast pocket and reached in to take out the folded piece of paper inside the white envelope. Unconsciously, he used a palm to slick down the sides of his short, chestnut-colored hair, straightening the premature wings of distinguished gray. Always neat, always presentable. A professional.

At the faux marble front desk the security guard sat up and greeted them with a cautious smile. "Good afternoon, gentlemen," the guard said, moving his glance like machine gun fire down the line of agents. "What can I—"

Craig slid the folded leather badge case from inside his jacket and flipped it open. His companions did the same. The guard reeled back at the barrage of IDs.

"Federal Bureau of Investigation. We'll be visiting

some of your facilities this afternoon," Craig said. "Thanks in advance for your cooperation."

The security guard gaped like a stranded fish and reached for the telephone. Craig intercepted him by slapping the search warrant on the gleaming marble surface in front of the guard.

"You'll see here that we have a search warrant duly signed by a magistrate of the U.S. District Court. I'd appreciate it if you wouldn't use that phone, sir."

His smile inched up a fraction of a degree—cool, cordial, uncompromising. He scanned up and down the corridors of NanoWare. Apart from the neutral carpeting—charcoal gray and sterling silver tweed—everything gleamed with white and chrome, high-tech with a vengeance. The curved halls had no sharp angles, like a 1960s science-fiction vision of the year 2000.

"I believe the IC processing labs are down there," Craig pointed. "Is that right? We can find them ourselves."

"But wait," the security guard said. "You can't do that. Mr. Skraling is out of town until tomorrow and I don't have the authorization to—"

Craig tapped the paper again with his forefinger and gave a Mount Rushmore smile. "I have all the authorization the law requires, sir. After we've secured the clean room, you're welcome to call"—Craig searched his memory trying to recall the name of the senior VP of NanoWare—"Ms. Ompadhe. And by all means, send her down."

"Daniel," Craig nodded to one of the men, "would you keep our friend company while we gain access to the clean room? Then please see that he makes the right phone calls."

"Yes, sir," Daniel said. He pulled up a chair and sat

next to the security guard. He nodded at the fidgeting man. "So, do you watch baseball?"

Craig motioned for the other three agents to follow him down the hall. Their shoes scuffed like muffled gunfire on the carpet. When they were out of earshot, one of the field agents, Ben Goldfarb, lowered his voice and spoke to Craig. "I thought we couldn't legally forbid them from using the telephone. That's not kosher is it?"

Craig stared in feigned surprise at Goldfarb, pointing to himself innocently, as if saying, *Moi*? "I didn't forbid him to use the telephone. I just said I'd appreciate it if he didn't. And I didn't tell Daniel to forbid him either. I just told him to stay there."

Goldfarb grinned, making small wrinkles around his dark eyes. "Yeah, but your meaning was implicit."

"Implicit doesn't carry the law, Ben." He sighed, then let his demeanor soften now that he didn't have to keep up the "tough agent" facade. "Look, I've been investigating these high-tech crimes long enough to know how little time it takes the bad guy to wipe the slate clean. Five minutes worth of warning, and people can delete all sorts of incriminating files. A diskette or two tossed into an incinerator will cause us months of reconstruction work, if not irreparable harm to our case. A surprise inspection means just that—surprise. Once we're in position and baby-sitting them, they can do whatever they want."

True, before his time several blunders had been made during overzealous investigations against supposed computer crimes. Most infamous was the Secret Service raid on a gaming company in Texas. That had been botched every way imaginable, from bogus charges to incorrectly filed paperwork, and had generated a lot of bad press. That sort of thing happened when technologically illiterate agents tried to investigate a high-tech case.

Craig specialized in that kind of work, though. It took a smart agent to catch a smart bad guy, such as in this case. And NanoWare was no innocent bystander.

Operatives in Malaysia and Singapore had traced bootleg microprocessor chips that had been flooding the market. The path led through several sham corporations, directly back to the Silicon Valley company NanoWare.

"Here, sir," Jackson, ahead, pointed to a double airlock door with a flashing light mounted outside. Through large, thick observation windows in the hall Craig could watch people in white garments, masks, and hair nets moving around cabinets of glittering microchip fabrication apparatus.

"Okay, let's go inside," Craig said, stepping up to the airlock door that led into the changing room. "I want you to suit up for the clean room. Everything by the book. Do minimal damage. Our primary objective is to secure this facility, not to damage it."

They stepped through the door to the outer clean room, walking across a gray mat of stickum to pull away loose dust from the soles of their shoes. They passed into the changing area and rummaged in the cubicles for spare outfits. A bin of dirty uniforms sat beside a sink. Wooden benches lined the walls near blue metal lockers. Racks of folded white jumpsuits stood next to a box full of nylon hair nets and bins of thin plastic booties marked SMALL, MEDIUM, and LARGE.

"Let's make it quick. They may have seen us."

Craig put on a facemask, adjusting the elastic at the back of his head and snugged on a hair net. He stepped into a white Tyvek jumpsuit and grabbed flimsy booties that billowed around his black street shoes. He smelled clean, new fabric and filtered air, cold from the increased air-conditioning.

Before sealing the Velcro straps on the jumpsuit, Craig took out his badge wallet and small camera and stuck them into one of the deep external pockets. He pulled on rubber surgical gloves from an open box, snapping the thin membrane against his wrist. Once finished, the four FBI agents gave each other a cursory checkover. "Good enough," Craig said. "Let's move."

They passed through the second airlock door together. Craig took the point; Goldfarb and Jackson fanned out. Holding his badge high, Craig raised his voice—firm, businesslike, no-nonsense.

"May I have your attention please? We're with the Federal Bureau of Investigation. All operations must cease immediately. Do not touch anything. Do not shut down any processes or equipment. We want everything nice and clean, just the way it is."

A storm of voices swirled around him in several different languages. He noticed for the first time the dark almond eyes behind many of the face masks, saw Korean and Vietnamese workers, probably at minimum wage, doing sophisticated high-tech labor.

"Goldfarb and DeLong, secure the lab. Jackson, round all those people up by the desk. I'm going to start taking pictures, get an inventory."

As confusion bubbled around him, Craig snapped a series of quick shots with the small camera, fumbling with the button through the rubber gloves. Then he set to work on the part that most interested him, the large X-ray lithographic chip-imprinting apparatus. The three-foot by three-foot negatives were used to burn patterns upon coated sapphire wafers—thin circular disks that looked like CDs. The process exposed incredibly reduced and intricate electronic circuits that would then be etched. Once imprinted, the thin wafers were chopped into small rectangles as individual chips.

Craig spread out the set of four overlarge negatives on a light table rigged next to a high-resolution X-ray camera. He flicked on the table and picked up a loupe the size of a postage stamp. As the white fluorescent light flooded beneath the negative, he squinted and scanned down the complex labyrinth of millions of circuit paths.

He ran his pen along one edge, counting grid lines, searching for the spot the original PanTech designer had told him to look for, the small signature of PanTech's own design: a tiny circuit loop connecting nothing, difficult to find and impossible to deny. Like the intentional mistakes on copyrighted maps, this signature proved the identity of the original designer.

Craig found it without much difficulty, proving that this set of masks had been stolen from NanoWare's primary competitor. Then the negatives had been altered—sabotaged—to make the bootleg chips malfunction frequently.

"Dead to rights," Craig said, snapping off the light table and rolling up the negatives. He raised his voice, calling attention to himself.

"Goldfarb, Jackson, DeLong, you all saw me take this set of negatives out of their apparatus." Craig rolled up the large dark sheets, placing an IMPOUNDED sticker on the side.

The inner door of the clean room burst open. A dark powerhouse of a woman barged in without bothering to put on the entire clean-room outfit. Craig paused only a moment, noting to himself that with all of NanoWare's difficulties, a contaminated clean-room environment was one of the most minor things the company had to worry about right now.

The woman was short, stocky, and filled with an energy born from contained fury. She had dark Indian skin and bright flashing eyes under glossy black hair cut short like a man's. "Just what the hell do you think you're doing?"

Craig refused to be intimidated, though, standing up and meeting the brunt of her anger. "Are you Ms. Ompadhe?" He removed all the appropriate documentation one piece at a time. "I'm Craig Kreident from the Federal Bureau of Investigation. These are my agents. This is my search warrant. I think you'll find everything is in order." He narrowed his gray eyes and tapped his finger against the rolled up lithographic negatives.

"What—" she started to say, but Craig decided he didn't want to let her finish a sentence.

"Alleged bootlegged chips, stolen circuit design, industrial sabotage, market fixing. I could go on." He held up his hand again before she could say anything. "I know you're probably going to say you don't know anything about this, Ms. Ompadhe. For your sake, I hope that's true. But for the moment I would advise you not to say anything at all. Unless you'd care for us to read you your Miranda rights here and now?" He stared her down. Finally Ompadhe succumbed and followed his advice, saying nothing.

"When is Mr. Skraling supposed to be back?" Craig asked. "We have a subpoena for him."

Ompadhe flinched, stared at the floor, then looked up to meet the eyes of all the non-English-speaking line workers herded into an open area beside one of the workstations.

She looked squarely at Craig. "He should be on a plane right now, flying back from Bermuda. We expect him to come in to San Francisco International late tonight, and he plans to be back at work tomorrow. When I see him, I'll tell him you're expecting him."

"Thank you," Craig said with false levity, "but I think I'd rather you gave me his flight number. We'd prefer to meet him at the airport directly. Saves time."

Ompadhe's shoulder slumped just enough to let Craig know she realized she was defeated. "Come back to my office," she said.

Craig motioned for Goldfarb to stay and watch over the facility. He and the two others followed Ompadhe out of the clean room, shucking their white Tyvek suits and returning to their own FBI uniforms of a suit and tie.

As they followed the stout woman down the carpeted NanoWare halls, Craig had to fight to keep the springy bounce from his step. This entire investigation had gone well.

Tuesday

Building 433—T Program
Virtual Reality Chamber
Lawrence Livermore National
Laboratory

With their noise and bustle and unpredictability, little kids had a peculiar way of getting on Gary Lesserec's nerves, no matter how understanding he tried to be. It wasn't so much the incessant whining, the tear-filled eyes, or the blatant refusal to obey simple commands—it was more the indefatigable lack of logic. Children didn't make sense, and that scared him.

Still, he had a role to play as the T Program deputy, now that Michaelson had left him in charge. Smile, put on a good face for the PR show. Associate Director José Aragon was watching as he led the tour group of "challenged" children for the Coalition for Family Values, happy as a dung beetle deep in his element. Aragon was going to get a lot of good coverage for this event.

Lesserec pretended to be happy as he greeted the visitors. The smile burned on his face to cover his alarm at the group of wheelchair-bound, emotionally disturbed, Down's syndrome, or otherwise crippled children. Even normal, rambunctious kids threw a complex situation into chaos, but this group created even stiffer problems, required more careful watching.

But it also gave him a marvelous opportunity, without watchdog Michaelson looming over him, and he could finally install those new NanoWare chips and give them a whirl. He took it as a challenge. If Lesserec intended to reach out to a huge market share with his own VR breakthroughs, perhaps children like these, who had so little to start with, had the most to gain from his simulations.

Lesserec watched the last of the children ushered through the open security door into the T Program exclusion area. Aragon stood like a cable-car conductor, motioning everyone to come forward. Escorted by nurses, attendants, or parents, the children moved into the common area. Upon hearing the first high-pitched tiny voices, the scuffling of feet, the bumping against wobbly modular office furniture, he thought, *Show time*!

He felt tense, unlike any time when he had stood up to Hal Michaelson or any of the other head-up-their-butts management types. The mob of children descended upon the Virtual Reality laboratory like a plague of locusts.

Lesserec scanned the room in reflex, seeing all the other T Program engineers who had slapped together Aragon's demo in record time. "Everybody ready?" he muttered, just loud enough for the technicians to hear.

Danielle, one of the programmers behind a workstation, punched in an access code, prepping the simulation run. "Equipment's all set up, Gary. You're the MC.

You know which buttons to push. It's your show . . . solo."

"Hey, where are you guys going?"

Danielle jabbed her fellow programmer in the side and motioned with her head for him to follow. "Errands. We skipped lunch today so we could head out to Lab supply this afternoon."

"Yeah, Gary," said Walter, the other programmer, nodding. "You okayed it, remember?"

"Hey, that was before we set up this tour!" Lesserec pushed weakly up from his chair. "You're not leaving me alone?"

"Of course not," Danielle said with a parting shot. "You've got all those kids to keep you company."

Lesserec muttered something he would never have wanted the children to hear, then looked up to see José Aragon extending a hand to him. He smelled of strong aftershave. His dark hair glistened with hair oil, sculpted in place like meringue on a baked Alaska. "Ah, Gary! It's good to see you again. Thanks for all your help."

Lesserec made sure his smile remained firmly in place as he shook the Associate Director's hand, squeezing firmly into the other man's clammy palm sweat. Aragon wore a leisure suit, as usual, and trousers just a tad on the short side.

"Welcome," Lesserec said to the audience, rubbing his hands together. "We've got a good show for you today. I'm sure the kids will enjoy it."

He cleared off the front of his computer console, leaving a small plastic model of Snoopy, a picture of him and his girlfriend Sandra standing outside their new condo by Lake Tahoe, and a small bumper sticker that said PORSCHE DRIVERS DO IT AT 150 MILES AN HOUR.

With a stage manager's bustle, Aragon continued to look around the workstation area, his dark eyes carrying a glazed shallowness. "So, Hal didn't stay to show us around?"

Lesserec erased his scowl before it could show. "He's in Washington for a high-level meeting. Don't worry, though, Mr. Aragon. I can handle it."

"Yes, of course." Aragon seemed flustered, as if he didn't know how to deal with a change of routine. "Glad you could find time to show the children around, Gary."

"My pleasure," mumbled Lesserec, meaning exactly the opposite.

"Excuse me," Aragon said. "I have to help the rest of these youngsters in." He patted Lesserec on the shoulder and moved over to help the group enter the secure facility through the unsealed emergency exit, though it looked as if he were only getting in the way. A Protective Service Officer stood watching the slow progress.

Lesserec watched, having no idea how many visitors they were expecting. It would take all morning long just to get a dozen of them inside. He wondered whose idea this crazy spectacle was anyway. Probably Aragon's.

Now alone in the control area, Lesserec turned to his computer console and called up a file from his private directory. He decided that would be best, and Michaelson wasn't here to breathe down his neck, anyway. Normally, he would have arranged for a computational physics simulation of one of the lab's new high-priority "dual-use" missions, something that would feed into the commercial sector, or perhaps even be used by the Pentagon.

He considered bringing up the jet fighter dogfight sequence—normal, red-blooded kids should get a blast out of that—but the thought of these handicapped children disoriented by Top Gun maneuvers made him pause. He couldn't think of anything more appropriate than the Yosemite simulation he had shot and dimensionalized himself last month. He hoped Aragon wouldn't squeal about his fooling with the VR chamber for other than "official" business; but if the kids were satisfied with the show, he didn't suppose that would be a problem.

Aragon seemed to be having a field day, walking around to each of the sixteen kids taking their places in the VR chamber, squatting down and speaking to them at their eye level, then standing and patting them on the top of the head as if they were puppies. A photographer seemed attached to Aragon's elbow; no accident, Lesserec supposed.

One scrawny little girl with patchy blond hair stared around the lab, her big eyes absorbing the sights. Her sinewy neck seemed to ratchet as she moved it, as if she were unable to control her muscles.

Computer screens as big as a school blackboard filled one of the walls; circuit boards from the patchwork control rack, optical fibers, and computer keyboards were stacked unceremoniously on one of the desks; a poster on the far wall displayed a futuristic scene with the words JEDI ACADEMY emblazoned underneath. The place looked much cleaner and more organized than it had the day before, sanitized of all classified information.

"You work here?" the scrawny blond-haired girl asked Lesserec in a solemn voice. "Must be fun."

"It is, sometimes," he said.

The little girl didn't speak further. Her eyes slowly panned the rest of the lab room. Her thin hands clutched the black padded armrests of the wheelchair, as if she were afraid of falling out at any moment.

"We'll show you something fun today," he said, "don't worry."

José Aragon continued to herd the children and their escorts into the enclosed chamber. They had to crowd around the row of motion chairs, though a few of the children were ambulatory enough to sit in them. Lesserec made a note to disengage the motion simulators, to keep the kids from puking all over the chamber. Aragon plopped down in a chair, fidgeting on the edge of the seat, then gave up his spot when another child came through.

Lesserec stood by the thick vault door as the last visitors filed in. Aragon obviously thought he controlled the show, so Lesserec let him talk. The dark-haired man folded his hands in front of him and spoke in an offensively patronizing voice, as if he thought he was the twin brother of Mr. Rogers.

"Boys and girls," said Aragon, smiling broadly, "this is Mr. Lesserec, the technician in charge of the Virtual Reality lab. He's going to show you something very interesting today."

Lesserec winced at being called a mere tech, especially by a incompetent "boob," as Michaelson called him.

"This is one of my most favorite places at the Livermore Lab," Aragon continued. Lesserec wondered if the man had ever set foot in the VR chamber before. "You know, our scientists are trying their best to help the people in our great nation live better lives."

Lesserec rolled his eyes. Next Aragon would be telling them that Livermore weapons designers were hard at work developing lawnmowers powered by neutron bombs. The Lab should dump this end-of-the-Cold-War martyr complex and move into new areas without the apologies.

He caught only the tail end of Aragon's comment: ". . . mind telling the boys and girls a little about your machine?"

"Sure." Lesserec stood outside the door to the VR chamber. Every tiny face watched him. "Anybody know what virtual reality is?" He didn't wait for a answer, though a chubby boy on crutches raised his hand. "It's like playing a smart videogame, one that can respond when you twist a dial, pull back on a lever, or even touch a screen. Virtual reality is going somewhere that you've never been before—without leaving your room."

"Like dreaming," interrupted the blond-haired girl to his right.

"Kind of like dreaming." Lesserec pointed around the VR chamber where they all waited. "This room is about the size of a typical living room—twenty feet on a side. But inside this chamber we broadcast computer-generated images, like what you see on TV, except these are much bigger, three-dimensional holograms, and a lot more real. We've got special technology that lets you feel some of it, too."

"Like the holodeck on *Star Trek*," one of the children said.

Lesserec smiled. "Exactly, in principle at least. I think the *Enterprise* system might be, uh, a little more advanced than ours. But ours is real—and that alone makes it a lot more interesting."

The kids chuckled. Lesserec sighed with relief, happy that things were going well enough. "Still," he continued, "we can transport you to places nobody can ever hope to go—say, to the center of the Sun or to the center of an atom."

"I hope to go to Disneyland," said one boy.

Before Lesserec could figure out how to respond, Aragon stepped up. "Mr. Lesserec has a demonstration to show you how his special chamber works. Would you like to see it?"

The room buzzed with a great deal of enthusiasm. Aragon whispered to him, "No problem. I'll accompany them." (As if that comforted Lesserec one iota.) "Just show the kids something they'll remember."

"I think they'll remember this. Just hang on. I've got to push the auto start."

Leaving the vault door open, he hustled to the banks of workstations inside the large control room and punched the run command. The images would begin projecting as soon as he sealed the chamber door behind himself. This would be a perfect test run.

Inside the chamber, the gray-white walls remained featureless as the door clicked closed. "This'll be better than any movie," he promised, killing time as the images loaded up. "Just don't touch the walls—that's where the pictures are made." He lowered his voice to Aragon. "If you think anyone's getting motion sickness, I'll stop the simulation."

Aragon looked suddenly worried. "You're not going to use that fighter plane sequence are you?"

Lesserec smiled. "No—this is a little more benign than that. We used this as one of our first sensor tests. I took the images myself during a long hike this summer."

He suddenly found himself transported to the top of a rocky mountaintop, along with the room full of children and their escorts.

Sheer granite walls plunged down thousands of feet in front of them to a green valley below, where a languid river snaked along the centerline, flanked by a thin gray road and tiny vehicles that flashed sunlight. Overhead the sky was crystal clear, blue, showing the blurred white line of a jet trail. A soft wind blew through the chamber, bringing a sharp ozone smell mixed with pine needles.

In tactile response the rock itself was smooth, a blister of whitened granite with flakes of loose shingle flanking sinkholes where murky water collected. Dazzling waterfalls, ribbons of white, danced down the rugged gray walls of the sheer valley. The scene took Lesserec's breath away, as had the original sight of Yosemite Valley as seen from the top of Half Dome.

Inside the chamber, the children responded with a collective gasp. No one spoke, as if afraid they might break the spell, until a small voice—which he realized belonged to José Aragon himself—said, "It's *beautiful!*"

The words unleashed an excited chatter. The children pointed to tiny cars and buses parked around small buildings far below.

The image moved forward with a change in perspective from the sensors, edging toward the dropoff. Several children cried out in alarm. Lesserec stepped into the center of the chamber. "It's all right. Remember, we're still in the lab. This is just pretend."

Just as the words left his mouth, the room seemed to drop as they went *down* the steep cliff, gliding along the images from the deployed sensors. Lesserec felt a small hand reach out and brush against his arm twice before clutching his shirt. Lesserec patted the hand in reassurance.

He looked down to see a young boy, about ten or twelve, with the obvious "stranded marionette" look of cerebral palsy. Lesserec flinched, but did not pull his arm away. The boy was not trying to speak, but the delight shone on his face. With waving hands, he tried to touch the image.

"With virtual reality we can take you places you would never get to visit." The room stopped its descent down the cliff face and hovered next to two brightly clad rock climbers who were intently—and insanely, Lesserec thought—groping their way up the impossible cliff face.

Lesserec turned to the small boy still grasping his sleeve. "And you can feel it, too."

Reaching down, he nudged the child's wheelchair closer to the cliff wall, closely shadowed by a stooped, worried-looking man, who seemed to be the boy's father. The boy's scarecrowish arm smacked against the hologram that had been solidified with three-dimensionally patterned microspheres suspended in electrostatic fields.

The palsied boy's expression changed, though Lesserec could not read subtleties in his uncontrolled facial muscles. Lesserec took hold of the small hand and brushed it back and forth against the illusory rock.

Other children moved forward to parts of the images, making sounds of amazement as they touched the mountain. José Aragon wandered the circumference of the chamber, prodding and stroking, a fascinated grin on his face.

"Just don't press too hard," Lesserec warned.

The simulation paused a moment, before dropping toward the ground in a gut-wrenching fall. Several of the children cried out, but the plunge slowed until they reached the rocky, forested ground below. Hikers and people in cars started moving toward them, all wearing puzzled expressions.

Lesserec popped open the chamber door, disengaging the simulation and letting a wedge of fluorescent light spill into the room. Yosemite vanished like a snapped rubber band, and the tour group found themselves sitting in a featureless VR chamber. The children and their escorts sat stunned and breathless for a moment, looking around in disbelief.

"That's all for today. Be careful on your way out," Lesserec said, pointing toward the door. "Please keep away from the walls—we don't want you to harm the sensors."

Aragon bustled over to him. He seemed genuinely moved. "Gary, thank you for allowing us to experience this magnificent demonstration! I will speak with Hal about opening this up as part of a general Lab tour." He nodded at the excited children on their way out of the chamber. "This is just the type of thing we need to improve our image with the community."

Lesserec smiled tightly, aware that Aragon was looking at more than pure community relations: if pitched properly, this would ensure Aragon's directorate wouldn't be short of funds as well. Well, they all fed out of the same trough.

"I'm sure Dr. Michaelson would enjoy that," he said without the slightest trace of sarcasm.

He kept his smile in place as the children made their way out, each one thanking him in their own way. He felt like a flight attendant watching passengers file out of an airplane. The last pair out the door was the boy with cerebral palsy and the slight man with stooped shoulders. The boy seemed delirious with happiness.

The tired-looking man nodded to him and extended his hand. "Thank you, sir. I'm Duane Hopkins." He fingered his green Livermore badge as if to prove it. "I just wanted to thank you. Stevie, my son—I've never seen him so happy. This was really special for him."

"No problem," Lesserec said. He was pleased by their reactions. The simulations seemed very marketable.

Hopkins looked down at the floor, then back up, as if he were afraid to meet Lesserec's gaze. "Stevie has been sick for . . . well, he's always been sick, and I just can't take him out very often. I work in the plutonium building, and we don't get to show off—"

"Mr. Hopkins, we're leaving now," interrupted the woman from the Coalition for Family Values. "Come along." The others had made their way out the emergency exit door where the security guard continued to watch. The woman from the community group gave a stern smile and raised her eyebrows, motioning for him to hurry.

Hopkins mumbled his thanks again and rushed after the others, pushing Stevie's wheelchair.

As the chaotic tour group left, Lesserec relaxed back in his chair, thinking how well received the simulation had been. He ran over the possibilities, wondering how people might respond to something really exciting, exotic, not just a vacation snapshot. He couldn't wait to test out some of the stuff he had been developing at home.

Through the dollar signs in his daydreams, he saw a real chance to make it big. He had Aragon snowed—leaving only Hal Michaelson.

CHAPTER FOUR

Tuesday

The White House
Washington, D.C.

Looking up and down the street, nondescript, Hal Michaelson decided to enter the White House through the most inconspicuous entrance. He doubted anyone would recognize him, despite his height and large frame and distinctive moustache; but the paparazzi permanently stationed by the south entrance hungrily scanned everyone who entered by more obvious means, and Michaelson avoided them on general principles. Most of the reporters wouldn't care, or understand, the International Verification Initiative; they wouldn't even carry the news conference live.

He entered through the Old Executive Office Building, a five-story gray granite structure that would have looked more at home in eighteenth-century France than next to the White House. The blocky, Gothic-looking building held most of the 1,500 staff members who actually served the White House. Two of the entrances were on 17th Street, allowing Michaelson to slip inside.

Once he passed the Secret Service checkpoint, Michaelson still felt conspicuous. As he walked along the black-and-white checkerboard halls, he fingered his laminated badge that prominently displayed a large V for visitor. Nothing was more likely to attract attention. He had to concentrate on his speech, on his meeting, and not worry about pestering interviewers.

He elected to take the circular stairway instead of chancing the elevator where he might run into some desperate reporter. God, he hated stupid questions. He climbed the stairs to the ready room off to the side of the fourth-floor auditorium, where the conference would take place at eight.

Usually Michaelson didn't mind the attention, since he had made his name through bluster and unorthodox showmanship. More often than not, he had used the press to discredit the tedious boors that infested the bureaucracy, embarrassing them into passing his proposals—as he had done with the Laser Implosion Fusion Facility.

But not now—now was the time to play his cards close to his chest. He had kept the IVI secret from Lesserec and the rest of the staff at T Program; he certainly wasn't going to spill everything to a random reporter he happened to encounter in the tiled halls of the Old Executive Office Building.

He huffed up the stairs, remembering the last time he had been interviewed at the White House, during the previous administration. His biting denunciation of the fossils running the space program as "the gang that couldn't shoot straight" had, in part, eventually resulted in the successful testing of a new class of rocket vehicles that had been delayed through red-tape snafus for years.

But today he needed to stay out of the limelight. It was the President's show, and he would get enough secondary glory from it. As difficult as it was for him,

Michaelson needed simply to be present, not to make troublesome statements or stir up controversy. Today, people would be throwing darts at *him*, rather than the other way around. He ran over the words in his mind again. The main question was whether the ignorant public would understand the significance of the IVI, or if they would miss the point altogether.

As he moved along, lost in his thoughts, business-suited young men and women clicked past him on the stairs. He watched them, glad he had spent most of his life in California where everybody wasn't wound up so tight and mummified in business clothes. The White House staff was always in a hurry, but their sense of urgency was inversely proportional to their position in the hierarchy. The men wore dark suits, white shirts, modest ties, and expensive black wing-tips; the women slid by in smart high heels and soft skirts swirling against sheer panty hose.

Michaelson sighed wistfully. The sight of these focused young women made up his mind for him. He made a mental note to cancel his "meeting" with Diana and call Amber instead. He needed a real break tonight, a celebration after the interview. Amber would be enthusiastic and refreshing. He looked forward to it. Diana was getting too rigid, too matter-of-fact.

Out of breath at the top of the stairs, Michaelson paused before making his way to the ready room. The hallway towered twenty feet high, wide enough for several cars to pass through. Recalling T Program's cramped, modular cubicles, he resented the irrelevant opulence. All of this decadence could have been better spent on additional scientific research.

Two Secret Service men stood outside the ready

room door, their dress indistinguishable from the White House staffers, except for the radio wire running from collar to ear and the slight bulge from automatic weapons under their jackets. A stream of reporters entered the auditorium from down the massive hall, carrying cameras, lights, and video equipment, trailing long strands of cables behind them.

"Mr. Michaelson?" The Secret Service man's voice echoed in the hallway.

He breathed deeply, still catching his breath from climbing the stairs. "Dr. Michaelson. That's correct."

"Have a seat inside, sir."

Checking Michaelson's name off a roster, the Secret Service agent gave him a nod to enter the ready room. He stepped inside, but saw no one else in the high-ceilinged room. He relaxed to note that he was early. He needed some time to settle down.

A pitcher of ice water and several plastic cups, each silk-screened with the presidential seal, had been placed on a table next to a mirror. He poured himself a cup and gulped it down. The water tasted fresh and clean with a slice of lemon.

Michaelson turned to a full-length mirror. Although this room was air-conditioned, the humidity and the walk up the four flights of stairs caused beads of perspiration to form on his brow. He mopped his forehead with a handkerchief and started to comb his hair.

The door swung open, and a Secret Service woman glanced over the room. She stood against the wall like a robot. Michaelson set down the water cup and waited. Seconds later, the President himself entered.

"Hal, glad you could make it!" He flashed a smile and extended his hand.

"Mr. President." Michaelson shook the man's hand as the Secretary of Energy, the President's chief of staff, and the press secretary squeezed into the ready room.

"You know Renee, of course."

Hal nodded and shook the Energy Secretary's hand. "Of course. How do you do, ma'am?"

"I have a lot riding on your technology, Hal," the President said. "The Pentagon brass can't stop talking about your flight simulation demo. You must have pulled out all the stops."

"It's easy to impress people with impressive technology, Mr. President."

"Well, no matter what you say, the DOE hasn't had this much support from the military since you guys designed the neutron bomb." He cocked an eye at Michaelson, who sat down on the ready room's sofa. "You all right?"

"Just a little winded. Instead of the elevator, I took the stairs. A bit too quickly, I think."

"They're set, Mr. President." The press secretary appeared at the door to the auditorium. "Any time you're ready. The heads-up teleprompter will be on either side of the podium."

The President placed a hand on Michaelson's shoulder. Not a small man himself, the President still looked tiny beside Michaelson's six-and-a-half-foot frame. "I might ask you to make some comments after the initial announcement."

"No problem, sir." Michaelson nodded to the Secretary of Energy. "I've coordinated my remarks through Madam Secretary."

"Good." The President straightened and turned to the press secretary. "I'm ready."

The young woman stepped through the door. Michaelson heard her voice ring out over the buzz of background noise in the auditorium. "Ladies and gentlemen—the President of the United States."

Michaelson followed in the wake of the Energy Secretary and took his place standing behind the President. He squinted in the bright media lights and tried to recognize the reporters as the applause died down. The President got right to the point, reading from the heads-up teleprompter.

"Today, I am pleased to announce the formation of an exciting new initiative. The end of the Cold War has allowed the United States to turn away from producing nuclear weapons. Now we can peacefully embrace the future. This is a time to ensure that no country will be in a position to inflict the nightmare of a nuclear holocaust. There are few occasions in our country's history that denote a decisive turning point in human events. Today is such a day.

"In 1945, under the secrecy of the Manhattan Project, our nation developed an unprecedented technological marvel. In three short years, in a crash project that brought together the free world's greatest minds, our ingenuity brought about the terrible weapon that brought an end to World War II."

Michaelson's thoughts wandered. *Why do they always say nuclear weapons were terrible? Didn't they prevent another world war from starting? Why doesn't anybody remember that?* But Michaelson wasn't a political type. He didn't have time for all that baloney.

"In 1960," the President continued, "our scientific elite was once again called upon, launching an ambitious project to take a man to the Moon and back. And today is another such day."

Michaelson figured the reporters would consider most of the words to be mere hyperbole, and they wouldn't understand the subtle consequences of the new project. But then, that was their problem.

"Today, I officially announce the formation of the International Verification Initiative—the IVI—an ambitious program to use our national labs once again to radically advance science by using virtual reality technologies. The IVI will enable a representative from every country to be 'present' at any location that uses sensing devices: during an underground atomic test, at nuclear weapons storage sites, on-board a missile launching into space—anywhere an electronic sensor is used. These Virtual Inspectors will be the watchdogs of the world during these tense times of gradual disarmament."

He turned and motioned Michaelson to the microphone. "I've appointed Dr. Hal Michaelson, whom some of you know from his work heading up our disarmament teams in the former Soviet Union, as the first director of the IVI. Hal, would you like to make a few comments?"

"Thank you, Mr. President." Michaelson coughed to the side, then looked down at the reporters, trying to gauge their interest. For the moment, he had their attention, and now he had the limelight—right where he belonged.

As he prepared to tell the world, he just hoped that boob José Aragon was watching.

Tuesday

Livermore, California

Duane Hopkins left his job at the Plutonium Facility at precisely 4:30 in the afternoon, as he did day after day. He got in his old blue station wagon and drove home, picking up his son Stevie from the day nurse on the way.

The routine had been unbroken for as long as he could remember. Duane had no one else to take care of Stevie, and his entire life was an endless sequence of eight hours a day plodding through his job and the rest of the time tending to the boy.

In his small two-bedroom house, Duane situated Stevie comfortably in his chair while the boy cooed and made happy nonsense sounds as his scarecrow arms waved in uncontrollable directions. His head lolled from side to side.

Stevie had spoken no intelligible words during his life, and Duane had stopped expecting to hear them long ago. But even with severe cerebral palsy, Stevie could communicate a great deal with his emotions and expressions. Duane could tell when his son was happy, and right now the boy was glad to be home in the familiar, comfortable surroundings with his father.

Duane turned on the television and let Stevie watch

cartoons. In the kitchen he set a pot of salted water to boil and tore the top off a cardboard package of macaroni and cheese, which he would spoon-feed to Stevie while his own portion remained warm on the stove.

When dinner was ready, he wheeled Stevie to the Formica dinette table. He used a damp rag to wipe the drool from around the boy's mouth, tucked a napkin under his shirt as Stevie's bright eyes fastened on him. The boy opened his mouth to receive the creamy orange macaroni.

Duane listened as highlights from the President's news conference were aired on the local news broadcast in the living room. He pricked up his ears, turning to look when he heard the Lawrence Livermore National Laboratory mentioned. He paid attention to some talk about the Lab's Virtual Reality program, and he smiled.

"That man, Stevie," he gestured toward the television, "he's the one in charge of that sight-seeing chamber you went in yesterday."

Stevie seemed to understand and made more noises, but then he smacked his lips for another bite of his supper. Duane fed him and listened again, smiling as he thought of the tour the day before.

He had never seen Stevie quite so happy as when the illusion had transported them to Yosemite. Duane had never been to the mountains himself, though he had lived in California all his life. He had gone to high school in Livermore; his high school diploma, proudly framed, still hung on the mantelpiece next to the faded old photo of Rhonda, his wife, who had left him years before.

He had enlisted in the Army for a couple of years, received some training on the GI Bill, and came back to his hometown, where he began working at the Lab. He had been there for more than twenty years.

Now as he watched, Dr. Michaelson was saying many difficult technical things that Duane couldn't quite follow.

". . . hot topics in electronics include solid-state lasers, radio frequency and optical devices—devices typically smaller than a pinhead. By ganging them together, you can imagine solid-state sensors no bigger than a postage stamp being able to transmit sound and pictures. Hang a postage-stamp-sized sensor on a wall, or scatter several of them in an area, and you'll be able to monitor . . ."

Duane nodded, as if Michaelson were talking to him directly.

". . . the actual chamber is lined with solid-state lasers, able to be phased, or coordinated, with each other. If you phase these guys right, you can create a 'true' hologram—one you can actually walk around, not just move back and forth in front of. The possibilities for remote surveillance are . . ."

Duane wandered into the living room to watch. As he saw the image, it startled him to see Dr. Michaelson standing next to the President himself, talking about their big initiative. It sounded as if some major work was going to come to the Lab. Dr. Michaelson sure sounded optimistic about it. That made Duane feel good and relieved.

After all the talk about the Cold War ending, budget cutbacks, program shutdowns, and layoffs, Duane had been uneasy for some time. Even with his high school diploma, at his age he doubted he could find another decent job if he got laid off from the Plutonium Facility.

The house was mostly paid for after twenty years, but Stevie's medical bills continued to eat up Duane's paycheck, not allowing him to move an inch ahead, barely letting him keep running in place. Duane didn't like his job, and had few friends among his coworkers, though he had worked quietly beside them for years.

After supper he spent an hour in the nightly ritual of dunking Stevie in the warm running bath. The boy splashed around in the water. He seemed to enjoy the heat and the buoyant freedom the bathwater gave his tortured body.

Duane noticed that Stevie's cough was getting worse, phlegmy and congested-sounding. After toweling the boy off and swaddling him in his nightgown, he forced some cough syrup into Stevie's mouth, wiped the red residue from the boy's grimace, and put him to bed. Stevie rocked from side to side and continued to make noises long after Duane went back into the living room.

Duane crouched in the old rocking love seat, leaning over the Mediterranean-style coffee table. He pulled out a worn deck of playing cards.

For the rest of the evening the TV played a blurred succession of sitcom after sitcom, and Duane knew from the laugh tracks when he was supposed to chuckle at the jokes. He shuffled the cards and spread them down one by one in a line for another game of solitaire.

He stared at the cards, moved the appropriate ones and turned over new cards, studying for strategy, looking up at the sitcom when the laugh track grew particularly loud. He considered peeking under the two piles of cards that remained, wanting to see which would give him the best advantage, but he did not do it. If you cheated at solitaire, you were cheating no one but your-self.

In the bedroom Stevie coughed, then fell silent with sleep.

Duane considered changing the channel, but realized that it probably made no difference. He dealt out another game of solitaire and continued playing.

Tuesday

**Building 433—T Program
Conference Room
Lawrence Livermore National
Laboratory**

Not one of the programmers in the Virtual Reality project said a word about staying late to watch the President's news conference on CNN.

Over the past two years Michaelson had brainwashed them all into believing they were part of something as important as the old Manhattan Project, coercing them into working ninety-hour weeks. They drove in red-eyed at dawn, stayed past dark, ate a steady diet of junk food bought in bulk from the local Costco warehouse store, and generally erased their families—if they had them in the first place—from their lives.

Wearing a Captain America T-shirt, Gary Lesserec lounged back in a chair at the head of the table, while Danielle—a black undergrad from Caltech on summer loan to the Livermore Lab—fiddled with the TV set that stood on a metal rolling cart in the corner of the conference room. All Danielle seemed to find were scrolling Livermore Lab Television Network announcements for upcoming technical talks.

"CNN is on Channel 12, Danielle," Lesserec said. "At least I think so, unless they changed it."

The other T Program technicians came into the room chatting with each other, passing Diet Cokes all around, aluminum cans clanking on the table. Someone crackled open a big bag of nacho cheese Doritos and dropped it on the tabletop as hands reached in from all directions to grab a few chips.

Danielle finally got the station right as the CNN announcers were discussing the "President's major new policy announcement, right after these messages."

"Whoa," said Walter Shing, the bespectacled Korean programmer who squinted through thick lenses at the image on the TV. "Hal's rubbing elbows with important people."

"We already knew that, Walter," Lesserec said. "I just want to know what he's going to spring on us." He lounged back and waited during the CNN preamble and commentary that promised, as usual, that the President's every word had some bearing on the ultimate future of the nation. None of the networks had bothered to broadcast the conference live, but CNN covered it.

While Michaelson was away, Lesserec had enjoyed his freedom to follow up on a few discreet phone calls to industrial partners. He could copy some of the files he needed to bring to his slick new home, where he would put in a few hours on his consulting work. He enjoyed sitting there in the evenings curled up in a saddle chair with the laptop propped in front of him, pecking away at a few codes and simulations, as he stared out the huge picture window overlooking the southern slope of Mount Diablo.

While listening to music on the stereo, he would incorporate new results and bundled routines that he had used the supercomputers to crunch during working hours at the Lab. At home, Lesserec stayed up late, drank plenty of cappuccino, and took pride in the fact that he needed no more than four hours sleep a night.

Some of that time Lesserec had to spend keeping his girlfriend happy; but what kept Sandra happiest was the influx of extra money that allowed her to buy the clothes and jewelry and limited-edition art prints she liked to hang on the walls. Satin sheets, fancy stereo systems, unusual kitchen appliances with European brand names: all the trappings of the American dream, Yuppie style.

It kept getting better all the time.

Lesserec lounged back in his chair and reached forward to grab another handful of Doritos. A few of the techs made catcalls as the President approached the podium in the White House press room. Looming beside him, next to the heads-up teleprompter, stood Hal Michaelson himself, a half-foot taller than the President. Michaelson's steel-gray hair was neatly brushed back, his Clark Gable mustache like a line of mascara above his self-satisfied, barely contained smile.

The President launched into an explanation of the International Verification Initiative, or IVI. Hearing it, Lesserec suddenly remembered hearing Michaelson talk about "ivy," and now he knew what the big man meant. Damn him for keeping something this big a secret!

Lesserec reached for his can of Diet Coke and brought it to his lips, but found that it was empty. He couldn't get up now to get himself another one. Everyone else watched the TV intently.

Michaelson spoke with a self-assured superior confidence. He seemed to be staring right through the television out at the vast American public, and stabbing his words right through his T-Program underlings.

"The President has authorized me to grant full disclosure of all of our virtual surveillance technology to a select group of foreign nationals, including representatives from the former Soviet Union, China, Japan, Israel, Great Britain, France, and Germany. With a suite of highly sophisticated sensors, we can conduct on-site inspections anywhere, at any time, without notice. The President is prepared to place sanctions on any country that does not allow us equal access.

"To prove our goodwill, representatives from the administration have spent the day discussing with officials of the foreign governments. Each nation has agreed to send a special envoy out for an important open-doors meeting at the Lawrence Livermore National Laboratory, where we will demonstrate the virtual technology and provide them with all the answers to their questions."

Lesserec leaped to his feet, spinning the chair around. "What the hell!"

Other technicians began chattering in disbelief while some sat in silence with puzzled frowns.

"What demonstration?" Walter Shing asked.

"Looks like we're going to be working late nights," Danielle commented. "So what else is new?"

"How dare he do something like this," Lesserec said, standing up and flushing, as if he could argue with the television. Michaelson kept talking smoothly, and Lesserec angrily motioned for the others to be quiet.

"My team at Livermore is already hard at work

preparing a spectacular demonstration of the nuts-and-bolts workings of our plutonium handling facility, and I'm pleased to announce the President's decision just this afternoon to implement the most appropriate use of this virtual reality technology." Michaelson turned and nodded to the Secretary of Energy, waiting to his left.

The Secretary approached the podium and spoke: "For the first time in many years, we will conduct an underground nuclear detonation using one of the devices that has been kept mothballed as part of our stockpile stewardship program. The Department of Energy's Nevada Test Site has been placed on alert this afternoon."

Standing next to the Energy Secretary, Michaelson leaned into the microphone. "The entire team of international delegates will remotely observe this underground detonation from Livermore, California, using our virtual reality sensors. They will be down hole, on the spot, seeing what no human eyes have ever seen before." Michaelson seemed to glow as he said his words.

"What the hell is he talking about?" Lesserec said, looking at the other amazed techs as if they might have an answer. "He won't even let us talk about this technology to *American* manufacturers, and now he's going to hand it on a silver plate to . . . to the competition! He's nuts!"

"Gary," Walter Shing said blinking behind his thick eyeglasses, "we always knew Michaelson was nuts. What's the surprise?"

This deflated Lesserec, and he found no other response but to smile. He shouldn't have been surprised. Michaelson enjoyed pulling the rug out from under T Program's feet, seeing how his team scrambled to change the proposals, to modify their work to meet suddenly changed goals.

On the news conference the President opened up to questions from the reporters in the audience, who didn't seem to grasp the significance or even understand the implications of the International Verification Initiative. They spent more time grilling the President about the scandal *du jour*.

Lesserec didn't wait around to hear the CNN rehash and commentary about the speech. He understood the subject more than the reporters would, anyway. He stood up, feeling his knees shaking. His mouth was dry and too salty from the Doritos.

"All right, everybody," he said. "Call home or call your baby-sitters, whatever you need. Michaelson's upstaged us. Again. You all know how to deal with it."

He switched off the television and went to find himself another can of Diet Coke.

Tuesday

The White House
Washington, D.C.

Hal Michaelson slipped out of the White House the same way he entered, through the Old Executive Office Building and onto 17th Street. Men and women bustled past him on the sidewalk, seemingly intent on their own versions of urgent business, no one making eye contact, everyone trying to outdo everyone else in their hurry to get where they were going.

Rush hour in the capital had started four hours before, and the traffic was finally dying away as evening approached. A truck hauling a trailer with a hand-painted sign proclaiming IMPEACH THE SOCIALISTIC BUMS blared its horn and turned in its slow circle of the White House.

Two young men dressed in crisp blue suits handed out pamphlets by the stoplight. A bald middle-aged woman played a rambling French horn solo next to the White House fence. Smells of steamed Polish sausage washed over him from a corner food stand. Flares of late twilight colors settled over the historic monumental buildings that glittered white under drenching spotlights. A city bus rushed past with blue curls of diesel exhaust, drowning out honking cars and yelling people.

Michaelson decided to walk back to his room. Cab rates were obscene, and there would be no telling how long he would wait in the traffic for the mile ride to his hotel. *Damn the humidity*, he thought and set off, wishing he could strip down to a polo shirt and slacks instead of this damned Washington-mandated suit and tie.

For the first time in years he didn't have to catch the next flight back to Livermore. He could get a good night's sleep—or at least a good night's bedroom exercises with Amber: the perfect way to unwind.

As he walked around the fence surrounding the White House, a news crew from a local station filmed a group of twenty people carrying signs for yet another demonstration. Ho hum. Every person in America had the right to protest at the nation's capital, but the fact that so many of them *did* only trivialized their tedious complaints voiced hour after hour, day after day.

Michaelson tried to read the signs, but when he saw the cameraman moving to get him in the picture, he hurried past. No use lending the protestors a bit of his credibility garnered from the recent press conference.

Minutes later, after passing the Treasury building, he turned right and spotted the George Washington Hotel. The traffic abated on the side street, but the cacophony of automobiles still echoed off the stone buildings that surrounded him. Once inside the stately hotel, Michaelson inhaled deeply of the air-conditioned air and felt the tension loosen, his shoulders relax.

His heart fluttered from the exertion of the mile walk; this just wasn't worth it. He'd overdone it today, first by taking the stairs, and now a damned sprint in the sticky heat. He'd had enough, and he could certainly afford the luxury to lounge back. No more cutting corners. Maybe he could join a health club, or maybe he should just soak in the jacuzzi—perhaps with Amber.

Inside his room, Michaelson turned up the air-conditioner, hung up his jacket, and turned on the television. He searched the channels, but was on the wrong side of the hour to catch any response from today's IVI announcement, even from CNN. He thought about calling Lesserec and the team back at Livermore to get their reaction, but decided against it. He wanted to give them time to cool down. He'd walked the tightrope on this Virtual Inspectors project for too long.

Right now all he wanted was to relax and savor the moment. He had scored his points for today; he would deal with transitioning the Lab's work when he flew back to Livermore. Even putting up with Lesserec's self-importance and constant questions wouldn't be too bad, since T Program would be getting a new leader anyway, once Michaelson took the reins of the much larger International Verification Initiative. And the new T Program leader sure as hell wasn't going to be Gary Lesserec.

He laughed at the image of José Aragon trying to explain to Lesserec why the red-headed kid couldn't be appointed group leader. All that, however, could wait until tomorrow. Tonight, he'd invite Amber to dinner, perhaps a nice French restaurant; according to his schedule this wasn't an opera night, so the *Le Rivage* might not be crowded.

His cellular phone rang. He thought about ignoring it, but not many people had his number. The caller must have a good reason for bothering him, though it was probably someone wanting to congratulate him about the IVI. Michaelson grumbled and padded across the suite to his jacket. He dug the phone out of his suit pocket and flipped it open.

"Hal, this is Diana."

"Diana." *Oh shit.* He lowered himself to the chair with a sigh, trying to keep his voice bright and happy. Years ago Diana Unteling had worked as his executive assistant at the Laser Implosion Fusion Facility. Even back in the old days on the Russian disarmament team, she'd had an uncanny knack of catching up with him when he didn't want to be bothered. Previously, he'd found her prescience and attentiveness to be unbearably sexy. But it was getting old, as were they both. Amber was so . . . young and energetic.

"Hal, I thought you were going to call me," Diana said.

"Sorry. Things have been hectic. I . . . forgot. You saw the press conference?"

Silence. "I'm at the office. Can we meet tonight? I'm free for dinner, and afterward. My husband's working late to arrange one of his Coalition retreats. He won't notice."

"Sorry, Diana. I'm heading back to Livermore—the Lab's going apeshit over the IVI announcement."

"You can't stay? Not even for a few hours?" she said sourly.

Michaelson leaned forward, breathing into the telephone. "You know I can't. Things are moving fast. I . . . I'll see you next time I'm out on the East Coast."

"Hal . . . we need to talk, and this would be a very good time." Silence again, tinged with desperation. This was really turning him off. Michaelson waited. He knew she wanted him to ask, but he maintained his silence.

Finally she said, "The Secretary's offered me a political appointment—the Assistant Secretary position—and I need to ensure we've got our story straight. They're going to ask me questions about Livermore, and probably about the time we were on the disarmament team. You know how they dig into everything." She hesitated. "You could take a later flight and we could meet in Crystal City, the Sheraton—"

So the rumor's true that she may be in line for a top job at DOE, Michaelson thought. How quickly things change. He shook his head.

"Look, I'm in a car now, on my way to Dulles airport. I'm expected to get home late tonight." He ran a hand through his steel-gray hair, trying to think, to give her a good enough excuse. "Listen, make up whatever story you want me to follow, and I'll go by it. The committee's probably going to ask me those same questions when I come up for confirmation as head of IVI. We've got plenty of time. I'll be back within the week. I've just got too many loose ends back at Livermore to tie up right now."

She settled into silence over the phone. Hal imagined her twisting up her face, as if in a battle with herself about what to say next. She'd be kneading a hand against her cheek, and her dark eyebrows would arch up against her short gray-blond bangs.

"Don't give me the brush-off, Hal," she finally said. "This is important."

"So is this," he said softly. "I'll call before I come out next time. Promise."

"You know how to reach me." Her words sounded bitter, and the phone clicked off.

Michaelson folded the phone and took several deep breaths. Diana's political appointment threw a new light on things. Right now he needed some time to think, to decompress.

No telling what would come out in the confirmation hearings. He knew the horror stories of the congressional staff digging up skeletons from the deepest closets, and senators ranting for hours about some trumped-up fantasy. But in the land of images and egos, he knew it was only the impression that counted, not the substance. VR had made him a master at that.

He wasted no more time before he picked up the phone again, punched up his electronic Rolodex to find the name Amber, followed by a phone number. He entered her number, and when a soft voice answered, he said, "This is Hal."

Ten minutes later, his face washed and suit jacket back on, Michaelson headed out the door to catch a taxi and meet his dinner date.

Tuesday

**Forrestal Building, DOE
Headquarters
Washington, D.C.**

The tinny HOLD music on the phone was meant to be soothing, but it had exactly the opposite effect on Diana Unteling. She tapped away at the computer keyboard on her desk as she listened, counting the seconds. She recognized the insipid music: an acid rock piece three decades old, deconvoluted and recomposed with a bouncy beat. It made her want to cringe.

While on hold, Diana put the time to good use, tapping away on the Department of Energy's e-mail system, zipping off messages tagged URGENT to her staff. Others worked into the evening hours, but the offices around her had fallen quiet for the night. Having sent her assistant home late before calling Michaelson, Diana was on her own, delegating tasks.

After years of practice, she found that parceling out the paperwork for a two-day trip took little time, but it demanded intense consideration. When assigning one of her staff members the job of tackling important agenda items, she couldn't make a bad call. Luckily, she had a lot of good people on whom she could depend.

That seemed to define her job nowadays—the higher she rose in the DOE hierarchy, the more her staff ran the show, coordinating meetings, preparing background papers, setting up appointments. She was merely the showpiece, the figurehead, bombarded with requests every minute; but by the time the problems got to her, it was only a matter of selecting options.

She zipped off her seventh message before the phone clicked and a live human being spoke. "Thank you for waiting. This is Sabrina at United Airlines, may I help you?"

Diana immediately switched gears, turning away from the e-mail message and focusing on her small personal calendar. "I need to make a reservation for tonight's nonstop flight from Dulles to San Francisco International. One of my coworkers, Hal Michaelson, is on the flight and I'd like to sit next to him if there's a seat available."

"I'm sorry, but I am not authorized to release any personal information about passengers without their prior approval," Sabrina said, as if relating a major tragedy. "If he made his reservation through your travel agent, you could contact them and arrange for the seating request."

Damn, thought Diana. "It's getting late. I don't think I'll be able to do that."

"Then may I take your reservation if you still want to leave on tonight's flight? You could always ask the flight attendant to exchange seats."

Diana raced through the possibilities. Hal always sat in an aisle seat, first class, as far to the front as he could manage, both because of his long legs and because he couldn't stand to wait for others to disembark.

Diana said, "Yes, I need an open-ended round-trip

flight—and I've got a Premier Card for First Class. I have a government transportation request I'll exchange at the airport for the ticket."

"Thank you. It'll be just a minute."

Once she had finished arranging the ticket, Diana terminated the call and pressed the speed-dial button. The phone chittered dial tones, rang once, then a voice answered: "National Coalition for Family Values. May I help you?"

"This is Mrs. Unteling. Could I speak to Mr. Unteling, please?"

"I'm sorry, ma'am. The director is in a meeting with the board for the start of our pledge-drive activities. May I take a message?"

Diana let out a silent sigh of relief. This would make things easier. "Yes, could you tell him I was called back to Livermore on an urgent matter? I shouldn't be gone for more than a few days, but I'll call him when I arrive in California."

"Yes, ma'am, I'll let him know. And please have a safe trip. With the amount of traveling you two have been doing lately, your marriage is a real example for all of us. "

Diana tightened her mouth, but tried not to allow any sarcasm to show. "Thank you."

Hanging up the phone, she eyed the clock. An hour and forty-five minutes before the red-eye was due to leave. No time to waste: even with a government driver, she would be pressed to make it out to Dulles in time. She could see the D.C. traffic from her office high on the fourth floor of the DOE's Forrestal Building; although rush hour was officially over, cars still inched along the wide downtown streets.

A call to the DOE transportation office confirmed that a government sedan would be waiting within minutes to rush her to the airport; rank indeed had its privileges.

She kept a nylon travel bag with a change of clothes in the closet by her private bathroom; she barely had time on the way out to run a brush through her hair and check that her makeup wasn't smeared. As she reached to turn off the lights, she caught a glimpse of the picture of her and her husband Fred and son James, taken ten years ago while they were still back in Livermore. Her blond hair had not yet taken to silver highlights, but her ice-blue eyes still dominated her features. Dark eyebrows, short, tousled haircut . . . that was even before James had decided to go to seminary, and Fred hadn't dreamed of making his coalition go national from its modest beginnings in a midsized California town. . . . But times changed, and so did people, even though the majority of people never realized it.

Diana glanced from side to side, surveying the waiting area, looking for a big man with steel-gray hair and pencil moustache. But Hal Michaelson was nowhere to be found. Just like him, waiting until the last minute, grandstanding even in this little manner, expecting the world to get out of his way. Diana searched the faces as baggage-laden crowds stepped off the shuttle from the main terminal.

It seemed that every man was dressed in a business suit, carrying a briefcase, holding an umbrella in anticipation of the rain, and had a folded copy of *The Washington Post* tucked under his arm; a line of lemmings, streaming from the nation's capital to infiltrate America.

Diana was sure she hadn't missed Hal. He would have stood out like a basketball player at a midget's convention.

"Ladies and gentlemen, we're ready to start boarding families with small children and those needing assistance. Main cabin passengers will board momentarily. First-Class passengers may board at their leisure."

Diana took one last glance around the boarding area. Still nothing. Firmly grasping her ticket, she turned her portable baggage carrier around on its wheels and stepped to the head of the line. She wasn't going to wait any longer for Hal to make his grandiose entrance, not when she could relax and prepare herself for the five-hour trip that lay ahead. She had to rehearse the things she needed to say to Hal. They had to clear the air, get things straight.

Sitting in her spacious, padded seat in the DC-10 First-Class cabin and sipping a glass of white wine—her husband would have disapproved, of course—Diana watched the cattle-car class passengers struggle on board. One by one they filed past, some of them staring, a few flashing her an envious look for having so much room to herself.

Before takeoff, she finished her second glass of wine. The flow of passengers thinned, then ceased. The flight attendants worked the door mechanism, and Diana leaned forward, expecting to see Hal barreling his way down the jetway at the very last moment. But the door was sealed and she found herself stranded on a plane, going somewhere she didn't want to go, with no sign of Michaelson.

"Damn you, Hal," she muttered.

Ignoring the work she had brought with her, Diana ordered a double Scotch on the rocks once they were airborne. She settled back in her seat, going over and over in her mind just what she would say and do to Hal Michaelson the next time she saw him.

CHAPTER NINE

Tuesday

San Francisco International Airport
San Francisco, California

Rather than make a scene, Craig Kreident and Agent Goldfarb stood discreetly in the nonsmoking waiting area of Gate 24; Jackson waited outside at the curb with the car. A kaleidoscope of people flowed around them, making it easy to become invisible among the friends and family members greeting those disembarking from TWA flight 2922 arriving from Bermuda.

Goldfarb looked again at the photo of Miles Skraling, but Craig knew he would recognize the executive the moment he saw him: close-set indigo eyes, wispy reddish-blond hair thinning at the top, jowly cheeks, medium build but thick at the waist, and pale skin—by now probably sunburned from his week in the tropical sunshine.

"Bingo," Goldfarb said, nodding toward a man emerging alone from the airplane—one of the first off, naturally, because Miles Skraling, CEO of NanoWare, Inc., would always fly First Class.

Announcements droned over the intercom as the crowd buzzed around them. Skraling seemed intent on setting his course straight for the baggage-claim area. Craig was afraid that Ms. Ompadhe would try to page him at the airport, give the CEO a heads-up—if she hadn't somehow contacted him on the flight. If that happened, Craig and Goldfarb would have no choice but to close around the man as he answered the white courtesy telephone.

It would still work out, Craig knew, but the search and arrest wouldn't be as smooth that way.

"Okay, clean and easy," Craig said. "We'll be back home in time for the eleven o'clock news."

They approached their quarry from behind, on either side. "Good evening, sir," Craig said. "Mr. Miles Skraling?"

Skraling looked startled. "Yes—"

Craig snapped open his badge wallet and held his ID with a firm hand. "FBI. We'd like to ask you some questions."

He looked at Craig, stared at the out-thrust badge and photo ID card. Skraling's close-set indigo eyes opened wider and wider as if they were about to pop out of their sockets. His face crumpled like a car windshield hit with a rock; a network of spiderweb cracks spread throughout his composure as his carry-on bag dropped to the floor with a dull thud.

"We have a search warrant for your home," Craig said withdrawing the appropriate paper. Goldfarb stood motionless beside him. "We'll need to search your premises and confiscate your personal home computer equipment, and we will have to go through all of your private files."

Skraling staggered backward as if Craig had suckerpunched him. "My . . . personal—"

"We'll escort you home, sir," Craig said, slipping his hand around Skraling's forearm, steering the man away from the flow of people. "Mr. Goldfarb, would you read Mr. Skraling his Miranda rights, just in case he decides to say something to us?"

Goldfarb did so in a low voice, saying the memorized words in rapid-fire succession. No one stopped and gawked, the exchange was kept that quiet.

"I . . . I need to call my attorney," said Skraling.

"You're perfectly welcome to as soon as we reach a phone," Craig answered. "But you'll find that everything is completely in order." He again presented his papers. "Would you like to make the call here, or would you rather wait until you reach your home, where you can have more privacy?"

Skraling shuddered in panic. "I want to go home. I want to think about this." He looked from side to side. His right hand kept twitching convulsively in a strange tic.

"This way, please, sir." Goldfarb picked up Skraling's carry-on bag as they walked down the concourse. Craig kept Skraling close beside him, directing him down the escalator and out to the busy entrance where Jackson waited with the car. Craig opened the door and motioned Skraling in the back; he and Goldfarb sat on either side of the man.

"I was supposed to rent a—" Skraling began.

"That's already been taken care of sir," Craig cut him off. "We've canceled your reservation."

They drove in silence, casual but intent at the same time. In tense silence they crept along the freeways, down the peninsula to the South Bay and the posh upscale community of Los Gatos in the forested hills southwest of San Jose. Twinkling lights studded the dark hulking hills under the light from a first-quarter moon.

Craig felt his pulse speed up as it always did when he

made a bust—though it had never been as exciting as shown on television. In seven years with the Bureau, he had only ever drawn his handgun at the firing range.

The same had been true of his apprentice years working as an assistant for a private investigator in the East Bay. Nothing like *Spenser* or *Magnum PI*. Craig had spent most of his days sitting in a nondescript car or van watching a mark's house to see if a man claiming disability benefits and supposedly laid up in agony actually slipped outside to play tennis down at the local court. During those times Craig had read an enormous amount, flipping through books on patent law as he studied at Stanford, absorbing information, filing it all away.

Jackson turned into the steep driveway of Skraling's tall, shake-shingled house built into the side of a rugged hill. Under automatic mercury lights a smooth black asphalt driveway wound up to a flower-bedecked carport.

Outside lights blinked on from motion detectors. The four men climbed out of the FBI car and walked up the driveway to the front door. Craig turned Skraling around. "Where are your keys?"

"In . . . my pocket." He fished out the keys, but Goldfarb took them from him and tried the lock. When the door swung open they entered the sprawling custom-built house. The marble floors gleamed. Craig smelled furniture polish and cleaning chemicals; a housekeeper must have spruced up the place while Skraling was on vacation.

A beeping sound came from down the hall. "What's the combo on the burglar alarm?" Jackson asked.

Skraling didn't answer. Craig sighed. "Look, Mr. Skraling, all you'll accomplish is to alert your neighbors that you're in trouble. What do you think the police are going to do when they find you here with three FBI agents?"

Skraling closed his eyes and whispered, "9-9-2-7."

Jackson disappeared around the corner and down the dim hall to find the numeric keypad on the wall near the thermostat. Seconds later the beeping stopped.

Craig heard a crash, then Jackson cursed. He reappeared around the corner, brushing off his pants. "Ran into a table," he said. "The phone's on it. I think I bumped the answering machine." Craig looked at the agent and knew Jackson had done the "accident" on purpose.

In the background a telephone answering machine started playing back recorded messages.

The answering machine clicked twice, then a voice started speaking in fast, excited tones. Craig recognized the syrupy accent of Ompadhe.

"Mr. Skraling, some gentlemen from the Federal Bureau of Investigation came here today. I know you won't be arriving back until tonight. I hope this gets to you before they arrive. Sir, they have shut down our operation, confiscated everything. They had a search warrant and they say they found a great deal of evidence."

Skraling opened his eyes. He seemed about ready to cry. "My lawyer," he said hoarsely. "Let me make a call."

"That's right," said Craig. "Go right ahead." Turning on the lights, he led Skraling past the hall which opened up into a kitchen with a living room beyond. "Goldfarb, Jackson—get moving on his files."

Skraling grabbed the portable phone and punched in the number for what must have been his lawyer. Craig noted that it was programmed into the speed-dialer.

The CEO waited, listening. "This is Skraling," he said. "I need to talk to Stein right now. I know it's late." He paused, then his shoulders sagged even more. "Wednesday! Well, how can I reach him? There's got to be a way to reach him." He listened again. "No, I don't want a damned junior partner."

He gnashed his teeth, as if he wanted to bite the antenna off the phone. "Oh, dammit all!" he said and, without hanging up, hurled the black plastic phone across the room where it struck the tile counter, rebounded once, and slammed to the floor. It splintered and broke apart, the battery pack bouncing across the floor.

"Hey, take it easy," Craig said, stepping toward him.

Skraling breathed deeper and deeper, hyperventilating. He froze and then forced a glassy, hollow expression on his face as if he were layering it on with thick plaster.

"Please excuse me, I feel ill," he said and walked stiff-legged down the hall.

"Just a moment, Mr. Skraling," Craig said. But Skraling moved faster with a jerky, hypnotized walk. He ducked into one of the side rooms, a large study with a desk and computer and leather-bound books on display along a back wall.

"What's going on?" Goldfarb appeared behind him, his dark hair mussed. Then, realizing Skraling was gone, "Oh, shit."

"Mr. Skraling, I can't allow you to—" Craig said, but the heavy oak door slammed in his face. He heard Skraling push himself against the other side of the study door and the metal-on-metal scrape of a deadbolt lock clicking into place.

"Hey!" Goldfarb shouted. Craig pounded on the door. Inside, he heard desk drawers rattling, papers tossed about.

"Mr. Skraling, destroying evidence will only make things worse for you. It can increase your sentence by as much as ten years, if convicted."

"Make it worse?" Skraling hooted through the door, then he just laughed and said nothing else.

Feeling stupid for letting himself get into this situation, Craig pounded on the door and rattled the knob, but it was shut tight. He looked at Goldfarb; the other man spread his hands helplessly.

Craig pulled air through his teeth. "Okay, let's break it down."

Together, they stepped back and took turns kicking at the deadbolt. Craig slammed the heel of his black street shoe with all the force he could muster, then stepped back, feeling the jarring pain through his shin.

Goldfarb cracked with his own shoe at the door. Craig tried again with his other foot. Goldfarb tried a second time, and the jamb finally began to splinter. The noises inside the study ceased.

"Come on out of there, Mr. Skraling," Craig said. "We can talk this out."

He listened for an answer as Goldfarb poised himself for another kick at the door. The only response he got from Miles Skraling, though, was a loud, high *pop*, then a loose *thump*.

"Oh, my God!" Craig said. Goldfarb let loose with all his strength, slamming his heel into the deadbolt. Wood splintered. The brass deadbolt protruded from the jamb. Craig threw his shoulder against the door, and finally the lock broke away. The door popped open, letting him stumble into the too-silent study.

Craig caught his balance. Goldfarb pushed in beside him.

Skraling lay slouched backward in the stuffed leather desk chair studded with a decorative rim of brass buttons. His hand dangled beside the desk. A small pistol lay on the hardwood floor, where the recoil had knocked it out of his hand.

The bullet had entered the back of his mouth, throwing him backward. Red spatters were sprayed across the fine leather-bound volumes neatly arranged in his study library.

Jackson came running up. The three agents spent a long time staring before they said a word to each other.

CHAPTER TEN

Wednesday

Building 332—Plutonium Facility Lawrence Livermore National Laboratory

Sitting alone at a table in the break room of the Plutonium Facility, Duane Hopkins opened his black metal lunchbox and withdrew a thermos of coffee. After carefully unscrewing the cap, he poured himself a cupful. He rummaged in his lunchbox, taking out a peanut-butter-and-jelly sandwich and a Twinkie. He always ate half his lunch during the 10:30 break and ate the rest of it at noon. He never spent money in the soda or snack vending machines.

He poked around to double-check what he had packed for himself, as if somehow hoping he would find a surprise there. When he had first gotten married, Rhonda had always packed his lunches, but she had stopped putting in surprises after six months. After Stevie was born a year later, she had gone away altogether, packing only a suitcase, taking the contents of their savings account, and leaving him a simple but eloquent note: "I have my own life to live." She hadn't signed it "Love, Rhonda," or anything. Just left it on the gold-flecked Formica dinette table. He had never heard from her again, not in ten years.

Sitting in his bright orange lab coat, Duane sipped some of his coffee and carefully unfolded the waxed paper surrounding his sandwich. He took one bite of the sandwich, feeling the sweet stickiness *goosh* on the roof of his mouth.

Then Ronald and his caveman buddies came in, talking too loudly, laughing like gorillas at each other's stupid jokes. Duane looked away and tried to become invisible, but Ronald headed directly over to him.

"Hey, Beavis, glad you could come to work today. No special missions for the CIA? No extra credit work for T Program?"

"Stop calling me that," Duane said.

"Calling you what, Beavis?"

"That," Duane said. "It's not my name."

"Well, why not?" Ronald answered with a gap-toothed grin. "You're a butthead, aren't you?" The three other guys with him laughed at that.

"I was just at T Program for a tour. I took my son to the Virtual Reality chamber."

Ronald raised his eyebrows. "Well, excuuuuse me," he said, lolling his head from side to side and raising his eyebrows in a sickening parody of Stevie's cerebral palsy.

Ronald had bristly dark hair and a blurred blue tattoo of an eagle on his left forearm, visible because Ronald always rolled up the sleeves of his orange lab coat. He flaunted his former Marine image, knowing full well Duane's service in the Army. Ronald occasionally made up stories about his days in 'Nam, though Duane and most of the others knew that Ronald was too young ever to have been in the Vietnam war—but no one would challenge him on it.

Ronald leaned forward; his breath stank of sour tobacco smoke; he was probably lighting up again in the bathrooms, even though the building was a no-smoking facility.

"You sure they didn't want to just run some secret experiments on you, Beavis? Maybe run a special analysis to see why you're such a wuss?"

"It was just a tour of the simulator chamber," Duane said, putting his sandwich down. In fact, that nice man Gary Lesserec had called him this morning, and Duane had been delighted to hear from him, remembering how much Stevie had enjoyed the VR demonstration. He hadn't understood Mr. Lesserec's request, but Duane felt he owed the T Program man a big favor, so he was happy to promise the material Lesserec wanted.

Ronald picked up the Twinkie from Duane's lunchbox, tore open the cellophane and stuffed the sponge cake into his own mouth, dropping the wrapper to the floor. Duane sat silently fuming.

"The Virtual Reality Simulator," Ronald mocked with his mouth full and his voice high pitched and woman-like. "Next thing you know our friend Beavis here is going to be talking with the President on another news conference."

"Yeah," one of Ronald's cohorts said. "NIB—the National Initiative for Buttheads." They all guffawed.

Duane hated every single one of them, jeering in their blue jeans and orange lab coats. "Cut it out and just leave me alone," he said. He put his sandwich back in his lunchbox and closed it up.

"Hey, Beavis, where's your badge?" Ronald said. The

others looked around in mock horror. "Oh my goodness, he doesn't have a badge!"

Duane checked and saw that he had left his green badge clipped to his flannel shirt draped over the chair at his workstation in the metallurgy facility. He was supposed to have it with him at all times, though occasionally everyone grew lax once they had passed through the rigorous security checks to get into the plutonium building in the first place.

"What are you, some kind of a Commie spy?" Ronald said. "You'd better get your badge, or I'm going to call security right now—and get you fired!"

Seeing an excuse to get away from the taunting, Duane left the break room and pushed through the swinging double doors that served as an airlock. He hurried across the linoleum floors in the brightly fluorescent-lit open areas of the Plutonium Facility. Metal lockers stood against parts of the walls, with equipment carts or large rolls of thin sheet plastic to be taped down on the floor in the event of a spill.

Piping lined the ceiling—electrical conduits, water lines for emergency shower stations, thicker pipes for house vacuum or hissing continuous air monitors that sucked air through filter paper hooked up to radiation counters.

He shuffled down painted cinder-block halls, his plastic booties scuffing on the linoleum, until he passed through another airlock door into his glove-box area. It was part of the metallurgy and fabrication lab, though most of the glove-box labs looked the same, regardless of whether they were recovery stations, machine shops, laser welding boxes, or inventory chambers.

The lab room had six glove-box stations, each one relatively new, with the metal painted a dark blue. Circular metal ports were spaced evenly across the transparent angled window; Duane could unseal the port he needed and slide his hands into the thick gloves mounted to the metal walls, doing his work without getting contaminated. Large exhaust chimneys sucked air out of the glove boxes through thick, squarish high-efficiency particulate air filters. Fire-suppression sprinklers dotted the ceiling.

Duane went over to where he had left his flannel shirt, but saw to his dismay that the badge wasn't clipped to the collar where he always left it. He looked around, cold and angry. His knees trembled. Ronald must have done something.

Duane felt like a genuine Charlie Brown. And every time he went to kick that football, someone snatched it away from him at the last instant. The only peace and solitude he got at work was when he could huddle in the bathroom. Some people had noticed just how much time Duane spent hiding in the stall in the men's room, enough that a few had blessed him with the awful nickname of "Diarrhea Duane."

Right now Duane wondered what Ronald and his friends had done with his badge. If Duane lost his badge it would be a security infraction on his record. It was his fault for not wearing it, for giving Ronald the opportunity for his stupid pranks. He was supposed to wear his badge at all times, and he had screwed up. For all his years at the Lab, Duane's record was spotless, though unimpressive. He didn't want to risk a black mark on it, especially when people were talking about cutbacks and layoffs.

He fumbled in the pocket of his shirt draped across the chair, found a small hard lump. He pulled out the black plastic nuclear accident dosimeter that had been clipped to the back of his badge. Why had Ronald taken out his dosimeter? What were they doing?

Feeling cold sweat, Duane looked around his chair and his small worktable, then suddenly rushed forward to his glove-box station. He pressed his hands against the tilted glass and looked inside to the contaminated area, seeing squeeze bottles of chemicals, the grinder, the grit-caked balance and counterweights, small plutonium strips sealed inside acrylic disks, pliers, a screwdriver—and his own green photo ID badge smiling up at him from within the glove box, sitting in the horrendous invisible storm of radiation.

Ronald had bagged it through the access port on the end of the glove box, unsealing the metal hatch and sticking the badge through into the attached plastic bag. Then, reaching through with the gloves at Duane's station, he had unsealed the badge to leave it sitting exposed.

The plastic square itself had no dosimeter on it, but Duane shuddered to see his own picture there inside the hazardous box. A fully exposed dosimeter would have brought down a full-scale investigation from DOE headquarters in Washington, D.C. Ronald had covered his tracks, and Duane couldn't prove anything.

Working frantically, he pulled on a pair of rubber surgical gloves and uncapped the circular metal coverings to a pair of installed thicker gloves mounted to the interior of the box. He slid his hands inside, groping for his badge. After several tries, he picked it up, a thin plastic rectangle the size of a playing card.

He felt his heart pounding, his stomach knotting, but he followed procedure as best he could, wrapping the badge in a plastic baggie, then undogging the access port to slide the contaminated bag through into another sealed bag, which he pulled through the access hatch inside out.

Duane kept his rubber gloves on and got a set of tongs from the outside tool locker so that he wouldn't have to touch the badge. Every second he just knew that his badge absorbed more and more of the deadly stuff. His vision fuzzed from terrified tears.

Using the tongs to hold the double-plastic bag, Duane raced over to the bathroom. He held the bags under the running water in the sink, trying to rinse off the radioactivity, not caring what contamination flushed down into the drain. He didn't know if this would work but it seemed like it should.

After a few minutes under the cold water, he tore off the outer plastic bag, rinsed the inner bag even longer, turning the tap to hot, and then tore the bag again to pluck the thin badge free. He held it under the water for a long time, getting rid of the contamination.

To make extra sure, Duane decided to use the liquid pink soap in the dispenser. With his gloved hand he pushed up on the metal plunger hanging at the bottom of an old translucent plastic container, pumping it several times to squirt soap over all sides of the badge. Still wearing the surgical gloves, he lathered his badge and rubbed that under the running water again, until finally Duane felt he was safe.

He dried the badge carefully with a brown paper towel to make sure he wiped off all traces of the radioactive water. Then he pulled off his surgical gloves and threw them in the wastebasket.

Still shaking, partly from anger, partly from fear, he

clipped his badge back to the collar of his orange lab coat, trying to keep it as loose and as far away from his body as possible.

He couldn't wait until he got home to spend the evening with Stevie. At least his son loved him with an unqualified affection. As Duane rocked his boy in his arms, he could think only of the good things, forgetting his nightmarish days on the job.

. . . .

CHAPTER ELEVEN

Wednesday

Building 433—T Program
Lawrence Livermore National Laboratory

Daydreaming during the hour drive from San Francisco International airport, Hal Michaelson felt his eyes growing gritty from too little sleep and too much traveling. He wanted to go back home and sleep it off until his body caught up with the time zones, but he had to get back to work. It was noon already, and he had to put all the wheels in motion for the upcoming IVI demo. The nap he had snatched on the plane was all he was going to get.

He could have slept more the night before, but Amber hadn't given him much chance—not that he minded.

His brain on autopilot, Michaelson automatically turned off the interstate after a numbing drive across the San Mateo Bridge, through the East Bay lunchtime traffic snarl, and finally over the grassy hills into the Livermore Valley. He turned off the Vasco Road exit, but the Westgate Drive entrance to the Lawrence Livermore Lab came as a surprise.

Michaelson snapped out of his funk and turned left into the sprawling, fenced-in complex of the government research installation. When the gate guard stepped out of his kiosk into the road, Michaelson rolled down his window and fished for his badge. He extended it to the guard, who tapped it without much interest and let Michaelson drive through the gate onto the site.

The Lawrence Livermore National Laboratory looked more like a university campus than one of the nation's primary nuclear design facilities. People bicycled past, some riding their own ten-speeds, others pedaling battered red Schwinn bikes the Lab kept for employee use. Wind rustled the tall eucalyptus trees that stood over bike paths and buildings.

It was lunch hour, when the scientists, administrators and support staff suddenly became health conscious, shucking their work dress for shorts and colored spandex tops. Men and women jogged in groups of two and three just inside the gate around the par exercise course, running from station to station, performing calisthenics suggested by the fitness placards, then running to the next stop. The sun shone down, and everybody enjoyed the fine weather—a big switch from Washington, D.C., Michaelson thought, where it was just too damned hot and sticky to be outside.

Michaelson rubbed his eyes and fought back a yawn, wanting nothing more than just to be back in his office. He clipped the badge back onto the chain around his neck as he drove onto the mile-square site, straightening the badge over his tie, a leftover from his D.C. trip.

Even with the five uninterrupted hours he'd spent on the plane going over the management plan for the International Verification Initiative, Michaelson was still far behind. And thanks to Amber he didn't know how he was going to manage to squeeze in the rest he needed.

Amber—the sweet memory of their lovemaking—

how could anyone wearing a formal staffer's uniform and so much meticulous makeup be so wild and uncontrolled in bed? He grinned as he used his special car pass to drive through a second gate, behind another wall of chain-link fence into the RESTRICTED area where the T Program trailers were located.

Beyond these were a series of two-story aluminum and dark-glass structures resembling a futuristic movie scene. A white satellite dish, thirty feet in diameter, stood in a grassy clearing to the south; construction crews worked on another new building to the north.

The executive parking lot next to building 433 was big enough for only a few cars. Hal guided his aging Oldsmobile into the slot marked DIRECTOR and walked the sycamore-lined path to the white lab trailers, large portable buildings that had been given so much landscaping that they would never be moved anytime soon. Built from money originally designated for the Laser Implosion Fusion Facility, the Virtual Reality lab stood in the shadow of the towering LIFF, now used primarily for low-level laser experiments and equipment storage on the other side of the RESTRICTED area fence.

Well, with the IVI they would have an extravagant budget, enough money to build themselves a slick new facility, design fancy logos, get wooden desks instead of lab-standard modular furniture and fabric cubicle dividers. *Give it time*, he thought. But they had a great deal of work to do for the international delegates, who would have to be totally wowed by the VR capabilities.

Entering the Virtual Reality lab through the badge-reading CAIN booth, Michaelson found himself the only person in the cluttered small building. He looked around and frowned. *Where the hell was Lesserec?* Noontime and the place looked like the *Mary Celeste*. T Program workers weren't supposed to take lunch hours. Lunch was for people who weren't doing anything important.

The heavy vault door stood open, and the smooth-walled, featureless VR chamber looked the way he had left it two days before; but in all that time the team-members should have been able to show something for their efforts.

In the wake of that shock, Michaelson expected the place to be filled with bodies scurrying around, preparing for the high-level foreign visitors that would arrive here in only four weeks. He'd have to come down on his deputy, get Lesserec to start taking things more seriously, make sure his priorities were appropriately established. He wondered if Lesserec knew his days were numbered.

Michaelson grumbled to himself and made his way through the tangled nerve center with its control racks and monitor screens, stepping over bundled fiberoptic cable. He scanned the rows of empty workstations, discarded Diet Coke cans, and stacks of technical papers and software users manuals that cluttered the lab area. At least his own office would be clean and neat. Whenever he went away on travel, his administrative assistant, Tansy Beaumont, took the opportunity to file away the debris he left scattered around his office.

Tansy had her own cubicle now; her former office, tucked away in the far corner of the open hall, served as a holding area for the electronic equipment and spare parts that Lesserec's people insisted on keeping around. With the growing success and visibility of T Program, though, Michaelson had needed to establish his "moat dragon" in a prominent position to act as a buffer for all the administrative bullshit so he could get some work done.

Once the IVI got off the ground, this place would turn into a bureaucratic frenzy, with everybody trying to push their mouths in the same watering hole . . . he'd have to give Tansy a special briefing on how to handle it. But he wouldn't worry about that for at least another month, given the usual ramp-up time. There were just too many things to do right now.

Michaelson glanced at the yellow phone messages on his desk. Other than the usual queries for information and pestering calls he could ignore, he found a terse memo from José Aragon—did that man want his fingers in *everything?*—requesting that Michaelson meet with him at the Plutonium Facility by the end of the afternoon. Michaelson snorted; that could wait, though it probably had something to do with the IVI demonstration. At the end of the day he was scheduled to have a meeting with the Lab Director himself, which was more important; but Michaelson knew he'd probably be chastised for springing such a surprise on everyone. Oh well, that's tough. He had thought there would at least be messages from the local press, requests for interviews. He hoped Tansy hadn't squelched them.

Michaelson shuffled through the yellow notes, tossing the entire wad into the wastebasket. Then he logged onto the Quickmail system and methodically went through his electronic messages; still nothing of consequence. Finally, he punched up his home phone number to access his private messages. The thing he hated most about constant travel was all the tedious catching up once he got back.

When his home answering machine activated, he keyed in his private code and pulled up the messages. Finally, two reporters requesting interviews. He smiled. The delivery service telling him they had stocked his pantry. The next caller, though, caused him to rock back in his seat.

"Hal—this is Diana. Pick up if you're there." A pause. "Where *are* you? I got into Livermore last night and you're not home. I thought you were catching the red-eye. Give me a call when you get in. I'm staying at the Pleasanton Sheraton. I must have missed you on the plane."

The answering machine beeped for the next caller. "Hal, this is Diana again. Dammit, it's ten o'clock in the morning and you *still* haven't gotten in—or you're not returning my calls. What the hell's going on? The Lab says you're not due in until later this afternoon. You bastard—you *knew* you weren't coming back!" There was a long pause on the recording, a disgusted sigh. "Hal, we've got to talk about your confirmation hearings for the IVI. You might think this is all a big joke and you'll be able to breeze past this senate confirmation, but you're not bulletproof. Get that through your thick, arrogant skull. If they ever find out about us, it's going to be one hell of a ride for you. And for me, as well. I'm in line for a promotion here, you know.

"These guys are out for blood. You've been taking potshots at Congress and the administration for years—this is their chance to get even. They can taste it, and they'll stop at nothing to discredit you. People have had their careers ruined for far less than fucking administration officials. Talk to me—or do I have to threaten you?"

Michaelson punched the buttons on the phone, cutting off the recorded message.

Rocking forward in the chair behind his desk, he tossed the lightweight plastic phone back into its cradle.

Diana was becoming a bigger pain in the ass then he had imagined. Well, screw it. It's over with her.

Bothersome details filled his days, forcing him to work late hours just to get his job done. It was going to be another long night—alone again.

But first he had to clear up the stack of administrative requests. He sighed and plucked one of the yellow slips out of the wastebasket. The meeting with Aragon and the Lab Director was first on the list. It was probably one of those butt-kissing circuses he couldn't get out of.

He heard several people arriving, passing one by one through the CAIN booth, slipping their badges into the reader, keying in their access number, and pushing open the heavy door. The tightly knit group of technicians returned from lunch, but it sounded as if they had spent their entire time talking about work-related problems. Michaelson expected nothing less.

"Hey, Dr. Michaelson, that was some press conference!" the young black woman from Caltech called out, raising her hand in greeting.

"Yeah, does this mean we can move to a real lab facility now?" said someone else. Michaelson had forgotten his name.

He waved them off and growled as he picked up the phone to call Aragon. "Tell Lesserec I want to see him in my office as soon as he gets back," he called. "We've got to change these banker's hours and accomplish some work around here. That international team will be here before you know it."

Not waiting for a reply, he punched the number to call Associate Director José Aragon and acknowledge the meeting in the Plutonium Facility for that afternoon.

Wednesday

Building 332—Plutonium Facility Lawrence Livermore National Laboratory

Looking both ways, Duane Hopkins peeked out of the bathroom door in the Plutonium Facility. He hoped no one had noticed how long he had hidden inside the rest room. He had already spent a lot of time that morning washing his badge and recovering from the shakes, hoping never to see Ronald and his mean friends again.

He had vowed to get even with them, but it probably wouldn't work, and then they would be on his back even worse than before. So he had hidden there during the afternoon break, avoiding any chance at another confrontation.

He hesitated when he heard someone come toward him, almost turning around to rush back into the rest room, but he forced himself to keep going ahead. He stepped away and tried to regain his composure before somebody else hooted after him.

"Hey, it's Diarrhea Duane!" He looked up and saw Ralph Frick chuckling next to two other guys. Ralph had been an okay guy, ribbing him instead of openly insulting him—but lately Ralph's teasing had taken on a more bitter, harsher tone, and Duane just couldn't laugh it off anymore.

He tried desperately to think of a come-back line, but all he could manage was a red face. Duane hurried back to his glove box station in the metallurgy lab. He had to stay away from the bathroom, at least for the rest of the day.

He looked at his digital watch. Hours to go yet, with each second passing like a blacksmith's mallet hitting an anvil. His stomach had been knotted all day long. He wondered if he had time to get the stuff for Gary Lesserec.

Duane flinched every time he looked at his badge, afraid that invisible radiation kept pouring out of it into his body, streaming through his chest and lungs.

After all the years he had worked in the Plutonium Facility, Duane had a healthy respect—no, a mortal terror—of radiation. He was playing with fire every day he went in to work.

His biggest scare had come early in his career at the Lab, back when it had been called the Lawrence Radiation Laboratory, long before the strict handling procedures had been put in place, before anybody knew any better. It had been shortly after his marriage to Rhonda, when Duane had walked with a spring in his step fresh from leaving his short stint in the Army, aglow with his training under the GI Bill.

He was happy then. He hadn't known the world was so full of nightmares. He used to smile. He talked openly to people because he hadn't realized how much better it was to remain quiet, never to open up to everybody.

Back then, the group of bullies had been led by a man

named Bodie. A different group from Ronald's gang, but just the same, nevertheless. No matter where he went, they seemed to target Duane Hopkins.

Duane had talked to everyone about how wonderful it was to be a newlywed, all the plans and dreams he and Rhonda had. They had wanted to have kids, three or four of them. He said that a lot; he talked about it at the lunch table where everyone could overhear.

Duane had been stupid, unsuspecting.

Bodie and three of his wise-ass friends were standing outside one of the materials vaults. The halls of the huge Plutonium Facility echoed. Back then yellow lines had been painted on the floor showing allowable separation distances between carts that contained sealed sources or canned parts: *follow the yellow brick road*! Yellow and black radiation alarms were mounted on the wall with neutron counters. The harsh white fluorescent lights washed away all shadows, all softness of color. The building really hadn't changed much in fifteen years.

Duane had been going about his business, pushing his cart along, probably even whistling to himself. He had his inventory card hooked to the bottom of it, returning a sealed sample to its appropriate lead-lined can on its appropriate shelf in the vault.

"Hey, Duane," Bodie called from inside the otherwise empty vault. "Come here, we've got a wedding present for you."

Duane raised his eyebrows. "A wedding present? I got married months ago."

"Yeah, so we're late," Bodie said. "Come here," he gestured for Duane to come into the vault.

Even now as he thought about it, Duane winced. He wished he could go back in time and change what he had done. That one act of stupidity may have doomed him for the rest of his life, and all of Stevie's.

Inside the vault Bodie said, "Heard you want to have kids. That's nice." It was Bodie's favorite phrase, Duane remembered. *That's nice*. "We wanted to warm up your sex life a little bit, Duane."

Even then, Duane had been more baffled than afraid. Nobody else was in the corridors. The Plutonium Facility was a big, ugly building with a maze of halls and corridors, but not a bustle of people inside.

"What do you mean?" he asked. Bodie looked at his two companions and they each grabbed one of Duane's arms, yanking him into the vault.

"Hey!" he yelped. "What's going on?"

Bodie unclipped one of the quart-sized metal cans and reached in, wearing his rubber glove. He pulled out one of the small nickel-plated plutonium buttons from its wire cage bin—a small hemispherical disk about as big as a silver dollar. He flashed it in the light. "Hoo, it's still warm. That's nice." Bodie made a great show of tightening his rubber glove. He held the metal button up to Duane's face.

"Plutonium," he said in an evil whisper. "Valuable stuff. This is what they make the atomic bombs out of. Highly radioactive. You can feel the heat from the radiation." He smiled, then reached forward to yank the waist band of Duane's trousers, reaching through the open flaps of his lab coat.

Duane squirmed. "Stop it!" he said, but Bodie just snickered, grabbed the elastic of his briefs and dropped the slick plutonium button down into Duane's underwear.

Terror flowed like lava through him. He couldn't believe what Bodie had done. He could feel the plutonium button, heavy metal dropping down into his crotch. *It was warm*—it was warm, hot with radiation!

He screamed.

He could feel the crackling neutrons or gamma rays or whatever they were called sizzling around his testicles. He yowled another soul-wrenching scream and writhed, thrashing about like a snake. The plutonium button still clung to his groin. Duane howled as if he were being eaten alive.

In sudden shock, Bodie's two friends simultaneously released his arms and stepped back, looking confused. Bodie also lurched backward and slapped Duane on the face.

"Criminy, Duane! Can't you take a joke? That's not nice."

Duane reached his hand down his pants, still sobbing, frantically grabbing for the hot piece of metal, which he tore out of his waistband and hurled to the other side of the vault where it clanged and clattered against the metal cages. He tried to shout obscenities at Bodie, but his mouth would make only wordless noises.

"Come on, Duane," one of Bodie's friends said. "It's all right, for Pete's sake. The thing's shielded. Nickel-plated. You didn't get any dose. It's safe. Jeez, what a baby."

But Duane never believed any of that. He fled the vault leaving his cart in the hall. He ran down the corridors turning left and right, not sure where he was going until finally he stumbled to the lunch room. He grabbed his jacket and left the facility, taking sick leave for the rest of the afternoon. He did receive a reprimand from

his supervisor the following day for not logging and se-
curing the radioactive samples on his card.

Again being stupid and naive, he had reported the incident to his supervisor. Because of a long list of other
infractions, Bodie was fired, and his goon friends were
placed on temporary suspension.

And Duane's car had been smashed with a sledgehammer in the middle of the night, a brick thrown
through his living room window, threatening phone
calls for weeks—and the police wouldn't do anything.
He never told everything to Rhonda, just that one of the
guys at work didn't like him. Rhonda couldn't believe
he would let some bully terrorize them, and she kept
mocking his manhood.

Later, when Rhonda had gotten pregnant, Duane
spent many sleepless nights biting his nails, afraid that
some lizard-faced mutated monster might be growing
within her womb. He tried to convince himself that
would never happen.

At first, baby Stevie had seemed normal, and Duane
had felt frigid relief for a few months . . . until the mysterious symptoms of cerebral palsy started to show up.
The doctors insisted that Stevie's condition had nothing
to do with exposure to radiation in Duane's job at the
Plutonium Building. In fact, they were *too* quick to say
that, no doubt to prevent Duane from suing the Livermore Lab for wrongful exposure to harmful substances.

But Duane *knew*, no matter what the doctors said, no
matter how safe everything supposedly was, he
knew . . . and now Ronald had been playing games with
radiation again.

Duane looked down at his green laminated badge.
Year after year he had put up with this torture. No one

would ever leave him alone. He wasn't as big or as tough or as confident as any of the others, but Duane wasn't helpless.

He kept telling that to himself as he went back to his workstation still shaking, still afraid, hoping to get even with Ronald, or his buddies, or even Ralph Frick, or any of the other ones who preyed on him day after day.

It didn't really matter to him. He just had to prove that he wasn't helpless. He kept telling it to himself.

I'm not helpless!

Wednesday

Building 332—Plutonium Facility

Five minutes late, Hal Michaelson drove a government-issue vehicle—a cream-colored Ford Escort—to the small portal building that granted access into the Superblock, the section of Lawrence Livermore Lab encased within double ultra-tight security fences. Passing deeper and deeper through tightening rings of Lab security, he felt as if he were penetrating one of those Russian dolls-within-dolls he had picked up during his time on the disarmament team in the former Soviet Union.

At this level of security, though, the guards were heavily armed and authorized to use deadly force.

José Aragon was already waiting outside the gate, pacing back and forth in his dark-green leisure suit and maroon tie. His hair had been slicked back immaculately and his face beamed, stretched back in a huge grin as if his face were made of plastic.

The Associate Director motioned him toward a vacant "Government Vehicle Only" parking spot and hurried over to open the door for him. Aragon was an *AD* for God's sake, Michaelson thought; he didn't have to act like a bellboy.

"Thanks for coming, Hal," Aragon said breathlessly.

"Let's go right in. I've got the paperwork finished. We can give you a full-fledged tour of the Plutonium Facility. You'll see everything you need to know for your demo."

Michaelson extricated his large body from the small Ford and stood looking down at the much shorter man. "I thought Lesserec was taking care of all this. Why do I need to waste my time here?"

"Oh, Hal!" Aragon said, "It'll be good for you to see things firsthand. It's been a long time since you've been in this area, and I want to show you all of the improvements we've made."

"Improvements?" Michaelson said, then snorted as they walked toward the tan portal building that stood in front of the chain-link fence. "I thought the Plutonium Facility was shutting down."

Aragon raised a hand. "Not shutting down—defense conversion," he said. "Dual-use technologies. Ways we can take advantage of what we already have in place, even after the end of the Cold War. The Livermore Plutonium Facility is one of only two of its kind in the entire country. We can't afford to lose this one."

"Right, right," Michaelson said. "Save the patriotic speech for later. I don't have much time. Got a meeting with the Lab Director at 4:30."

They entered through the door, passed their badges to the guard sitting behind a glassed-in enclosure, and then walked through a sensitive metal detector before retrieving their badges on the other side. Then they stepped through a second set of doors to the outside, inside the Superblock fence now.

The Plutonium Facility itself was practically featureless, the ugliest building in the entire square-mile lab: gray concrete splotched with age discolorations, veined with electrical and ventilation conduits running up the flat cement sides. Flashing yellow and magenta lights announced alarm or preparatory conditions inside the building. Crash-out escape doors allowed emergency exit from the inner laboratory rooms if a criticality alarm should sound.

"Just a sec," Aragon said as he scurried across the asphalt courtyard to one of the building's side doors. "I have to check something. Wait for me here."

As he ducked inside, Michaelson stood under the warm afternoon sun, frowning. It was just like Aragon to make *him* wait. The boob could never get things right. He'd proven that amply enough in the past.

Fifteen years earlier Michaelson had made his name at Livermore by launching the prestigious, big-budget Laser Implosion Fusion Facility: a groundbreaking, technological demonstration project that had implications for cheap and safe power generation to meet the nation's needs for the next century or so.

Michaelson had built the LIFF into one of Livermore's flagship projects with the full press treatment, brochures, tours, demonstrations, and high hopes. But as had happened so often throughout his career, Michaelson encountered severe difficulties with top management. At the peak of the LIFF project, Michaelson had become incompatible with the then-Director of the Lab.

He had found himself quietly transferred to a new position as the head of a high-visibility on-site inspection team in the former Soviet Union. As a disarmament expert who dominated the news, Michaelson again captured the public spotlight; but in the eyes of Livermore management, their loose cannon was safely distant in the Ukraine, working with his dedicated team of inspectors, including his personal deputy, Diana Unteling.

The LIFF had been left in the untried hands of José Aragon, a bright-eyed "yes-man." Michaelson suspected Aragon had climbed up the ladder simply because of his minority status, and had continued to rise as people promoted him to get him out of their hair.

It had taken Aragon only a few months to trash the LIFF. Because he was not a scientist, because he did not understand the real issues behind the project, Aragon had unknowingly misled Congress, made impossible concessions and unrealistic promises, and mixed up details—all of which led to missed deadlines—and the bad luck began to spiral. *Any* non-scientist might have screwed up just as much, but Aragon had been in the hot seat.

While in Kiev, Michaelson had gotten a tip-off from one of his former workers about how badly Aragon was screwing things up. Enraged, Michaelson had flown back directly to Washington, leaving Diana Unteling in charge of the disarmament team. He rushed like a hero to the rescue, barging into Congressional hearings, pulling strings, making phone calls, shouting at the right people, pleading with others, trying to save the LIFF funding from being canceled—all to no avail.

The ripples of scandal had caused a great shakeup at Lawrence Livermore. The Director himself was "promoted" to DOE Headquarters in Washington. Michaelson was removed from the disarmament team because of his "notorious lack of responsibility and blatant abandonment of the inspection team." And the huge and expensive LIFF, nearly completed, was mothballed without ever being switched on.

Aragon, the incompetent boob who had caused it all, found himself promoted to Deputy Associate Director, then Associate Director. *Would miracles never cease?* Michaelson thought.

He himself had been demoted to group leader, but Hal Michaelson had enough pull and enough connections so that even starting from scratch he created a new project based on his on-site inspection experience halfway around the world. With a mere scrap of discretionary funding from the Lawrence Livermore overhead budget, Michaelson had launched the groundbreaking work for his virtual reality on-site inspectors. Now T Program had the enormous prestige of full presidential backing with an upcoming landmark demonstration.

And he was stuck waiting outside the Plutonium Facility, looking at his watch, and cursing José Aragon's name.

As Michaelson looked on, a beat-up gray government pickup drove up to the double gate outside the portal building. A uniformed security guard came out and opened the outer chain-link gate. Metal bollards automatically sank down into the ground like giant steel teeth, allowing the truck to drive into the compound.

The guard closed the fence behind him as the driver ran around to pass his badge through the reader. The guard took out a long angled mirror on a pole and began inspecting underneath the chassis of the old truck. He opened the doors, looked under the seats, popped open the glove compartment, and rummaged around in the bed of the truck. The driver came back through the portal building and waited for the guard to finish his search.

Michaelson tapped his feet as he watched the tedious process. *What a pain in the ass*, he thought.

When the guard signaled that he was finished with his search by slapping the hood, the driver hopped back into the truck. The second set of metal bollards lowered to allow the truck access to the Superblock.

"Okay!" said Aragon, coming out the side door and rubbing his hands together. "Just had to reset the software. We're ready to go in. Follow me and we'll get you suited up and checked through."

Aragon continued to chatter during the entry process. They passed through another metal detector, then into the locker rooms where Michaelson had to squirm into a tight-fitting orange lab coat, clip on a nuclear accident dosimeter, and finally enter the Radioactive Materials Area.

The building was as ugly inside as it was on the outside, Michaelson thought: 1960s prison-barracks style . . . or worse yet, public schools from the fifties with linoleum-tiled floors, white-painted cinderblock walls. More metal junk and pipes than could possibly be accounted for ran along the suspended ceiling and along the walls.

The workers seemed busy, like a bunch of good-old-boys who catcalled to each other, with a lot of back-slapping, punching in the biceps, as friendly joshing. It annoyed Michaelson. They seemed like a bunch of high school football studs playing grab ass. Even though the workers seemed on good terms with each other, no one appeared to recognize Aragon; however, that didn't stop him from smiling and greeting each person he passed.

Michaelson felt bone tired, thanks to Amber, thanks to the long flight. Traveling did little more than upset his stomach and make his eyes burn. He'd been running on adrenaline for days before the presidential press conference, and now that it was over he felt exhausted, let down. He had little patience for a boob like Aragon.

"Just what exactly did you want to show me?" Michaelson asked as they walked down the hall, passing the third identical-looking glove-box lab.

"Well . . ." Aragon shrugged. "We need to discuss the best place to set up those VR sensors of yours. That's a fabulous chamber you have, by the way. I witnessed a demonstration of it when Mr. Lesserec gave a wonderful tour to those kids from the Coalition for Family Values. We want to bring them in here for a tour next, show them some nuts-and-bolts work."

"Glad you were impressed," Michaelson said in dull voice. "It means a lot to me. A hell of a lot."

Aragon beamed, then faltered, not knowing how to take Michaelson's comment. The Associate Director took great pride, and a great deal of time, to show Michaelson the new array setups in the radioactive materials vaults, the forced separation of samples of fissile material, the careful accounting and security methods.

They passed the fabrication facility, then the welding and recovery lab. Waving his hands, Aragon seemed euphoric as he showed off the new barrel counters, large neutron and alpha detectors that assayed barrels of mixed radioactive waste and suspected contaminated materials. Aragon led him to the door of another lab area filled with more glove boxes, grungy like a bad high school metal-shop project and just as uninteresting as the first three similar rooms.

Michaelson felt his brain turning into mush. His eyes itched from lack of sleep, and he just plain did not want to be in the company of José Aragon, or inside the Plutonium Facility. He either wanted to be home in bed or back at his T Program office.

Before they could enter the glove-box room, Michaelson held up his hand. "Hold on a second." He walked across the hall to the bathroom. "I'm calling a halt to this crap."

Shocked, Aragon followed Michaelson like a puppy into the rest room. Michaelson stood at the urinal, staring at the wall and ignoring Aragon. Finally, he turned to the smaller man and said, "So what did you really bring me here for? All this tour-guide baloney is a bunch of bullshit."

Aragon didn't seem to know how to answer. "I, uh, just wanted to show you some of the things we do here in the Tech-Transfer/Defense Conversion Directorate. You *are* part of it, Hal, even though you don't participate in any administrative activities."

"Thank God for that." Michaelson finished, zipped up, and glared at him. "Look, I've got the President and a bunch of foreign dignitaries coming here in a few weeks. I've also got a ton of catch-up work to do—and you're playing show and tell with me. I don't have time for it. No way, José."

He looked at himself in the mirror, sighed at the red-rimmed eyes and the haggard face. He turned the water on in the sink, hit the soap dispenser, and lathered up before stooping over to splash the cold running water on his cheeks, in his eyes. It felt good, refreshing. He splashed again.

Aragon started to say something, but the running water drowned out his words. Michaelson shut off the faucet and stood up, flinging droplets from his hands.

"What I'm trying to say, Hal," Aragon said, sounding

panicked now, "is that I know we've had difficulties. I'm trying to build a bridge between us—to bury the hatchet, or whatever you want to say. I'd like us to make peace if we're going to make this International Verification Initiative work together."

Michaelson stepped back and looked at the AD in scornful amazement. Aragon fled to the sink, hit the soap dispenser briefly, and washed his hands just for something to do.

"Look, José, the IVI Project is *mine*, not yours. Not anybody else's here. I'm the only one who had the vision and the foresight. *I* developed the technology. *I* created this alone, in spite of the mess you've made out of just about every single thing you've touched.

"I don't want to make peace with you. I don't want to talk to you. I don't want to see you. Delicate instruments have not yet been calibrated to measure how *little* I care about what you think of me."

He dried his hands, dabbed his face with a brown paper towel and tossed it in the wastebasket.

"Now, if you would escort me the hell out of here, I need to get back to work." He turned and narrowed his eyes at the befuddled Aragon. "Or do I have to write a few more memos about your poor performance?" He smiled coldly. "Maybe this time I could send them to the President directly, since I've got his ear."

José Aragon scuttled after him as Michaelson took long strides down the corridor of the Plutonium Facility, finally feeling good for the first time that day.

Wednesday

Oakland Office
Federal Bureau of Investigation

"Craig, could I see you for a minute?"

Craig Kreident looked up from the paperwork to see his supervisor, June Atwood, standing outside the doorway of his small office. Slim and in her mid-forties, June gave him a broad smile that halfway succeeded in masking her expression of concern. Her skin was the color of polished walnut wood, with the same sheen; her black eyes seemed too big for her narrow face; her close-cropped hair lay like felt against her head.

"Sure, June. Your office of mine?" said Craig.

His windowless office was cramped, bookshelves laden with old criminal law books, electrical engineering and computer science texts, and cardboard bankers' boxes filled with handwritten notebooks from his patent law days. June's slender form was nearly blocked out by the two long metal drawers yawning open from his file cabinet and exposing a disarray of papers.

June looked around, saw no place for her to sit, and gestured out the door. "Let's go down the hall."

He pushed up from his desk, surprised that his body

felt so fatigued. Coffee just hadn't done it this morning. As a field agent, he wasn't used to sitting for hours on end anymore, poring over reports and going over obscure facts. But he had to tie up all the loose ends of the NanoWare incident. Being intently involved in a case always made his body realize there were other priorities in life than paperwork. As usual, he just didn't have the time.

He had spent the entire previous day answering questions, being grilled by Internal Affairs personnel, filling out form after form, documenting exactly what had gone wrong with the Skraling arrest. Jackson and Goldfarb had confirmed everything Craig had said, and the evidence against NanoWare was overwhelming. But the CEO's suicide had thrown everything into a whirlpool.

June Atwood's office was as clean and spacious as Craig's was cramped and sloppy. Two pictures of her family sat on the credenza to her left; an undergraduate diploma from Grambling and an MBA from Harvard hung on either side of a cluster of framed government Superior Service awards. A squeaky overstuffed chair waited for him on the opposite side of her wooden desk as Craig plopped down his lanky frame, then adjusted his suit. June closed the door after him.

"Don't worry, this conversation's not being recorded," she said jokingly.

He forced a grin. "That's a first." Craig drummed his fingers on the arms of the chair, feeling uneasy. "This looks serious, June. I've nearly finished all the reports you asked for—"

Instead of hiding behind the barrier of her desk, June sat in the visitor's chair opposite him, a colleague and a friend rather than a boss speaking to a recalcitrant employee. She smoothed her khaki skirt. "We haven't talked for a while, Craig. Whenever I'm back in the office, you're out in the field or testifying."

"You're telling me," Craig said. "I suppose the CIA folks are all taking early retirement after the Cold War, but unfortunately, we've still got plenty of bad guys to catch inside our own borders."

June looked away, distracting herself. "Call it job security. So, how are things going? How's Trish?"

Craig shrugged, then looked annoyed. "It *has* been a long time, hasn't it? Trish has been gone for over a year." The memory hurt—she had been a medical student with something like a pre-midlife crisis. "Had to follow her own path, left for the East Coast to take up residency at Johns Hopkins. I hear she goes by the name Patrice now."

June sighed. "Sorry to hear that, Craig. I didn't—"

Tired of the small talk, Craig interrupted her. "June, what's going on? I appreciate your concern, but something's the matter, and you're not doing a very good job at hiding it. Am I going to be placed on administrative leave for the NanoWare mess?"

June nodded slowly while keeping her big, dark eyes on him. "Okay, I'll come right out and say it. I think it would be a good idea if you took a day or two off. Let us finish going over the paperwork."

Craig blinked. "What are you looking for?"

"We want to let the dust settle, that's all. I know you, Craig, and I know your work. So does everyone else here. And with the clear-cut evidence you've uncovered, nobody is going after your hide. But our investigations don't usually end up with the prime suspect dead."

"That wasn't my fault—" Craig began.

"Just sleep in tomorrow morning. You'll keep drawing your salary and have all benefits, but I'm sending you away from the office, to keep you out of sight for a few days. Consider it a vacation."

Craig's heart pounded, his stomach roiled, oscillating between shame and anger and disappointment. A prickle of sweat washed over his skin. He narrowed his eyes. "This doesn't mean I have to hand you my badge or anything crazy like that, do I?"

"No, of course not. Your file is clean. No reprimand, honest. For the two years you've been assigned to this office, your performance has been flawless." She sighed and leaned forward in the chair, smoothing her skirt again. "I can't say I understand how you feel—I've never been in a situation like this before."

"Like what—being put on administrative leave for something out of your control?"

June was quiet for a long moment, avoiding his gaze with her big, dark eyes, then she spoke softly. "You'd be surprised at what I've been through, Craig. The things I've been accused of doing. You should have heard the whispers when I was appointed to run the Oakland bureau. Nobody seemed to consider the possibility that I might actually be *competent*, a good candidate for the job. No, it was either because I was black, or a woman, or sleeping with someone."

She drew air through her teeth, as if trying to keep her own reactions under control. "No, Craig, I've never had a suspect shoot himself right in front of me. But you do have plenty of support in this office. I won't blow any smoke past you. Just take a little time off."

Craig finally nodded. *Why did everything seem to*

happen at once? he thought. He was either on top of the world, or down in the dumps. The last few years had been going pretty well. He had graduated from Cal Poly with an engineering degree, then continued at the Stanford law school, before starting as an assistant with a firm in patent law. Being accepted as an FBI agent fulfilled a lifelong goal. His relationship with Trish—while she labored her way through med school—had seemed rock solid. It had seemed that nothing could go wrong.

Craig shook his head. Time to get things back on track. He had to step away and take control of his life, get a little perspective. "Okay. Thanks."

"I understand."

Do you? he thought. He studied her for a moment, and decided he couldn't tell either way.

June Atwood smiled tightly, showing even white teeth against her red lips. "Take advantage of it. You know you'd never take time off to kick back and relax. Doctor's orders. If it makes you feel better, we're through with the backlog of high-tech investigations for the moment, so I wouldn't have anything to keep you busy even if you did stick around. I'd end up giving you some of *my* paperwork to do."

Craig pushed up from his seat. "No thanks. Got to keep the bureaucrats busy back in Washington. Better you than me. Will you call me if something really hot comes up?"

"Promise," June said. "If we need you, your phone starts ringing."

Craig walked out the door, somewhat numb but surprised at how relaxed he already felt, as if a weight had been removed from his shoulders. He hated desk work, anyway.

Strange how things worked out. All through school Craig had concentrated on subjects that demanded intense study—engineering, law. He'd even studied while working part-time for that private investigator during law school. And yet he found that he no longer enjoyed sitting still and reading. Maybe June was doing him a favor, taking him off the paperwork for a while. Yeah, and if he clicked his heels together and said that three times. . . .

Craig stepped into the hall, dodging a secretary wheeling a metal cart piled high with legal briefs, dossiers, and case files.

He returned to his small office and slammed shut the metal file drawers he had left open. With a long sigh, he surveyed the mess. His desk was completely covered with triplicate forms and manila envelopes, scrawled notes to himself, an empty spot where Trish's picture had been.

Time to get the hell out of Dodge, go home. He hadn't logged onto his computer bulletin boards for more than a week, and he needed to catch up with surfing the net. If getting tossed out of the office was the only way to get caught up, then so be it.

Grabbing his lightweight jacket, he stopped by the sign-out board and wrote HOME in big black letters by his name. Maybe by the time he returned, the paperwork would have evaporated all by itself.

•
•
•
•
•
•
•

Wednesday

Building 433—T Program

Gary Lesserec contented himself with the lap of luxury while Hal Michaelson wallowed in the armpit of politics.

Lesserec sat back in the ergonomic chair next to one of the workstations linked to the VR chamber. He looked at his fingernails, polished them on his Incredible Hulk T-shirt, then reached forward to grab his second can of Diet Coke.

Hal Michaelson was the one full of thunder and bluster. He hobnobbed with the President and senators and industrial executives. He grabbed the microphone every chance he got and won his funding more through intimidation than technical merit.

Michaelson knew all the right words, knew how to bully his squad of artists into providing the flashiest viewgraphs, the slickest videotapes. He knew how to make his project sound Impressive with a capital "I"— but, Lesserec thought, Michaelson didn't know *squat* about the real VR technology, about the sophistication possible through the nested real-time simulations and the suspended microspheres in the chamber itself. He saw none of the broad applications of the hardware at his fingertips, only his narrow-minded, cockeyed Defense Department scheme. The International Verification Initiative—what a trumped-up joke!

If Michaelson had bothered to be there for the demo he had given the handicapped kids from the Coalition for Family Values, he would have seen for himself. Though he had been annoyed at the time, Lesserec had discovered a whole new possibility for VR therapy, if only Michaelson would get his big, ignorant face out of the picture.

Thinking of the kids' demo reminded him to call that Plutonium Facility technician, Duane Hopkins, to see if he had managed to get the material Lesserec wanted. He hated to wait once he had an idea in his head.

On his workstation Lesserec punched up the status of the routine that T Program's dedicated parallel computer had spent the afternoon concatenating. Danielle, Walter, and Lil were busy debating the best method to set up the Plutonium Facility demonstrations, studying blueprints of Building 332. The Laser Isotope Separation increment was the newest and cleanest-looking part of the facility, though somebody would have to doctor-up a bit of actual work to be done in the area, since that program had slowed down in recent years.

Lesserec cracked his freckled knuckles and rocked back in the chair, staring at the big-screen terminal. The whole Plutonium Facility demonstration seemed a bogus and boring example of VR capabilities, but Lesserec supposed it was a viable example of the actual surveillance techniques the virtual inspectors could use in a foreign nuclear weapons fabrication facility.

Of course, that assumed Michaelson's concept was not fundamentally screwed up—yet it was. Anyone could see that, except Hal Michaelson was too dense—no, too *proud*—to admit it.

Certainly, the microsensors and the sophisticated virtual reality technology made possible the concept of invisible inspectors, who would be able to watch from a distance and see everything. But of course that assumed someone else with sufficient skill and computing power couldn't *alter* what the sensors showed. Lesserec knew how to do that. Michaelson could have put two and two together himself if he'd bothered to understand the implications of his sales pitch.

Some of the T Program people chatted in their cubicles while patching up the minor demo routines, enhancing the Yosemite simulation and the Air Force jet dogfight; but Lesserec worked alone. He always worked alone. That gave him the freedom to concentrate and to add his own enhancements without anyone watching over his shoulder.

Hal Michaelson took all the credit and made the headlines, but Lesserec had developed the core technology himself. Sometimes Michaelson forgot about that.

And he needed to be reminded.

Lesserec had hoped to go up to his new condo with Sandra this weekend and spend a couple days up at Lake Tahoe, where they could enjoy their place, sit in the Jacuzzi, or make love in front of the fireplace. That's the way it should be, now that he could afford the finer things.

The salaries of everyone at the Livermore Lab were a matter of public record; and Lesserec had checked on Michaelson's earnings. Though he was only a group leader, the big man was one of the highest paid employees in the entire complex. Michaelson's ability to bring in outside funding for enormous and prestigious projects made him indispensable.

But his salary was peanuts compared to what one could earn from VR patents and spinoff technologies. The medical benefits, the entertainment possibilities, and a thousand other applications made it asinine to keep the technology locked up in tight security, devoted to a lame and hollow spy system. Lesserec wondered if Michaelson's overbearing enthusiasm had caused a slight case of brain asphyxiation.

Lesserec watched the progress on the terminal screen. The entire file was enormous, maxing out the capabilities of the parallel processor. He had been working on it for months, developing modules at home, fusing them at the Lab, creating something so absolutely mind-blowing it would knock Michaelson flat on his ass. The big man wouldn't know what hit him. Lesserec smiled at that.

He was one of the few people who dared speak his mind to Michaelson. The T Program leader intimidated everyone else, including the Lab Director and a number of prominent congressmen. But Lesserec had been around since the program's inception. He had been one of the bright-eyed boys sitting at the table, kicking back on Michaelson's ranch, brainstorming what they could do.

Lesserec had been younger then, incredibly bright and talented—and wet behind the ears—his own enthusiasm unbridled by the bureaucratic reality of working in a government lab abiding by shelves full of DOE "Tiger Team" regulations and coping with managers more interested in timely reports than in actual progress.

Back then, Lesserec had viewed the entire Virtual Reality project as a thought experiment: *Given appropriate funding and appropriate talent, what is it possible to do?*

He had not realized then that those two assumptions were practically impossible. As a result, T Program preyed on the enthusiasm of starry-eyed students and new graduates—like Walter Shing and Danielle Fawcett—who came in and dumped their brainpower into the project, working incredibly long weeks. T Program squeezed them dry and then tossed them aside to pick up another batch of bright young researchers. That technique kept the project working at a frenzied level at all times, producing the impossible and gaining a grudging respect from those others who operated in a normal routine. *Nothing was truly impossible.*

And now Gary Lesserec had created his masterpiece: a simulation that went far beyond anything Michaelson had imagined in his most gushing presentations to Congressional subcommittees, far beyond even the Yosemite simulation. The new NanoWare chips he had installed made the capabilities an order of magnitude more sophisticated. The tactile response, canned smells, ultraphonic sounds, accelerometers, and the boggling graphics made this the best, most-intense experience ever produced on Planet Earth.

The mainframe took several hours, eating enough of the parallel machine's capacity that a handful of other T Program workers came out to Lesserec to bug him about how long he was going to be. Everything else was running as if the disk drives were full of molasses, but Lesserec had finally compiled the entire simulation for the VR chamber. The chips could handle it.

He had never run anything like this before, but he

was going to save it for Hal Michaelson. Michaelson, unsuspecting, would think he was just going to see himself floating above the clouds again while fighter jets zipped about below him.

But this was more, much more.

Michaelson wouldn't know what hit him.

And *then* he'd believe.

Wednesday

Building 433—T Program
Virtual Reality Chamber

Another wasted day. Hal Michaelson bitterly wondered what he had to show for it.

Hours thrown down the toilet to tour one more program that boob Aragon would eventually muck up; then he had been called to the Director's office for another meeting, a recap of the IVI and arrangements for the visit from the foreign nationals. The Director didn't seem to know whether to rage at Michaelson for going behind his back or to beam in awe at the amount of funding Michaelson's project would bring to the Lab. More hours down the toilet.

Lack of sleep was catching up with him; he would have to work through dinner, grab a sandwich at the cafeteria, pull an all-nighter before he'd feel caught up enough to go home. He'd have to return to Washington within the week to hold hands there, too—and he couldn't put off the meeting with Diana any longer, either. He asked himself for the thousandth time if the glory was worth all the bullshit.

He turned the government car into the empty lot outside the T Program trailer complex, dismayed to see that most of his workers had already left for the evening. He himself hadn't even been back to his house, coming straight from the airport. What the hell gave them the right to go home *on time?* Heads would roll in the morning, Michaelson vowed, and he would enjoy letting off some steam.

In the gathering darkness, parking-lot lights radiated yellow circles of sodium light. The Lab's thick-tired red bicycles lay abandoned on the sidewalk where they had been left by employees during the day. Behind dark miniblinds, lights burned in three offices of the T Program trailer complex.

In the big-budget glory days during the Cold War, many buildings on-site would still be lit up, researchers working through the night refining nuclear designs, directed-energy weapons, and sophisticated space sensors.

Michaelson went up to the mirrored CAIN booth door that guarded access to the restricted T Program area. Closing the heavy door of the booth behind him, the lock clicked and the badge reader waited for him. Michaelson fumbled with his laminated green badge. He sneezed, feeling uncomfortable and itchy all over. *Damned allergies starting up again,* he thought.

The LCD display in the badge reader blinked as Michaelson slid the badge into the slot, magnetic strip down. He punched in his PIN code 0-1-3-7, the inverse of the fine structure constant. *Access approved.* The inside lock clicked open, and he shoved the door wide, stepping into the dim T Program trailer offices. Empty and quiet, a few lights burning but nobody home.

Out of habit, he snagged his special blue T Program badge from the rack on the wall, clipping it to his shirt. He set his mouth, steamed to find no one present. Long lunch breaks, going home early—these people were getting lazy.

He had faxed explicit instructions to Gary Lesserec, but

apparently his deputy didn't care about meeting deadlines or providing specific milestones. With the President's speech Michaelson had launched T Program on the most exciting phase of its existence, a history-making mission. The place should have been pulsing with excitement, hackers busy pumping up simulations, engineers installing modifications to the VR chamber, techs distributing the tiny sensors for appropriate visual input. To make the IVI succeed, a thousand pieces would have to come together smoothly—all at once—and *right now.* The multinational task force would arrive within three short weeks to observe the first full-blown demonstration.

Heads wouldn't just roll, he thought—he'd launch them into orbit!

Gary Lesserec was bright, but not as bright as he thought he was. His talent didn't excuse him from shirking his duties. Michaelson already planned to recruit a replacement for the young upstart as soon as he could, but now he reminded himself to stop wasting time. He needed to get another hotshot enthusiast fresh from grad school who would be glassy-eyed and happy for the chance to work eighty hours a week if it meant he could play a role in the IVI.

Michaelson worked his way through the cluttered tech cubicles back to his own office. He snatched at the yellow sticky note taped on his door and read: HAL—I SENT THE TECHS HOME EARLY SO I COULD RUN A FULL SYSTEM BACKUP OF THE CHAMBER. I'LL REINITIATE THE CHAMBER EARLY TOMORROW. UPGRADED CHIPS INSTALLED. GOT A NEW SIMULATION READY TO RUN IF YOU WANT TO TAKE A TEST DRIVE—GARY. Lesserec had drawn a little smiley face at the bottom of the page as his stupid signature.

Michaelson crumpled the note and tossed it into the

green metal trash can. *System backup?* he thought. *Upgraded chips?* What the hell was Lesserec doing? They wasted time on full-system backups only before making a substantial modification. With the IVI announced only yesterday, Michaelson had allotted a good two weeks of upgrading before the system was ready for a backup; more wasted time, wasted effort, a poor administrative decision.

Want to take a test drive? Lesserec was goofing off, oblivious to the importance of his own project. That did it—no one was indispensable.

Fuming, Michaelson unlocked his office and powered up his workstation, thinking of the words for a new job posting. He rubbed his palms on his slacks, feeling tingly and itchy again; this time his face felt hot, scratchy. *Damned kid is getting to me.* He wondered if somebody had messed with the thermostat.

Scooting his chair up to the keyboard, he tapped out a terse memo describing Gary Lesserec's job position. Tansy could clean up the wording, and he'd cram it through the Internal Transfer office in the morning.

Michaelson sat back to think, though, and the ergonomic chair creaked with his bulk. What he really needed to do was find the perfect person for Lesserec's job first, *then* post the notice; if he didn't have the right replacement in mind, it could turn out to be another disaster.

Besides, thanks to the Lab's prehistoric hiring procedures, Michaelson couldn't just fire Lesserec outright. He had to play along with policy just to make everything appear fair. That would mean another delay.

Michaelson viewed the Livermore rules as obstacles to get around, blockades thrown up by incompetents. Bureaucratic rules, made up by beancounters who had nothing better to do: boobs like José Aragon, who had been promoted beyond their capability to do any real job.

Michaelson printed a copy of the memo and stuffed it into his upper desk drawer. He would have to make phone calls in the morning, ponder who might be a good replacement. The smart-ass kid who always wore inane superhero T-shirts had outlasted his usefulness.

Deciding he could do no more tonight, Michaelson shut down, rubbing his hands and face again. Damn, that burned—he wondered if he had picked up some kind of rash. He thought of how good it would feel to go home, mix himself a drink, take a long shower, then go to bed.

But as he headed out of his office, he stared down the long back hall at the empty VR chamber.

Got a new simulation ready to run if you want to take a test drive. Even though Michaelson had complete access, he saw that the door was propped partly open, inviting. The chamber was dark. He glanced around, seeing only the glowing phosphors of Lesserec's workstation and other terminals blinking as the main system computers crunched away.

A test drive? Michaelson had no idea what Lesserec had been developing, probably another one of his "consulting projects" instead of doing IVI work. "This better be good," he muttered.

He scanned Lesserec's desk, seeing at the clutter of scratch paper, code printouts, technical reports, and a toy Snoopy model. Michaelson frowned at a photo of Lesserec and his model-beautiful girlfriend standing on the rocky shore of a deep-blue lake.

Michaelson picked up the photograph. Lesserec sported a wide, goofy grin; his red hair and white legs made him look like a bloated fish just pulled from the icy depths. The girlfriend was dark-haired, sleek, and tan, making the couple an unlikely pair. Michaelson snorted and placed the picture down. What did she see in a twit like Lesserec? But he knew very well how appealing some women found quick-witted young men. His own attraction to Amber, Diana Unteling, and all the others rose in his mind.

After all, despite his faults and screwed-up priorities, Lesserec *had* developed the algorithms that turned the virtual reality chamber into a playground for the gods. But that still didn't excuse Lesserec's arrogance and lack of responsibility. He wondered how far the little dweeb had gotten with the IVI prep while he had been gone.

Michaelson hunched over Lesserec's workstation. In the primary window tiny icons dotted the layout as a flowchart of the VR chamber appeared on the screen.

Fidgeting, rubbing his hands and cheeks, Michaelson glanced over the modifications to the virtual reality software, trying to decipher what Lesserec had done.

By now the burning sensation had spread over his palms and the backs of his hands. He looked down, expecting to see angry red skin, but found instead a whitish pale appearance to his hands. He must have gotten into something.

He punched in the final loading procedure for the new VR simulation. The icon of the small jet fighter denoting the Nellis AFB simulation had disappeared, replaced by the stylized drawing of a tiny mountain with smoke around its top. Lesserec had gotten rid of the aircraft simulation! What the hell?

A few taps on the keyboard confirmed that no other routine remained in the parallel processor, only one new memory-hogging simulation. Michaelson stared at the workstation screen, appalled.

Distracted from the fiery itching that continued to spread, Michaelson angrily used the menu-driven directions on the screen to power up the chamber. A minute passed and the screen blinked green, indicating that the simulation was ready.

Michaelson straightened and stomped down the hall toward the open vault door. "This had better be damned good, Lesserec or I'll rip off your head myself."

A red glow pulsed from inside the VR chamber; light streamed onto the floor from the door. Michaelson entered, holding a hand up to shield his eyes from the ruddy brightness.

He closed the heavy door, and instantly gray curls of holographic smoke swept around him. He couldn't see through the illusion, but he could smell burning sulfur, one of the packets from the scent-simulators. "What the hell is that?" he muttered.

Shapes drifted in and out of focus through the dull red smoke, as if the software running the chamber had somehow gone awry. He wondered if Lesserec had made a forest fire simulation. What a waste of time!

A loud rumble came from within the walls and floor, the big wall speakers and vibration panels. With a blast of hot air, the smoke cleared. Hal Michaelson found himself transported to another world, one far more realistic than he had ever seen.

Leafy fern fronds towered over him as red sunlight speckled across the earthy ground. A breeze ruffled the plants, sounding like scratchy fingernails, bringing a stench of methane and keratome-impregnated gas. The air dripped with humidity, and the light seemed grainy and thick.

A ratcheting sound just to his right made him jump. A dragonfly the size of a model airplane bore down with chainsaw wings and angrily buzzed around him, its green eyes as large as oscilloscope screens. Michaelson swatted the giant insect away as it dive-bombed in, smacking his hand against a hard exoskeleton. *Damn, that hurt!*

The rash on his hands seemed to ignite with pain, and his face felt as if it wanted to peel off. He tried rubbing, then digging deep with his fingernails, but the burning grew worse. He felt as if he had fallen into a pit of glass fibers, and he couldn't make the itching go away.

His heart raced, and he remembered the times in Washington he had overexerted himself. He looked for the door. Enough of Lesserec's smoke and jungles and giant bugs.

Something crashed through the towering palms behind him with a deep-throated roar. Michaelson heard armored tree trunks splinter, and he felt the ground shake as a thick swatch of smooth gray rumbled past, blocking the low orange sun. Looking up, and up, Michaelson saw long, razor teeth set in a steam-shovel-sized reptilian jaw. *A dinosaur?*

He backed up. *This isn't real—it's just a simulation!* The wall of teeth turned toward him and the mouth opened in another subsonic wail. Beady, coldly intelligent eyes locked on him.

Michaelson caught a sickening blast of keratome as the teeth moved closer. The reptile thrust its head through the dense foliage above, breaking branches and ripping trees from their roots. A shriveled head, outlined with gray outer skin and set apart by two eyes the size of grapefruits, thrust down. The head was as big as a chest of drawers; the yellowed teeth were the size of baseball bats with chunks of red flesh hanging between the incisors.

Michaelson fell into the peaty mud, stunned. He clawed backward, trying to get away, but his hands and face seemed to explode with the burning pain. The monster's breath made him sick to his stomach.

Still moving away, Michaelson closed his eyes, but the red pulsing light wouldn't go away. The burning . . .

It's not real! Damn you, Lesserec!

He backed against a spiky fern tree. The dinosaur heaved its entire body into the clearing, thudding on piston legs. Its head swung back and forth, sniffing, searching for Michaelson, jaws agape.

He screamed, searching for the door to the chamber to shut the thing down. The images might just be simulations, but the pain was definitely real. He couldn't breathe . . . the agony in his hands was fire now, his face started melting, dripping off and pooling to the prehistoric earth.

With a hissing explosion, a volcano split the ground and erupted nearby, geysering molten rock. The dinosaur shrieked and honked as burning rock pelted its hide. It fell, writhing and burning. The primeval forest burst into flames.

Michaelson still couldn't find the door. With a great blast, the volcano showered him with incandescent lava, searing—

Tearing at his face with liquid metal hands, Michaelson tried to rip out his eyes to stop the pain. . . .

CHAPTER SEVENTEEN

Thursday

Building 433—T Program
Virtual Reality Chamber

Four hours of sleep and a lot of coffee was all Gary Lesserec needed to start the day.

Showing up at 6:45 A.M. at the Lawrence Livermore National Laboratory, he was able to claim the best parking spot in the minuscule open lot nearest to the fence surrounding the T Program trailers. He enjoyed coming in even before the other early risers showed up, able to get more done in the first quiet hour than he managed to accomplish during the rest of the day with the phones ringing and the offices bustling.

Inside, the T Program trailer was utterly silent. As he passed through the CAIN booth into the Exclusion Area, Lesserec flicked on only a few banks of the fluorescent lights, leaving the trailer in a comforting gray gloom that emphasized the quiet.

The light in Michaelson's office was on, but the big guy was nowhere to be seen behind his desk. *Just like him,* Lesserec thought, *completely oblivious to the world around him.* The rest of the trailer completely shut down to conserve energy, and Michaelson happily went home, leaving his own lights burning all night.

Not maliciously, just not noticing and not caring. The world revolved around Hal Michaelson, after all.

Lesserec powered on his workstation and keyed in his password to access the parallel processor. When the system came up, Lesserec checked the log and saw that Michaelson had indeed gone into the VR chamber the night before and had activated the new simulation, Lesserec's masterpiece. He hoped the new chips had done their stuff.

But he didn't want anyone else to know about it—not yet. For now, it was just a small example to keep Michaelson aware of who really did the work around here, who was the true brains and imagination behind T Program.

Michaelson was just a mouthpiece. He and Hal had an understanding; and now, after having his mind blown by the incredible entertainment simulation, Lesserec was sure that Michaelson understood in a way that he had never done before.

Lesserec removed his entire package from the computer. He had a stack of the original disks at home, and it would take hours to recompile the simulation for use; but he didn't want it clogging up the machine, and he didn't want anyone else stumbling into it. The simulation was available to the right people, if they really wanted to see it; but for now Lesserec would play his cards close to his chest.

He stood up, cracked his knuckles, and went to the small kitchenette. He yanked open the white door of the refrigerator. A bright yellow Notice sticker insisted the refrigerator was to be used for food items only—no film, batteries, or hazardous chemicals allowed.

The bottom and middle shelves were filled entirely

with cans of Diet Coke, cases and cases bought from the local warehouse store, the cost of which was shared evenly by all T Program members. A few long-forgotten lunches lay tucked at the back of the top shelf, and a box of rock-hard sesame-carob fudge leftover from the Christmas party.

Lesserec snagged a cold can, popped the top and slurped a big mouthful. He'd had enough coffee before leaving his home, while Sandra continued to sleep.

Holding the can of Coke, he sauntered down the trailer's carpeted back corridor. The VR chamber was still sealed shut, and Lesserec worked the access panel, slipping his badge into the reader and keying in his PIN. The vault door popped open.

Inside the silent, featureless chamber he found the body of Hal Michaelson lying contorted and motionless on the floor.

Michaelson looked like a roadkill sprawled with his arms and legs bent at odd angles. His face and his hands had a sickly pale appearance like the soft white underbelly of a fish floating dead in a tank.

Lesserec bent over, his heart pounding. He looked into the expression of agony on Michaelson's dead face.

"Gross," he said, then hurried off to call Security.

The Protective Services Officer used his master keys to get into the emergency exit door of the T Program trailer, and Lesserec ushered him down the halls. The PSO didn't know what had happened, obviously expecting something like a security breach or a tripped alarm that had not shown up on the monitors.

The guard had short blond hair cut in a butch and wore a dark-blue uniform that fit like Spandex. His keys jingled, and the leather on the gun holster at his side squeaked as he strode forward; the walkie-talkie at his left hip squawked and hissed.

"Okay, so what's the problem?" the PSO asked. His face had the scrubbed pink appearance from sunburn.

"Right this way," Lesserec said, leading him down the hall toward the VR chamber. "I hope you like paperwork and publicity. This is going to be a real pain in the ass."

He swung open the heavy door to the VR chamber. When the PSO saw Michaelson's body on the floor, his jaw dropped as comically as a cartoon figure. He swayed back, grabbing the door jamb.

"Oh, my God," the PSO said. He froze, unwilling to step in farther.

Glad I could count on you in an emergency, Lesserec thought. *A real man of action.*

"What happened?" the PSO asked again.

"He died, that's what happened," Lesserec said scornfully. "Aren't you going to investigate or something?"

The PSO grabbed the walkie-talkie at his hip. "I'm calling for backup," he said. "Who is this guy?"

"You don't know?" Lesserec answered in disbelief. "I admit"—he looked down at the corpse's contorted face—"he's not very photogenic right now, but he has been in the news a lot. That's Hal Michaelson. The guy on TV with the President the other night?"

"You mean *that* Michaelson?" The PSO blinked his eyes. "Oh, boy."

The PSO clicked the button on his walkie-talkie and spoke rapid-fire into it: "We've got a situation here. A dead body in the Virtual Reality chamber over at T Program. It's apparently Dr. Hal Michaelson, the head of the project."

"Say again," the walkie-talkie said.

Lesserec reached out and grabbed the PSO's arm. "Do you realize you just blabbed all that over an open channel?"

The PSO blinked. "What?"

"Your walkie-talkie. Don't they drill you guys on operating procedures? Newshounds listen on the open-band scanners just to pick up a scoop like this. You just blew the story before we could put together an official Lab press release."

"But," the PSO said, still sweating, "it's too early in the morning. Nobody'll be listening."

"Get real. Those people watch like vultures to see if we've had another tritium release or a security breach or anything. You just told the whole world that the head of the President's new high-visibility initiative is lying here dead." Lesserec shook his head. "This place is going to be a circus in less than an hour."

The walkie-talkie squawked again. "Hello? Apparent cause of death? Please advise," the voice asked back.

The PSO wet his lips and looked at Lesserec. Lesserec put his hands on his hips and blew air through his lips. "Go ahead, the cat's already out of the bag."

"But . . . how did he die?"

"Do I look like a coroner? How should I know?" Lesserec said. "Heart attack, I think."

The PSO clicked the SEND button again. "Uh, apparent coronary arrest. Request backup. We need to get the body over to Medical. We're going to get a lot of publicity on this."

"Acknowledged. Backup on its way," the voice answered. "Will call Health Services and get them ready for an emergency inspection."

Visibly shaking, the PSO shoved the walkie-talkie back in its holder at his hip.

Lesserec looked around the VR lab. "A lot of this stuff is highly classified. I've already cleared the computers and locked up the classified documents Michaelson had lying around. We've got to put black cloth over all this equipment. Even just the shapes of some of this stuff is Secret National Security Information. Anybody who doesn't have a need to know can't get a glimpse of it—including *you,* so don't pay attention."

Flustered, the PSO said, "Uh, yes. Let's get to work and clean this place up."

The T Program members knew something was up when they came to work because of the flurry of police cars and the extra scrutiny when they entered the double gates into the T Program trailers.

Lesserec called a meeting at 9:00, although the hot-shot programmers pretty much came in at all hours of the morning, whenever they pleased. Lesserec assumed he would have to give the same information repeatedly.

He stood, crossed his pudgy arms over his T-shirt, and looked at the confused programmers sitting around the table. No Doritos this time. No festive atmosphere of making catcalls during the President's news conference.

"All right, listen up," Lesserec said. Rumors had been flying for the last hour, and some of the rumors were right by sheer chance. "You already know something's happening," he said.

Walter called out, "Now presenting, Gary Lesserec, Master of the Obvious!"

Lesserec ignored the catcall. "Michaelson's dead. I found his body this morning in the VR chamber. Look's to me like a heart attack while he was working late last night, but we won't know until the Health Services looks him over. He might have to be taken down to Valley Memorial Hospital for a full autopsy.

"Regardless of the cause, he's dead. And that means it's up to us to put together the whole dog-and-pony show our dear friend Hal set up for us."

He gave a short, barking laugh. "Knowing him, I almost think he did this on purpose, and right now his ghost is laughing at us. Michaelson was always shoving us into quicksand and walking off with the rope."

He sat back down again and looked at their reactions. "Lab management has to make everything tidy and official, but for the moment I'm still acting group leader. I don't want it, and they'll probably post the job, but you know the blinding speed anything official happens around here. They can't possibly get anybody else to pick up the reins fast enough to get this international demonstration done in time. It's going to be crazy to finish it, but a lot of the Lab's prestige rides on this.

"I'm open to your suggestions, but my gut feeling is we should not ask for a postponement, because a delay will look like we don't have our act together."

He lowered his voice and leaned across the table, meeting the scattered stunned expressions. "We don't need a whole lot of talking the next four weeks. We need a lot of work. We need to finish setting up the virtual presence inside the Plutonium Facility for the first-stage demonstration. I'll be coordinating with the folks out at the Nevada Test Site so we can rig up the full downhole simulation that Michaelson wanted us to show off.

"I've already talked to NTS this morning. They are in as much chaos over there as we are. Testing has been shut down for years, and just to get it up and running again is keeping them at Warp Nine. They're gonna set up a preliminary test detonation for us with two thousand tons of high explosive so that we can calibrate our sensors and get a good feel for what it's like to watch the explosion through virtual presence."

Danielle raised her hand and then stuttered as if she didn't know what to say. "But . . . but what about Dr. Michaelson? Shouldn't we . . . take a . . . take a day off or something?"

"And what?" Lesserec raised his voice. "People die, the program goes on. Any other questions?" He stared at them, pleased to see everyone flinch. "All right, then let's get back to work."

Thursday

Oakland, California

Loud ringing pierced a fuzzy-headed morning, shattering the vivid reds, yellows, and blues of an impossible dream. Rising through the depths of sleep, Craig Kreident knew he didn't have to go to work. If he waited long enough, the ringing would stop.

But instead of melting away with the dream, the noise continued until it bore through the fog in his brain. So much for sleeping in.

Craig rolled to his right and slapped at the speakerphone. "Hello?" His mouth tasted dry, cottony. Sunlight streamed through a window, illuminating a bright yellow rectangle on the hardwood floor.

"Craig, this is June. June Atwood." Her voice sounded loud and tinny from the speaker.

He lifted to an elbow and glanced at the clock, blinking 9:03 in red numbers. "Yes, ma'am. What's going on?" His mind started to clear from the sleep. "If I'd known you were going to call this early, I wouldn't have stayed up partying so late."

"Sorry to wake you. But you did make me promise to call if something came up."

Craig sat up and swung his legs to the side of the bed,

wrapping the sheet around him. "I can be downtown in half an hour. Did the NanoWare—"

"This is something different, Craig. A field job."

Craig's hopes dropped upon hearing June's matter-of-fact tone. What did she have in mind? Asking him to appear before a middle school assembly, speaking about his career as a G-man? "I'm listening."

"You're the most experienced agent I've got in high-tech investigations. This morning there was a suspicious death on Federal property—at the Lawrence Livermore National Lab. A bigwig scientist was found dead in a sealed area early this morning. The preliminary inspection from the Livermore medical department found high concentrations of some kind of acid on the body."

"Acid? Like the Phantom of the Opera?" Craig asked.

"Not quite so gruesome, but this guy . . . didn't have a pleasant time dying."

"Sounds suspicious to me," Craig said.

"It gets more complicated," June continued. "There's some sort of high-level multinational team coming out to Livermore in a few weeks, by invitation of the President himself. Couldn't be worse timing, so we've got to look good. Go in, talk to a few people, bless the scene so we can rule the death an accident."

"*Was* it an accident?"

"You tell me."

Craig's mind clicked into the problem at hand, focusing his full attention. June rattled off the details of how Gary Lesserec had found Michaelson's body, and the subsequent uproar. "Death occurred in one of their Exclusion Areas, whatever that means. Top-Secret place, I suppose. We're getting a provisional security clearance sent over there for you within the hour. Naturally our

FBI clearances don't mean anything to the DOE folks, so you'll have an escort at all times."

Craig thought fast: he still had to shave, shower and hit the can. But he kept plenty of clean suits hanging in the closet. "I can be there by ten-thirty."

June's voice sounded grim. "I sure hope you find out it's a straightforward, natural death."

"You know it never turns out to be as simple as that, June," he said with a sigh. "I just hope these scientists don't get confused about who's on their side."

CHAPTER NINETEEN

Thursday

**Sheraton Inn
Pleasanton, California**

It was a snobbish thing to do, really. Diana Unteling still had friends in Livermore, dozens of them, and longtime ties that went back for years, long before her husband had formed the Coalition for Family Values. She could have stayed in a nice home close to the Lab; she could have received a home-cooked breakfast after the hard night of traveling, had someone to chat with over morning coffee.

But this wasn't a social trip. Friends would ask too many questions, and she needed time alone to deal with Hal Michaelson.

The Sheraton Inn in Pleasanton, ten miles west of the Livermore nuclear lab, allowed Diana to blend in with other travelers. No one really gave a flip at the Sheraton if she was a Deputy Assistant Secretary of Energy or the Queen of France. She and Hal had met here a dozen times during their years-long affair, but now just the thought of him sent a wave of uneasiness and tension through her.

No one would notice her comings and goings this time, either.

Diana came down to breakfast with the freebie hotel copy of the *San Francisco Chronicle* tucked under her arm. She decided to skip the complimentary breakfast buffet and ordered a pot of coffee and a Danish. Sleeping in—and simmering anger toward Hal—had soured her appetite, and the three-hour time difference screwed up her metabolism.

Spreading the newspaper in front of her, she ignored the local "puff" news and turned to the national section. She was thankful that the Sheraton had stopped handing out *USA Today;* once she had moved from Livermore to Washington, she had grown too used to the *Washington Post,* or "Pravda on the Potomac," as Hal called it.

She scowled at the thought of him again: tall, imposing, with his pencil-thin mustache and domineering personality that made him seem like a grizzly bear on the outside, but a teddy bear on the inside. *Why hadn't he returned her calls?*

Arriving in Livermore late after taking the last flight from Washington, D.C., she had spent the previous day hanging out at Hal Michaelson's dim and empty ranch house. She knew where Hal hid the spare key, and she had slipped in and waited for him—and waited and waited—but he never showed up. She got more furious with him as the hours went by.

The success of his International Verification Initiative must have really gone to his head, not that Hal's ego had ever been small.

In the Sheraton restaurant Diana took a sip of her coffee and tried to concentrate on the paper, but her thoughts kept coming back to Hal. He wasn't at his home, and all the previous afternoon no one at the Virtual Reality lab would admit he was there. She had refused to leave her name or leave the number of the Sheraton, but no one could be that busy, not even Hal.

Yesterday, she had grown livid with him for making her waste an entire day. She couldn't afford to wait any longer, not if she had to prepare for her Senate confirmation hearing. She had fudged one too many imaginary business trips to Livermore already, and she had to get back to DOE Headquarters. If Hal didn't want anything else to do with her, that left only one thing to do.

She reassembled the paper and folded it, automatically tucking it under her arm. Diana smoothed her skirt, bumping the chair backward. Her deep-blue suit with white hose would stand out as too formal at the Livermore Lab, but here at breakfast among the high-tech entrepreneurs on the outskirts of Silicon Valley, she was just another hard-charging visitor to the Bay Area. She gulped her coffee, ignored most of her Danish, and left a tip that was more than twice the cost of her breakfast. She clicked out of the hotel restaurant.

Classical music played in the background of the hotel lobby, competing with the low tone of TV news from the lounge. A uniformed doorman, in a scarlet jacket, stood just outside the wide glass entry, waiting to open the door for guests. Diana fished in her purse for the rental car keys, but froze when she heard a reference to the Lawrence Livermore National Laboratory on CNN.

She was unable to make out what the talking head on the news program was saying. She left the doorman holding the door as she turned back to approach the television set. When Lawrence Livermore got mentioned on the news it was usually because of some kind of scandal, which made her work at DOE even more difficult. Therefore it was better to find out as soon as possible.

As she drew near, hearing more words than she wanted to, all the little details seemed to stand out in bright spotlights for her. Her steps came slower and slower. She gripped the newspaper under her arm, making the paper crackle. Her right hand clutched her purse, the rental car keys pressing a sharp indentation into her palm.

". . . to repeat, unconfirmed reports that controversial scientist Hal Michaelson, recently appointed director of the President's new International Verification Initiative, was found dead early this morning from unknown causes. Officials at the Lawrence Livermore National Laboratory, the nuclear design facility located forty miles east of San Francisco, have refused to make a statement, prompting rumors of politics and foul play. Also in the news this half hour . . ."

Diana stopped in the lobby, unable to move, afraid she might lose her balance. She was exhausted as she stared at the TV screen, unable to fully comprehend what the news anchor had said.

She wavered and held out a hand to support herself against a planter filled with plastic flowers. The car keys slipped from her hand and jangled to the carpet. A moment later the newspaper fell as well, fluttering into strewn sections.

Diana didn't know how long she stood in the lobby, as her eyes and mind focused on events in the past. Highlights from the last three years played over and over in her head, with Hal Michaelson cast in the starring role.

Diana felt pressure on her elbow. She turned to see a

young red-haired woman standing beside her, dressed in the ubiquitous uniform of the Sheraton staff. "Ma'am, can I help you? Are you all right?"

It took Diana a moment to recall where she was. "No, thank you. I'm fine."

The woman bent and picked up Diana's newspaper and held out the car keys. "Are you sure? Is anything the matter?"

"No." Diana shook her head and bit her lip, trying but unable to clamp down her customary ice mask. She couldn't stop the tears. "Everything is fine. Fine."

CHAPTER TWENTY

Thursday

Lawrence Livermore National Laboratory
Livermore, California

Off Vasco Road the Lawrence Livermore National Laboratory spread out before him, a square mile of office buildings, laboratories, trailer complexes, and gigantic experimental facilities, enclosed within a chain-link fence topped by barbed wire.

Although he had been an FBI agent for the past six years, Craig Kreident still felt a tension at the bottom of his stomach whenever he began a new case.

He switched off the cassette player in his car as he drove up to the triangular white building that housed the Lab's badge office, just outside the guard kiosk and the fence. He felt as if he were standing on the fringe of a different world.

The FBI had always been aware of COMSEC—communications security—and the all-too-real possibility of espionage. But these "Livermorons" routinely dealt with classified material. Even after the Cold War, Third World countries still drooled over U.S. national security information, since they had none of the large budgets, computer capabilities, or sophisticated manufacturing techniques to create the latest weapons of war.

Inside the badge office, Craig waited at the long white counter behind two consultants in suits and a woman in a white Navy uniform. Up front a man and a twenty-something businesswoman argued loudly with a stoic white-haired woman behind the counter; three others, obviously part of the same group, stood like guard dogs beside an assortment of gleaming cameras, folded silver tripods, leather cases bearing the call letters of a local TV station, and videotapes in black plastic boxes.

Sliding into an air of practiced patience, Craig took his place in line. Out of habit he straightened his tie and brushed the front of his dark suit, then folded his hands behind his back. He kept his smile well hidden behind a professional expression as he caught snippets of the heated battle between the reporters and the woman at the counter.

Before Craig could hear details about the squabble, he felt a touch at his elbow. "Excuse me, are you Mr. Kreident?" a woman's voice asked.

His FBI training for analysis kicked in as he turned and saw the deepest blue eyes he'd ever seen. The young lady was tall, at least five-ten, with hair the color of a sun-washed beach. She had a cheery but no-nonsense smile, someone who considered herself a colleague and equal until proven otherwise. He tried to guess her age—twenty-five?—before she held out her hand.

"I'm Paige Mitchell from the Protocol Office. I'll be your security escort and run interference if you hit any bureaucratic snafu."

Craig blinked and held out his hand to shake hers briskly. "Pleased to meet you, Ms. Mitchell." Then he pulled a dark brown wallet from his coat pocket, flipped it open and handed it to her.

She held the wallet between her fingers and took the time to inspect the ID. Unlike most people Craig had met, Paige seemed serious about studying the laminated card. "Good enough," she said, handing it back to him.

He let loose only a fraction of the smile his lips wanted to make. "I hope I don't cause you too many problems."

She turned, distracted as the man at the counter thrust his hands up in the air and stomped over to the video equipment. The twenty-something woman next to him continued to argue in a frostbitten voice as the badge office employee listened patiently but without any real interest.

Paige nodded to a room off to the side. "It's been a zoo here ever since news of Dr. Michaelson's death was leaked. Every TV crew wants to crawl inside to get shots of the virtual reality chamber, but we don't allow news cameras on site. It's going to get worse over the next few hours."

She sighed, tossed her hair back, and then smiled at him. "But at least we've got *your* paperwork all set. Follow me, Mr. Kreident. Once you get badged, I'll take you out to T Program, show you around, answer whatever questions I can."

Paige nodded to a small reception room off to the side. "Step over here. We need to set you up with a temporary photo badge and a dosimeter."

"A dosimeter? Do I need to worry about radiation?" Craig said, trying not to sound alarmed.

"We all wear one." Paige tapped her own green photo badge to indicate a small plastic case behind it. "I doubt you'll be going into any laboratory areas where radioactive materials are actually present."

"I was just curious, Ms. Mitchell," Craig said briskly.

Paige looked at him for nearly a full second. "Mr. Kreident, we're pretty informal around here. We'll get along a lot better right from the start if you don't call me ma'am and if you don't call me Miz. How about calling me Paige?"

Craig swallowed uncomfortably and, though it went against his personality to do so, he felt obligated to make the same offer. "Then I suppose you'd better call me Craig. Just to keep things even."

"Kay-O." Paige shuffled through green and yellow forms in a folder tucked against her right elbow and hip. She pulled out several for him to sign before handing him a green laminated badge that bore his full name, the block letters FBI, and an expiration date exactly thirty days in the future displayed prominently on the front.

Then she steered him to one of three bulky devices that looked like government-designed bathroom scales with a digital console and black foam-wrapped handles that extended to the floor.

"Go ahead and get on," said Paige. "When it asks, punch in a four-digit personal identification number. Whatever you want. That'll be your secret code." She smiled in a way that made him wonder how serious she was. He had the faint impression she was pulling his leg, but he maintained his professional cool.

Craig slid the laminated badge into the reader; the words WELCOME TO LAWRENCE LIVERMORE flashed across the tiny screen in sharp LCD letters.

After he had entered his PIN, Paige said, "You'll need to remember that number to get inside our Restricted

Areas and Exclusion Areas. You'll enter through a CAIN booth that has a scale embedded in the floor. If your weight is five percent different from what you've just been weighed at, the computer will deny your access. So don't go on a binge with all the fine Livermore cuisine during your assignment here." She laughed at his mystified expression. "Just a joke—we're not known for our overabundance of good restaurants in this town."

"Ah." He forced a smile. "Does CAIN stand for something?"

"Controlled Access by Individual Numbers. It's like a TV/badge-reading booth."

"Sounds like *Get Smart*," Craig said.

"That's the impression the general public has of 'top secret government research labs.' I think you'll find we're a lot like any other business park or campus." She handed him a copy of his forms, which he filed in his briefcase.

Craig kept focused on the matter at hand. "Won't there be any guards at these booths?" he asked.

"Normally they're just at the main gate and patrolling the site. Budget cutbacks. It's cheaper to have an automatic system than it is to keep guards in every building. Oh, and you should know that we don't call them guards—they're Protective Service Officers. PSOs."

Craig looked into her blue, blue eyes. "PSOs. I'll remember that . . . Paige."

"Very good!" She smiled. "And we don't have secretaries, either. They're all administrative assistants."

He rolled his eyes, just barely. "I see. I suppose you don't have janitors either?"

"Custodians."

"Gardeners?"

"Botanical resource specialists."

His eyes widened, and she laughed. "Just kidding. Come on, now that you're badged I can take you over to T Program."

Craig slid a small notebook out of his suit pocket and clicked a pen. "Could you tell me what the *T* stands for?"

Paige shook her head. "Not in a million years. A lot of our programs and divisions have letters, but nobody alive knows what they mean." She put a finger to her lips, and her face softened into a mischievous expression. "I think if you arrange all the letters into an anagram, you can spell the words to the *Mr. Ed* theme song."

"What?" Craig asked, completely baffled.

Paige sighed. "You don't have a sense of humor, do you, Mr. Kreident?"

"Not on duty, ma'am," he said.

They both chuckled lightly. "All right, that's a start," Paige said. "Let's go. I have a government van."

They passed the defeated-looking news crew on their way out; the group sat sullenly in the corner while the lead reporter spoke into a public pay phone.

Stepping outdoors, Craig fumbled in his shirt pocket to put on sunglasses. The glare wasn't too bad today with a high, thin overcast, but he knew he'd have a headache within minutes if he didn't filter the light.

Paige led him to an old-model Chevy van with a number 2 painted on the hood. "Climb on in. The T Program complex is halfway across the lab."

As soon as Craig buckled his seat belt, Paige pulled out of the small badge office parking lot and headed for the guard shack at the main gate.

"Ready for the standard visitor briefing?" Paige kept her hands on the wheel as they waited for several bicyclists to go by. "LLNL was originally an old Naval Air

Station. After Los Alamos built the first atomic bomb, Edward Teller—one of the scientists who developed the H bomb—wanted to establish a sister lab to compete in designing nuclear weapons, to serve as a 'peer review,' like in a normal university, only at the secret level, of course."

Paige pulled up to the badge checkpoint, and the guard—Protective Service Officer, Craig corrected himself—reached through the window to touch their badges and wave them on.

Driving off, Paige said, "The PSOs are required to touch each badge, supposedly to make sure they actually notice you. You won't find a real heavy security presence in here, though. It's visible but not obtrusive."

"Reminds me of Quantico," said Craig. "The Marines were always running around, training for one thing or another."

Paige threw him a sideways glance. "Quantico? You don't look like a Marine."

"The Bureau also has a training facility there," he said. He stared out the window. The Lawrence Livermore Lab looked like a typical university campus—plenty of green space, people oblivious to everything around them as they walked in deep discussion, bicyclists riding by on battered government-issue red bicycles.

"I've never been out here before, but I was expecting this place to look like a ghost town. The newspapers have been talking about the Lab losing its nuclear weapons work with the test ban moratorium and the end of the Cold War. It looks like a busy farmer's market in a small town."

Paige slowed at a traffic circle before answering. "Designing nuclear weapons used to be our flagship, but we saw the writing on the wall years ago. We've still got some of the best research facilities in the world—and that's no exaggeration.

"We've spent a lot of effort turning them to dual-use technologies, letting our researchers apply for patents, setting up CRADAs with industry—that is"—she paused a moment to remember the acronym—"Cooperative Research And Development Agreements for marketing our aerogels and multilayered materials and other breakthroughs. We've had big programs in biomedical research, computer code development, and fusion power.

"One of our biggest investments some years back was the Laser Implosion Fusion Facility, which should have been the cornerstone for cheap and clean energy. A billion-dollar program, overall, but thanks to the usual near-sightedness of annual budgets, the last sliver of funding was cut before the scientists could even turn on the machine." She sighed. "A lot of people here are bitter about that. It was Dr. Michaelson's pet project before he went to work on the disarmament team in the former Soviet Union, and then came back to set up T Program here."

As Paige talked, they drove to another badge checkpoint, a gate leading deeper into the Lab. "We were just out in the Limited Area, where no classified work is done. A lot of our programs don't require security clearances, and those employees wear red badges. Now we're going into the Restricted Area, where you need a security clearance to enter. Everybody who works here has a green badge.

"Inside the T Program central computer complex, our Plutonium Facility, and a few other heavily secure places, there's one more level of security. There's another CAIN booth that allows access only to those people with a programmatic justification to enter. Those places are called Exclusion Areas."

"I see," Craig said. "And Dr. Michaelson was found in an Exclusion Area?"

Paige nodded, and Craig thought of the highly unusual acid burns on Michaelson's face and hands and wondered how they could have gotten there. If Michaelson was indeed murdered, he supposed the Exclusion Area limited the number of suspects.

After the PSO at the second checkpoint touched their badges through the open van window, Paige drove into the Restricted Area, which lay beyond another perimeter of chain-link fence. They passed modernistic buildings with smoked-glass windows, but most of the facilities were low modular structures, inexpensive trailers hooked together into complexes. She pulled into a narrow parking lot filled with other government cars, trucks, and small white Cushman carts.

"Sorry I went into rah-rah mode about the Lab," Paige said as she parked the van. "It's just my canned speech. This is T Program here."

Craig climbed out and looked at a cluster of white modular buildings. Paige came around to meet him, then she led him down a bike path toward the T Program trailers.

A new sign with fresh blue paint stood in a flower bed outside the front trailer. T PROGRAM: VIRTUAL REALITY CENTER. A wide band of yellow plastic tape lay draped across the main door to the complex, printed with the repeating words DO NOT ENTER: CONSTRUCTION SITE.

Paige stepped over the fluttering tape and opened the door to the lobby. "It's the best we could do," she said. "We didn't have any police line tape."

"I don't see any security guards to keep people out." Craig looked around in dismay, thinking of all the damage that could already have been done.

"With the CAIN access, we don't need them, remember? Nobody but T Program people can get in here."

Craig took off his sunglasses and made a noncommittal sound. "But this is a potential crime scene. What if the T Program people are the ones we need to worry about?"

Paige looked at him long and hard, appraising him. "Do you really think there's a possibility that this wasn't an accidental death?"

Craig shrugged. "It's hard to imagine how somebody could have gotten acid all over himself and not sounded an alarm."

The T Program lobby was no larger than an oversized closet with a chair, telephone, and an LLNL phone directory. Set into one wall was a reflective glass door resembling an airlock. The words CAIN ACCESS had been stenciled on the front. The other walls held a safety bulletin board, an Equal Opportunity flyer, and a large green EXCLUSION AREA sign.

Paige opened the heavy CAIN booth door on the far wall and unclipped the badge from her blue blouse. "We do this one at a time, just like you did at the badge office. Stick your badge in the reader, key in your PIN, and the other door will open. You'll hear the click. Just watch me."

Paige's expression became stern as she stood with the door half open. "I should warn you that if you make a mistake with your PIN, the booth will flood with colorless but deadly nerve gas. Can't trust those old bomb designers, you know." She slipped in and closed the door.

Craig stood appalled, then realized she was joking. Paige Mitchell seemed to enjoy testing how stuffy he could be. He could see only her hazy outline inside the booth, but he heard a succession of beeps as she keyed in her PIN. After an unlocking clunk he lost sight of her outline as the door on the other side of the booth opened.

He pulled at the door and stepped into the booth as the heavy door shut, sealing him in. Behind a glass panel, two TV cameras peered at him. A silvery LCD display above the magnetic strip reader blinked PLEASE INSERT YOUR BADGE. Craig punched in his PIN and the inner door clicked, allowing him to join Paige.

He found himself in an open trailer space broken by islands of low office cubicles and offices with doors on the far wall. Randomly arranged tables served as holding platforms for computer workstations, bundles of wires, circuit boards, bound preprints of scientific papers, users manuals, and stacks of floppy disks. He could smell burned insulation, solder, and cleaning chemicals.

Down one carpeted hall in the back of the trailer, a large room stood partially open like a bank vault. He recognized instinctively the centerpiece of the laboratory area—the VR chamber—but he also saw the yellow CONSTRUCTION AREA tape that had once been stretched across the door opening to seal the crime scene—though now it lay discarded on the floor.

Craig stepped toward the chamber, anger sharpening inside him just as a man in his mid-twenties sauntered through the open vault door. The young man stepped on the yellow tape as if on purpose and moved toward one of the office cubicles, shuffling papers. Craig burned the image of the man into his mind: pale skin, red hair, and the beginnings of a paunch. He wore jeans and an ash-gray T-shirt with a garish drawing and the name Nexus, apparently some comic-book superhero.

The man looked up, noticed Craig and Paige, and altered his course to come over to them. "Oh. You the FBI guy? I can always tell visitors around here by the goofy suit and tie."

Craig stiffened within his dark suit. "Yes, I'm from the FBI. And you are—?"

The red-headed man held the sheaf of papers like a shield and did not offer his hand. "Gary Lesserec, the one who's trying to hold this program together in the middle of a shitstorm. I'm the only one who knows what's going on, now that Michaelson bit the big one."

"Excuse me, but was that the VR chamber I saw you exit?" Craig narrowed his eyes, feeling a growing uneasiness.

Lesserec said flippantly, "That's where we work, you know."

Craig nailed him with his gaze. "So you blatantly crossed a crime scene line. I see. Are you aware of the penalties you could now face, Mr. Lesserec?"

Craig didn't wait for the red-headed man to answer, turning to Paige. "The guards should have sealed this building the moment Dr. Michaelson's body was found, and it doesn't look like they did a very good job. If a felony was committed here, no one should have been given the chance to tamper with the crime scene. It's been hours since Michaelson was discovered—how much has been changed?"

"Wait just a minute!" Lesserec tossed the papers down on an equipment-strewn table, where they lay on top of the clutter. "This is my lab, Mr. FBI, and our whole team has an impossible challenge to meet, thanks to Michaelson. The President of the United States and the whole world is counting on us, and we can't just go on vacation because somebody wants to make a federal case over a heart attack."

Craig kept his cool with an effort. "I'm sorry you feel that way, Mr. Lesserec, but I've got a job to do. I am declaring the VR chamber off limits to *everyone* as of this moment. Paige, I want you to see that a permanent, uh, PSO is stationed right outside the door. Mr. Lesserec and his team members are not—I repeat, *not*—allowed to set foot inside until I have declared the area clear."

Paige bristled, but she glared more at Lesserec than at Craig. "I understand, Mr. Kreident. Let me make a call to Protective Services."

"Hey, you can't do that," Lesserec said with fading bluster. "I've got a simulation running, and I need to download some files. At least let me go in and get—"

"I'm afraid not, Mr. Lesserec. And if you doubt whether I have the authority to do this, perhaps you should speak to your Director. In the meantime, I'd like to set up an interview with yourself and each of your team members." Craig maintained a placid expression as he stared down Lesserec. It took Lesserec only about five seconds to glance away.

Craig spoke more quietly. "The sooner we can dismiss Dr. Michaelson's death as an accident, the faster your people can get back to work."

Lesserec ran a hand through his spiky red hair, stumped for a moment. Then, lifting his nose, he regained his composure. "Whatever you need to do, Mr. FBI, get on with it. We have only a few weeks to get a full-blown demonstration ready. Can't afford to lose a single day."

Craig worked his jaw to keep his temper under control. *Who did this clown think he was?* "Can you show me where you found the body, Mr. Lesserec?"

The question seemed to throw Lesserec. He shrugged. "Sure. Follow me."

Craig and Paige followed him around a table of equipment toward the vault in the corner of the trailer complex. Without waiting for them to catch up, Lesserec stepped over the torn yellow tape again. "Don't touch anything—the guards nearly ruined Michaelson's experiment."

Craig entered the darkened room. The ceiling was ten feet high, but the chamber seemed small because of its odd shape. The walls were filled with arrays of lenses, and two rows of movie-theater seats stood in the middle hooked to complex and unsightly hydraulics. A chalk outline of the body showed where Michaelson had crumpled to the floor. Craig walked carefully to the chalk and squatted down to squint at the rough carpet. He would have to get a forensic team in here to test for blood, saliva, fingerprints, chemicals and anything else they could think of. He expected to find traces of the acid to which Michaelson had been exposed.

Lesserec stood by the doorway with his pudgy arms folded. "After they hauled the body away, I held a meeting with my people, and they're at their workstations crunching code. Some of our mech techs need to get into the chamber to make modifications, but I'm keeping them busy at the Plutonium Building on another part of the demo. You'd better get what you need as soon as possible. Life goes on, you know?"

Craig clenched his teeth. "It seems we have different priorities, Mr. Lesserec. Until we rule out foul play in

Dr. Michaelson's death, practically everyone with access to this building is suspect."

Lesserec gave a snorting, bitter laugh. "Oh, don't limit yourself. Michaelson made enemies out of a lot more than just T Program people."

Craig refused to be distracted. "That makes my job even more difficult. And if you don't cooperate, I can have you held in jail for obstruction of justice—then where would your deadline be?"

Lesserec seemed frozen in place, breathing deeply and glaring at Craig. "All right, I understand, tough guy." He walked out of the chamber, leaving Paige and Craig alone. The click and thud of the CAIN booth door signaled Lesserec's exit from the Exclusion Area.

"Well, that was a good job of intimidation," Paige said disapprovingly.

Craig stood back to survey the chalk outline. Michaelson had been a large man, and had fallen face down, spread out on the floor. "I'm not going to let some smart-alec scientist walk all over my investigation."

He looked at Paige. "I'll get a more detailed coroner's report later today. Until then, I'm calling in a full FBI forensics team. That should have been done this morning. Maybe we can trace where the acid came from."

"Kay-O. What do you propose to do in the meantime?" Paige sounded curt, strictly business.

"Got to do a damage assessment, conduct an inventory of Michaelson's papers—first order of business. If you can show me his classified document repository, we need to see if anything's missing."

Thursday

Kaiser Medical Center
Pleasanton, California

José Aragon sat in the hard plastic chair of the waiting room, fidgeting, biting back tears as he clamped his lips together. He looked at his watch and saw the second hand travel in slow motion from one tick mark to the next. *Hurry, hurry, hurry!*

The center of his right hand burned, as if someone had fired a laser through it. His lower lip pushed out in a pout, Aragon repeatedly rubbed the circular spot with his thumb. But the pain kept getting worse and worse, drilling through his skin to his bones, crawling up his hand and arm. He felt that it would never end.

He had taken pain pills the night before, moaning to his wife Rona, who looked flustered, unable to help him. He had soaked his hand in cold water, wrapped it in ice cubes. Rona had bathed the oddly pale and dis-colored spot in the center of his palm with medicated cream, but nothing seemed to help, not hand lotion, not ice cubes. Now in the medical center, as usual, they were making him wait all morning.

He knew it didn't sound like much on their list of pa-tients: burning sensation in the right hand. But José

Aragon had never felt agony like this before. "Please hurry," he muttered, all alone. "Please hurry." He looked down at his hand again.

Rona had driven him to the Kaiser Medical Center the moment it opened. He had refused to let her take him to the hospital emergency room, and now he regretted that decision.

Rona had called him in sick, asking his administrative assistant to cancel his meetings. Rona had told the people in his office only that he had a medical appointment. Aragon didn't want to raise any alarm until he knew what the problem really was.

Aragon had been sitting here for over an hour, staring at the other people, all of whom squirmed waiting for their turn; he wished they would just go away, so the next available doctor could see *him*.

He hated taking days off of work when he couldn't plan ahead for it. His job was very important, and he had a great many meetings to attend, luncheons to arrange, memos to write. Granted, every worker thought he or she was indispensable, but José Aragon was the Associate Director for Technology Transfer and Defense Conversion! He couldn't afford to miss work just because of a sore hand—and it was his writing hand, too.

He stared down at it again and flexed his aching fingers. Oh, it hurt!

The medical center intercom played a soothing Barry Manilow song, but none of the other patients in the waiting area seemed to be listening. Aragon leaned back against the hard plastic back of the chair. His breath hissed between his teeth. "Come on, come on," he muttered and looked at his watch again.

Finally, a nurse emerged from the bowels of the clinic and read his name from her clipboard. Aragon fairly leaped out of his chair and hurried after her. His heart pounded with anticipation, relief of knowing that finally somebody would fix his hand.

But he found himself sitting in a doctor's examination room with the door ajar, his personal manila folder stuck in a plastic bin outside. He waited fifteen more minutes for the doctor to come in.

"This will sting a little," the doctor said as she popped off the plastic protective cap from the hypodermic. "It's a topical anesthetic, but the needle might hurt going into your palm."

Aragon sweated and looked up at her with a pleading expression. She had shoulder-length gray-brown hair, a soft face, and a quiet voice that gave her a gentle bedside manner. He couldn't remember her name. Every time he went to Kaiser, they assigned him a different physician. Right now, though, Aragon wouldn't have minded even Dr. Frankenstein if he could just make the pain go away.

"I'm not going to notice a horse needle right now," he said. "Just give me that pain killer, please!"

She jabbed the needle into the skin of his palm like a knight in a jousting contest. Despite her assurances, Aragon did feel the sting in addition to the burning. He closed his eyes and pressed his lips together, waiting for the medication to take effect.

"I've taken a biopsy," the doctor said, "and we're going to send it to the lab. I'd rather you stayed here, because if your skin is deteriorating as rapidly as you say, we'd better find out what this is."

Aragon opened his watery eyes again. "Yes, you'd better find out what it is! And quick. I can't take this much longer." He didn't feel any effect from the pain killer yet.

The doctor tossed her head, shaking her loose mane of hair back behind her shoulders. "Now, Mr. Aragon, your chart says that you work at the Livermore Lab. You're sure you didn't spill any chemicals on yourself or pick up radioactive material, or—?"

"I'm an administrator," Aragon said. "I don't work inside the actual labs. I can't imagine where I would have come in contact with anything hazardous. The things I handle all day long are pencils and telephones."

She pursed her lips and prodded the flat colorless skin of his palm with her fingertip. He winced. "Still looks like some kind of acid burn," she said. "Well, if you'll go back out to the waiting area, it'll be an hour or so."

Aragon hoped by that time the pain killer would have taken effect.

It actually took closer to three hours. Every time he pestered the receptionist, she didn't seem to know what was going on. Aragon had read all the magazines in the waiting area, even *Highlights for Children* and *Modern Maturity*. If it hadn't been for the returning pain, he would have noticed his boredom even more.

When the nurse finally called him again, she and a companion whisked him back to one of the larger rooms with more of an air of importance. Aragon was glad to see their concern, but as he thought about that, he grew even more uneasy.

When the nurse left Aragon in the room, he saw not

only his own doctor but two other consulting physicians already waiting for him. *What a switch!* he thought. One of the doctors, an older black man with a full moustache, stood up and said without preamble, "Let me see your hand, please."

Aragon held out his palm, then looked to the doctor he had spoken with earlier. "Have you figured it out?"

"It's very serious, Mr. Aragon," she answered in her soft voice. "I must say you've given us quite a puzzle here."

"Yes, yes," the older black doctor said, pointing to the second physician. "Just what we suspected. See the liquefaction necrosis of the soft tissue? It's probably spreading, and you can be certain the invisible damage is far worse than what we see here."

Aragon stiffened, feeling a shiver run down his spine. "What are you talking about? What have I got?"

"It seems you came in contact with a very nasty substance, Mr. Aragon," his own doctor said.

"It's hydrofluoric acid, or HF. It has a delayed but severe reaction because it eats down through your skin and begins to do nerve damage. You don't even feel it until sometime after exposure. Do you know where you could have come in contact with this?"

Aragon stammered. "Acid?" He looked wildly around the room. "Acid! But I don't handle any chemicals whatsoever. Can you give me something for it, treatment or—?"

The black doctor interrupted curtly, placing a hand on Aragon's shoulder. "We're going to inject you with calcium gluconate right away. That will arrest the continuing damage in the main area. But I suspect if you came in contact with it primarily here"—he tapped the center of Aragon's palm—"it may also have spread elsewhere. Do you feel burning sensations on the rest of your hand?"

At the mere suggestion, Aragon felt the skin on his entire body tingling and itching and burning.

"We're going to take some more biopsy samples," the black doctor said, "and I'm afraid the treatment is rather severe and painful—but necessary."

"Treatment?" Aragon said, relieved that at least there was something they could do. "What treatment? I need to get back to work. Can't you just give me another pain shot? That one seemed to work for a little while."

His own doctor shook her head. "That merely stopped the pain, Mr. Aragon. The damage is continuing."

"There's only one way to remove the acid," the black doctor said. "We must excise the surrounding tissue."

"What?"

"Get rid of it, cut it out."

"How do you do that?" Aragon said with rising alarm. "Do I need to schedule an operation?"

All three doctors looked at him with narrowed eyes. "We need to get you to surgery as soon as possible, Mr. Aragon. Today."

The black doctor seemed to take glee in watching his expression. "We must excise the skin from your entire hand."

For a moment José Aragon did not feel the pain from the acid burn in his palm as his vision turned into a closing funnel of black fuzz and he fainted.

Thursday

Building 433—T Program
Lawrence Livermore National
Laboratory

As she drove in darkness to the Lawrence Livermore National Laboratory, Diana Unteling thought of how familiar the attitudes had become. Whatever the verdict on Hal Michaelson's death, she knew that everyone from Congress to the radio talk shows would rip apart every strand of his life like medieval medical researchers with a brand-new cadaver.

A top political appointee always attracted sharks. She was used to that. But the feeding frenzy over Hal's death wouldn't be confined to the Beltway, and any scandal would send ripples into the lives of anyone he had known. It was the Washington Way—people *had* to have a scapegoat, and the Administration had already proved its willingness to drop controversial appointees at the first scent of trouble. Someone was bound to find out, and her career would be ruined.

Unless she could obliterate the link between herself and Hal. Having the affair exposed would not only trash any chance of her advancement in the Department of Energy, but would also cast a black stain on Fred's

Coalition for Family Values. She could stand the pain herself, but she wouldn't allow her husband to be hurt.

Holding the rental car's steering wheel with one hand, Diana unsnapped the DOE Headquarters badge from her neck chain, leaving the green LLNL badge, dosimeter, and master key. Showing the DOE badge might make someone remember her presence this late at night.

Only the main East Avenue gate remained open after hours. As she approached the guard kiosk, a PSO stepped slowly out of the shack. He held a styrofoam cup of coffee in his left hand and looked bleary-eyed as Diana handed over her green badge.

Diana smiled briefly, but said nothing. "Have a good one," the guard muttered, then waved her on as he climbed back into his chair.

Diana rolled up her window as she pulled onto the site. Back when she had started working here, in the frenzied days of nuclear testing, a regular subculture had developed from all the teams working through the night. She herself had been involved in some of those crash programs with impossible deadlines. Even with the work slowdown, though, enough scientists kept odd hours that she would attract no attention.

Under the orange sodium streetlights, the narrow tree-lined roads were deserted. She held out her badge to the PSO waiting at the gate for entrance into the Restricted Area around T Program. Few lights burned in the office buildings and trailers. Parking the car in the deserted lot outside the VR complex, she switched off the ignition and sat waiting in darkness. She breathed deeply, trying to gather the courage to go ahead.

Meanwhile, she knew her husband slept alone in their

large house in Arlington, busy but content. As his Coalition had grown, Fred had become more beatific, satisfied with the progress he had made, with the people he helped.

Diana attended all the appropriate social functions with him, but kept herself out of the limelight. Fred gave her everything she needed, but during a long and lonely assignment in the former Soviet Union she had let Hal Michaelson sweep her into an affair through the force of his will. They had been intense but infrequent lovers for years—and if Fred ever learned of it, the news would destroy him personally, and it would unravel the Coalition, his life's work.

She couldn't imagine what memorabilia Hal might have kept of their time together, but in light of his death, any thread pointing to Diana Unteling would be magnified. Within days the news would be plastered across the pages of *The Washington Post*—unless she could fix it.

She drew in a breath and opened the car door. The sound echoed against the trailer walls, very loud in the night stillness. She walked briskly to the main entrance of the T Program trailers. Yellow construction tape barricaded the entrance, but she ducked under the flimsy ribbon and yanked on the door handle. Locked.

She had never seen the facility locked before, and a rush of prickly sweat tingled against her skin. The fact that Livermore security would actually *lock* a door to an area already protected by CAIN access made her realize that they were treating Hal's death with an unusual degree of suspicion. Not a good sign. She fumbled with the key dangling behind her badge, access Hal had given her more than a year ago. She had to move fast.

Through the cramped "holding tank" lobby, Diana entered the glassed-in CAIN booth, slid her badge through the reader, and keyed in her code number. When the opposite door clicked open, she slipped into the dim labs of T Program.

She stood waiting for her eyes to grow accustomed to the dimly lit room. Only three of the fluorescent light panels in the ceiling shed a garish glow onto the clutter, throwing long shadows from the equipment-filled tables into the partitioned cubicles.

Even in the dark the place looked as it had the last time she had been here . . . what, over a year ago now? But the major advances had not been in the outer appearance of the VR chamber, or the supporting apparatus, but rather in both the software and in the microsensors that shuffled the information required by the chamber.

The Virtual Reality chamber itself stood sealed at the far end of the room, taped shut with more yellow construction area strips. She was relieved to see no guard standing bored and alone in the deserted lab. But she didn't need to get into the chamber itself—just into Hal's files.

She made her way slowly toward the back, bumping into discarded junk on the floor, catching her shoe on loose cords. She felt like a blundering drunk in an obstacle course.

She passed a table with three modern workstations, each more powerful than the Cray supercomputers that only a few years ago had been the flagship of the weapons design program. A glint of stray white light reflected off a framed photo on the table: Gary Lesserec and his bimbo girlfriend.

Diana's face clouded over. It wasn't right that this squeaky little man would still be alive when Hal, with all he had to offer, was gone. Lesserec should have been the one lying face down on the carpet in the VR chamber.

She hurried to Hal Michaelson's office door. Yellow construction tape blocked the entrance, but at least she had a key to his office door. She didn't hesitate to peel away the strips, allowing her access. She worked carefully, so that she could replace them when she was finished.

Diana squeezed through a gap in the tape and flicked on one half-bank of lights in Hal's office. She went to the window and fiddled with the miniblinds to block the light from alerting any outside observer wandering by.

Hal's office was, as usual, a disaster area. Volumes marked with yellow Post-It notes were shoved at all possible angles into the bookcases; stacks of journal articles, preprints, and unmarked floppy disks covered the desk and credenza. His bulky classified document repository stood behind the door, five feet tall and three deep, like a thick-walled black file cabinet.

Diana spun the dial and tried the first combination she could think of: her birthday. Seconds later she satisfied herself that no permutation of the numbers would work.

Bastard, she thought. Diana tried his birthday—it was more like Hal to think of himself instead of her, anyway—but still without any luck. A few more dates also refused to work: the date they met, the date the nonproliferation treaty he negotiated was signed, even the date they had first made love. Still nothing.

She thought of yet another place she could look for

the combination. Hal was always preoccupied, often forgetful; she felt sure that he would have jotted the combination down somewhere.

Diana pulled back Hal's desk chair and powered up his workstation. The dim room filled with the glow from the screen. When the request for a password came up, she hesitated. Same problem. No telling what he might have put in, but she didn't kid herself into thinking Hal would have used something from their relationship.

She racked her brain, trying to think what he found whimsical. He had taken pride in claiming that he had all the physical constants memorized, and she might be able to find them in the scores of books lying around the office. But she didn't have time to go scrounging around the room, looking up arcane numbers. Or maybe it was something serious, a mnemonic that he might base on an elegant formula, or event in history.

But Hal would have been wary about what he kept on his computer anyway, especially surrounded by a bunch of hackers who, once they knew the boss was away, might use roughly ten percent of the world's supercomputing power to dig out their boss's password. That would be just like Gary Lesserec. *No* password would be safe working in a place like this.

Diana sighed and slumped back in her chair. The words on the screen still waited for her: PLEASE ENTER PASSWORD.

It was a ridiculous request in a place where no password was safe. And then it hit her, just what Hal would have thought.

She reached out and tapped the ENTER key.

The word WORKING appeared in the center of the

screen, and within seconds she had access to his entire file base. *So he didn't use a password.* And it would have driven the hackers nuts trying to find it.

She rummaged through Hal's files and found a document titled IMPORTANT DATES. She found the repository combination at the bottom and recognized the numbers immediately, feeling a warm, bittersweet thrill. Hal had chosen their room numbers from the hotel in Moscow where they had started their affair. So gruff and arrogant Hal Michaelson had been sentimental after all! She felt tears stinging the corners of her eyes.

Diana opened the repository on the second try and started pawing through his files. Most of the folders were stamped SECRET/RD, NOFORN, or NO CONTRACTOR. Scarlet lines encircled the pages; dates, document numbers, and classifying authorities were rubber-stamped on the front.

She skipped past the technical reports. Lab overviews, stockpile numbers, and design criteria were all grouped together, but nowhere did she find any of the memos they had exchanged, the love letters from early in their relationship, sealed away in tighter security than any safe-deposit box. Except for now.

By the time Diana reached the bottom drawer, she was sweating—a deep, oily perspiration that seeped from her armpits, born from fear of not finding the dozens of documents that would incriminate her. Her knees and feet ached from the awkward position bending over the packed files, sifting through page after page.

She considered going through the pile of classified documents again, but she knew she had not missed anything. Hal's repository was not so extensive, and it only dealt with his latest interests.

Which obviously didn't include her.

She looked up, startled at a sudden noise. Had she really heard anything, or was it just nerves?

The FBI had already been called in to do a preliminary investigation on Hal's death. What if somebody had already been through this place and taken away the folders that didn't belong? What if, even now, the phone was ringing at her home in Arlington? Fred would roll over, answer it, and innocently tell them that she had gone to Livermore several days ago—before Hal Michaelson's death.

She struggled to her feet and nudged the heavy drawer shut with her leg. Her breath came in quick, laborious gasps. She ran a hand through her gray-flecked blond hair. *What did he do with those damned memos?* He could have shredded them, of course, but that wasn't like him.

At the time it had been a cute game Hal and Diana had played—passing classified love letters through the system, absolutely sure that no one else in the world would be able to intercept them.

She'd kept her own copies of the letters in her personal repository back in the DOE Headquarters building, but now she knew that was a huge mistake. She had to get back home and destroy them. Now. Right away.

She tried going through the files in his desk drawer, but still she found nothing. She turned off Hal's workstation, pushed the chair back to where she had found it, and flicked off the lights.

She felt sick to her stomach as she fought through the yellow construction tape back out of his office. Her fingers shook as she clumsily pushed the construction tape back against the door frame in a reasonable semblance of what it had looked like.

If the FBI had found the letters already, how long would it be before she was subpoenaed?

She stumbled through the obstacle course back toward the CAIN booth. Her elbow hit a stack of papers that hissed to the floor. Diana held a hand to her face and fought back a panicked outcry. She knelt and gathered up the papers, stacking them roughly on the table. Nobody could tell the difference with all this mess. Patting the top to ensure it was stable, she used her outstretched hands as a guide in the dimness until she reached the exit.

She didn't look behind her as she trotted to her car. No one would remember that she had come here; with 8,000 people working on the Livermore site, the night guard couldn't possibly know she wasn't a regular employee.

The drive back to the Sheraton seemed to take forever. She had to pack up and leave for Washington first thing in the morning. No one but Fred even knew she had come out to Livermore. Her DOE staff knew how to reach her through the Skypage, and they had left her alone. As far as they were concerned, she was visiting the San Francisco DOE office; and if she filed no travel voucher, no one would suspect.

Reaching the Sheraton and kicking off her shoes in the room, she called UNITED to make her reservation for the next flight departing for the East Coast. She couldn't stay here any longer. She was through with Livermore forever.

Thursday

Livermore, California

The bathwater pounded into the tub, but Stevie didn't seem to enjoy it as much as he usually did. Duane Hopkins tried singing one of the boy's favorite songs, "You Are My Sunshine," to no effect.

Stevie coughed, and kept coughing. He wore a strangely perplexed expression on his face, as if wondering why his lungs insisted on filling up with liquid that he couldn't spit out. The cough made a hollow, rumbling sound, a wetness deep in the boy's chest that Duane didn't like a bit. He had given Stevie the children's cough syrup he'd bought down at the drugstore, but it didn't seem to be helping.

Seeing the feverish red of Stevie's skin, Duane adjusted the temperature of the water, hoping it wasn't too hot. The boy made quiet, wordless noises. Duane reached over the rim of the tub to pull Stevie closer, hugging the boy tightly against his chest and soaking his blue-checked flannel shirt. The boy's muscles were hard and rigid like cables.

"I'm here, Stevie. I'll try to make it all better."

The boy cooed, a soft and trusting sound that communicated more to Duane than words ever could. He

shut off the running water and let the tub drain out as
Stevie splashed and rocked. Duane picked up the boy
and held him dripping.

Duane wasn't a large or a strong man, but his son was
so light that he could pick him up with ease. Stevie's mal-
functioning muscles drew his arms and legs up into a
fetal position like a newly hatched bird. Duane rubbed
him down with one of the old bath towels that he and
Rhonda had gotten as wedding presents years ago.

"Here Stevie, we've got to give you some more
cough syrup," Duane said and went to the mirrored cabinet, taking out the cherry-flavored medication. He had
bought the one with the most ingredients listed on the
side, which he decided must be the strongest medicine.
Duane poured a dollop into an old teaspoon and held it
to Stevie's mouth, but the boy's jaws remained clenched
and his eyes darted back and forth.

"Come on now," he said and pulled down on the
boy's chin, pressing the tip of the spoon into Stevie's
mouth. He finally forced the jaws open, spilling some of
the cough syrup down the boy's cheeks but getting most
of it into his mouth. Stevie smacked his lips. Duane
wiped his son's face with a wash cloth and then picked
him up, tugged his pajamas on, and put him to bed.

Stevie coughed again in his bed. Duane, concerned
enough now to call somebody, went into the kitchen and
plucked the thumb-worn card from under a refrigerator
magnet. For years now the volunteers at the Coalition
for Family Values were always helpful as Duane had
settled into the routine of how to care for a boy who had
cerebral palsy.

"Just call us anytime you need help, hon," one of the
women had said. Duane didn't like to take advantage of

their hospitality often, but now he picked up the phone and dialed the local office.

"This is Duane Hopkins," he said. "My boy Stevie has cerebral palsy. You've—"

The thin, whispering voice of the woman on the phone said, "Well, hello, Mr. Hopkins! I've talked to you before."

"Uh, yes," he said, then opened and closed his mouth, trying to decide what he wanted to say. "Stevie, my boy, has a cough. It seems pretty bad, and I'm worried."

"Yes," the woman on the line said and made a *tsk*ing noise. "There's a lot of colds going around right now. Have you taken him to see a doctor?"

Duane hesitated. "No, the medical center is closed."

"If it's serious, you should really take him to the emergency room."

Duane twisted his face. He hated going out at night, it was just too dangerous. He looked over to Stevie's room. The coughing didn't seem to be *that* bad. "No . . . no, I don't think it's that serious."

"Mr. Hopkins, listen to me. Do you need someone to come over and take you to the hospital? We can help."

Duane shook his head. "Please, no. We're all right."

The voice at the other end of the line was silent. Then, "Mr. Hopkins, please take your son in to see a doctor tomorrow. I'll put your name on our board here, and we'll all pray for you. We're thinking of you. We know you must have many trying times with a challenged child."

"Uh, yes," Duane said. "Thank you."

"Would you like us to bring a casserole over tomorrow? We can see that you have a good hot meal."

"That would be nice," Duane said. "Thanks."

A ringing noise sounded muffled on the other end of

the phone. "That's the other line, Mr. Hopkins. I've got to go. You take Stevie in to the doctor. We'll be praying for you and see you tomorrow around five-thirty, okay? But get to the doctor first! Bye-bye."

Duane hung up and listened to the quiet noises inside his house, the heavy coughing of Stevie down the hall. He went in to the living room to turn on the television. By now it was time for the ten o'clock news, and he liked to watch the weather report, though he never went anywhere and rarely even set foot outside when he didn't have to.

The main story taken from national news was about the sudden and unexpected death of Dr. Hal Michaelson. Duane sat back in shock. Though he had never met the man in charge of the International Verification Initiative, he had felt connected with the person responsible for all the new work that would come to Livermore, and the Virtual Reality simulations that had meant so much to Stevie. Now what would happen with Duane's own job? He bit his lower lip.

The Virtual Reality staff had nosed around in the Plutonium Facility, setting up some kind of demonstration, forcing them to work overtime to clean up the entire Radioactive Materials Area. Taking advantage of the building being "sanitized," the Coalition for Family Values had even set up a tour for some of the other kids, the healthy ones, to walk through the "super high-security" Plutonium Facility.

But now with Michaelson dead, Duane was concerned that all the new work would go away. The Livermore Lab would experience cutbacks again, layoffs. And Duane couldn't afford to be laid off. Right now he couldn't even spare the time to take a day off and take Stevie to the doctor.

Duane sat on the love seat with his chin in his hands, watching and frowning, letting his confused thoughts wash over him. His deep feelings were triggered by resentment because Stevie had been sick all his life and no news story had ever noticed *him.* He had never had a healthy normal day as a typical little boy, but that caught the attention of no reporter. It just wasn't fair.

But Dr. Michaelson's heart attack made the national news with many minutes devoted to his life, his background, his accomplishments at the Laser Implosion Fusion Facility, his work leading the disarmament and on-site inspection team in Russia. The reporter ended on a gloomy note, questioning whether Michaelson's crowning achievement, the IVI, could survive his sudden death.

Stevie, on the other hand, had never had his name in the paper. The boy could die and vanish without a trace—never appearing on the news, his name finally listed in an obituary notice.

Duane thought of his own work in the Plutonium Facility, and of how Ronald and his friends always picked on him. Long ago another bully had exposed him to the radiation which Duane *knew* was the source of Stevie's problems.

Nobody noticed Stevie or Duane's plight or any part of their lives. Why did some people grab all the glory, while others lived their lives as invisible people quietly hurting, year after year? It made no sense to him. He couldn't comprehend it. He sighed and stared at the TV as the story continued about the death of Hal Michaelson.

In the back room Stevie coughed again, louder this time.

Friday

Building 433—T Program
Virtual Reality Lab

"You could have met me at the VR building, you know," Paige Mitchell said, entering the badge office among the morning crowds. "You have access to the entire lab."

Craig Kreident looked up from his second cup of coffee to see her. He had arrived early, as was his habit. He squinted, and the morning light filtered around Paige from the large badge office windows, giving her a soft, angelic appearance—except for her bright outfit the color of sliced strawberries.

Craig's eyes widened. Paige's shoes, skirt, and jacket matched in stunning red, contrasted with a smart white blouse and *au natural* hose. She had tucked her blond hair back in a neat French braid that crowned the outfit perfectly.

Craig struggled to his feet from the deep cushioned couch, trying to keep the coffee from spilling as he extended a hand to her, but some of the black liquid slopped over the side of the styrofoam cup.

"Ouch." He shifted the cup to his left hand and sucked the side of his finger.

Arms folded, Paige watched him with an amused

smile. "See? If we had met in the T Program lobby, you wouldn't have burned yourself."

"And missed this great badge office coffee? It's been simmering to perfection for a few hours, I'm sure." Craig wiped his hands with a small white napkin, then tossed the coffee away without drinking any more.

She raised her eyebrows. "A joke from an FBI man? Very good—you're starting to sound like an insider."

Shifting to her curt business voice, she handed him a long printout that listed document titles. "This is Dr. Michaelson's inventory of classified papers, everything the document custodians recorded. I wouldn't bet money that Michaelson himself kept track of his work, but his administrative assistant, Tansy Beaumont, is like Attila the Hun. She wouldn't have let him slack off." She gestured to the door. "Let's go—we've got an exciting morning looking at numbered memo after numbered memo."

Craig stuffed the sheaf of papers into his leather briefcase, then snapped it closed. "Last night I watched the news and read the papers. Gave me a chance to read up on our friend Michaelson. He's had quite an . . . interesting and varied career."

Paige looked at him as they walked across the parking lot. "That's an understatement."

She directed him to a small forest-green MG sportscar. He glanced at her and smiled. "Nice. What happened to the government van?"

"No need to impress you anymore," said Paige. "It's either this or one of the clunky Lab bikes."

Seeing that it wouldn't fit on the floor between his legs, he swung his briefcase into the small area behind the passenger seat. He dug out his Visitor's badge as

Paige spun out of the badge office parking lot and approached the gate. "They provide bicycles here?" he asked.

"About two thousand of them are scattered all over the site. This is a big place. It cuts down on traffic and pollution. You'll also see a bunch of the little white Cushman carts."

Paige drove past the fences after the guard touched their badges. "Don't the bikes get stolen?" Craig asked.

She pointed to a bald and bearded man ahead of them, hunched over the handlebars and madly pedaling away. "Take a look at that bike."

Craig turned to watch as they zoomed past the bike. Paige's MG sounded like an overactive lawnmower. "Let's see, a wobbly reflector, thick tires, rusty basket . . ." He turned back to Paige. "Looks like the kind I had as a kid."

"Bingo. How many people would sneak past all this security just to steal a clunker like that?" She brushed back a few wisps of stray blond hair that the wind had whipped in front of her face.

"Can't argue with that logic," Craig said.

Paige's car permit from the Director's Office allowed her to drive the MG into the restricted area normally reserved for government vehicles. When they walked up to T Program's main entrance, he saw that the yellow tape had been torn down and lay in a wadded ball in one of the bushes.

"Where's the, uh, PSO? I thought you were going to have this place guarded."

Paige looked embarrassed and smiled wanly at him. "Well, we had a little problem."

Craig stopped, avoiding her gaze to dampen his own

reaction. He felt a gradually sinking feeling in his gut. What kind of red-tape muckup had they run into? "Don't make excuses, Paige. Just tell me what happened."

She shrugged. "Security has to go by the book. They agreed to keep an eye on the building, random spot checks, but they wouldn't station a guard here all night."

He made a disgusted sound. "Didn't you explain that this is a federal investigation site? Good lord, they've got a possible murder on their hands and they can't be bothered to enforce a little security?"

"We have plenty of security, Craig. We routinely keep stacks of highly classified material and enough plutonium to make a bunch of atomic bombs. Trust us to keep a crime scene intact, kay-o? We've been handling nuclear design information for decades."

Still upset, Craig stood next to her, trying to maintain a neutral expression. "But all of the T Program people have access. They could have come in last night—"

"Then we've got them. Anybody using their badge for access gets recorded. We'll run a computer check for a list of everyone who entered the CAIN booth here and the times they came in."

Craig slowly nodded. She had a point, and her comments placed things in perspective for him; in a way, this was like conducting an investigation in another country. "I'm sorry. I apologize."

"No offense taken," said Paige. "Well, not much." She entered the T Program lobby and Craig took his turn in the CAIN booth, following her through.

Inside the trailer complex, the programmers and electronics engineers worked intensely, shouting to each

other and conversing in a mid-level drone that seemed
amplified by the labyrinth of cubicles.

Just inside the main doors of the administrative offices Michaelson's secretary—administrative assistant,
Craig corrected himself—waited for them.

"Tansy," Paige said, "this is Mr. Kreident, FBI agent
in charge of the investigation into Dr. Michaelson's
death."

Craig shook hands. Tansy Beaumont was a wizened,
no-nonsense, dark-complexioned woman who looked
like a gypsy grandmother. Her black eyes bored into
him from a leathery face, and he saw an unyielding dy-
namo of personality, a dragon lady who could match
wills with someone like Hal Michaelson.

"Dr. Michaelson was a good boss, Mr. Kreident,"
Tansy said. "If somebody did this to him on purpose, I
want you to find out who it was. Understand?"

Craig nodded. "First step will be to check over the
contents of his document safe. How long will it take you
to open it?"

"Thirty seconds," she said with flat confidence. "Dr.
Michaelson never remembered his own combo and had
me do it for him all the time."

She had peeled away the wide yellow tape that covered the door to Michaelson's office. "I've been waiting
right here since seven A.M. Never can tell when one of
those clowns wants to stick his face in here and mess
everything up." She snorted in the direction of Gary
Lesserec and his hacker teammates.

"I believe I share your opinion, Ms. Beaumont,"
Craig said. "Do you have a copy of Michaelson's schedule for his last couple of days? Where he was, who he
met with?"

"We can get that out of his day planner," Tansy said, moving expertly to the avalanche of clutter on the work-table and, without so much as digging around, yanked out the single volume she wanted. She flipped through the calendar-marked pages. "He never would let me keep his schedule, no matter how many times he messed it up. Claimed that if he could manage to forget about something, then it wasn't all that important, anyway."

She paused for a beat as she found the right pages and handed them to Craig. "What I'm trying to say is that just because he wrote a meeting down here doesn't mean he actually went to it. And that doesn't mean these places are the only meetings he attended, either."

Paige leaned over to look at the schedule. "I've got another way to verify it, though. Remember that computer badge check I told you we could run, Craig? I've already started another one to trace the CAIN booths Dr. Michaelson used in the last couple of days. I'm also getting a record of all phone calls originating from and coming to his office, and an affidavit from the people he visited since returning from Washington."

He grinned at her. "Good work. I'm going to have to hire you over at the Bureau if you keep this up. Can you get that to me later this morning?"

"I'll work on it," Paige said, heading for the office door.

Tansy made a clucking sound to get their attention. "Meanwhile, Mr. Kreident, you've got your own work to do." She indicated the open repository crammed with haphazardly filed documents. "Everything's just the way he left it."

The black four-drawered safe seemed to grow larger as he stared at it. The repository fairly overflowed with envelopes and folders, each bearing a thick red border around the side and stamped with the initials SRD— Secret Restricted Data. The folders bulged with reports, typed papers, handwritten notes, and scribbled drawings. Opening the other heavy drawers, he found more of the same.

"Your list might not help much," Tansy said. "Dr. Michaelson's favorite stamp was SECRET WORK PAPER. That way he didn't have to document any of the classified memos or reports he wrote. He only needed a number assigned if he mailed them off-site through classified mail channels, or when I caught him being sloppy and rapped him on the knuckles for it." She sighed and turned away as her face seemed to crumple. "I'm going to miss him."

With a resigned expression, Craig pulled out a stack of documents from the top drawer of the repository and glanced at the title of the top report: (S) A 500 MEGA-JOULE DIRECT FUSION DEVICE and started flipping through the printout of classified document titles Paige had given him, checking off the number.

Slowly and tediously, he began to work his way through the folders.

"I think Tansy and I have reconstructed Dr. Michaelson's last day," Paige said, poking her head into the stuffy office.

Craig looked up from the pile of classified documents. Paige's strawberry-red outfit brought a much-needed brightness into the small room. Craig put down the folder filled with memos and notes describing something called "Rhoades-Alme diffusion" and rubbed his eyes. The inventory printout lay on his lap, dotted with check marks.

He glanced at the pile of documents on the floor next to his chair. "I'm about a third of the way through this top drawer and I can't find anything that looks out of place."

Paige picked her way through the clutter to the outside window on the far wall. "Why do you have the miniblinds closed? How about a little sun?"

Craig let out a sigh of relief when warm yellow light flooded the room, countering the harsh white fluorescents. Glancing at the clock, he figured he'd been sitting for nearly two and a half hours. Craig stood up and stretched. "Let's go over the schedule, then. I could use a break."

"Kay-O. Tansy has cleared a table for us."

They left Michaelson's office to see where Tansy Beaumont had, literally, shoved papers on the floor to clear a narrow table in one of the cubicles. Tansy scuttled back to her office as the phone rang.

As Craig looked over her shoulder, Paige spread out a sheaf of papers. "Michaelson arrived at Livermore back from Washington at around noon on the day of his death. They're having trouble downloading the CAIN booth records, but once we get that list we'll be able to have an exact time he entered and left the T Program complex.

"We know that Michaelson showed up at the VR lab while everyone was gone for lunch. He wasn't too happy about seeing the place deserted with all the new work he had just dumped on them.

"Michaelson then spent most of the afternoon in various meetings, making phone calls. He has something called a 'boob tour' written down for the late afternoon. I have no idea what that means—other than the crude implications."

Tansy returned just in time to overhear. "Oh, that was a tour of the Plutonium Facility with Deputy AD Aragon. Dr. Michaelson always called him a 'boob.' From what I hear, they had quite an argument during the tour."

"So Michaelson and this Aragon didn't get along?" Craig picked up the sheet and studied the notes.

"I'm not privy to all the facts," Paige said, "but I understand there was quite a bit of friction between them."

"One-way friction," Tansy interrupted. "Mr. Aragon was like a puppy dog, always trying to make friends with Dr. Michaelson, but Hal couldn't stand him."

Paige added, "I've already tried to call Mr. Aragon, but he's home on sick leave today."

Craig put down the paper. "Nice coincidence. Let's get back to that." He nodded at her notes. "What happened after Michaelson left the plutonium building?"

"He had a late meeting with the Lab Director. Dr. Michaelson was apparently under quite a bit of pressure from the President to get this verification initiative off the ground, so he was pushing the Director for a substantial increase in manpower. The front office is willing to schedule you with the Director anytime you want to talk to him, if you think that's necessary."

"What about after Michaelson left the Director's Office—did anybody keep track of him after that?"

"No, but once the CAIN records are available, we'll have the exact time he entered the VR lab for the last time."

"And the time that anyone else left the lab as well."

Tansy held up a yellow message slip clutched in her gnarled fingers. "Sorry for interrupting, Mr. Kreident, but you're supposed to call the FBI forensics lab."

With a rush of adrenaline, he took the note from Tansy's hand. "Can I use this phone?" He pointed to the phone beside the workstation in the cubicle.

"Dial 8 to get an outside line," Tansy said.

Craig punched in the numbers. "This is Kreident. What do you have?"

The voice of the woman lab tech sounded bleached and brittle, as if she had seen it all. "First cut on Michaelson's cause of death. We know he's had some coronary problems in the past, but no evidence of a heart attack here. Something a lot weirder."

Craig sat up in his chair, pulling out his notepad. "So what did they find?"

"Looks like HF poisoning—hydrofluoric acid caused those severe burns on his hands and face. According to our chemical toxicologists, HF penetrates the skin and begins eating away the nerves until it permeates the bones. Bad thing is, you don't even know it until too late. A five-percent bodily exposure is usually a fatal dose. Michaelson got it over fourteen percent of his body. Pretty nasty way to go."

Craig wheeled in his chair to look out the cubicle toward the VR chamber, its vault door yawning open. "Did the evidence techs find acid traces where the body was discovered?"

"No, but they weren't looking for HF specifically. We're sending a team back to Livermore to run a complete check."

After Craig hung up, Paige and Tansy both watched him, eager for news. "They've got a preliminary cause of death," he said. "HF exposure." He watched them both closely to spot any reaction. If the term meant anything to the two, it didn't show. "Hydrofluoric acid. You don't know if Michaelson had access to hazardous substances, do you?"

"Not that I know of," Tansy said. "They're all just computer jockeys here. Nobody plays in a real chemistry lab, especially not Dr. Michaelson."

Paige said, "If HF is a controlled or toxic chemical, we can get a list of all the places on site where it's used."

Craig nodded and stared at the VR chamber. The inside looked dark and foreboding. *Fatal exposure to hydrofluoric acid.* There seemed no further question about it: Hal Michaelson had been murdered.

Friday

Livermore, California

As Paige drove through the upscale residential section
of Livermore, Craig sat in the MG's passenger seat and
turned over the events in his head. Tall live oaks leaned
over the street, casting glossy green shade. The price
range of the homes probably climbed ten thousand dollars every block.

"Now, be careful not to say anything at all during
the interview," he said. "Let's see how Aragon reacts
first."

"Kay-O," she said, then turned left into a subdivision
of custom homes with expensive rock gardens and landscaping lavished on the front yards. She checked the address from Craig's note, and pulled up in front of a large
stucco house with a tile roof and a wisteria-clad arbor
overhanging the double front door.

Craig retrieved a pad of paper from his briefcase,
slipped a pen into his pocket, and drew a comb through
his hair before climbing out of Paige's forest-green
sportscar. She stood waiting for him in her strawberry-
red suit, ready to stride up the sidewalk.

He held his FBI wallet ID and Livermore Visitor's
badge out as soon as the left half of the house's broad

door opened. A petite dark-haired woman flashed an automatic smile at them. "Hello, Rona Aragon? I'm Craig Kreident with the FBI, and this is Ms. Mitchell from the Lab. We called earlier?"

She nodded. "Please come in, my husband is expecting you."

Craig flipped his ID wallet shut and gestured for Paige to precede him into the two-story home. A polished tile foyer extended to a formal living room with an empty fireplace flanked by two small crucifixes; arrangements of dried flowers sat on several smoked-glass end tables and shelves. Beyond, he could see a carpeted family room with a TV buzzing in the background. White walls were covered with family photographs from the local budget studio, high school pictures, and paintings of bucolic mountain scenes of the type usually displayed in cheap hotel rooms.

A dark-haired man not much larger than his petite wife rose from a reclining chair when they entered the family room. He smiled broadly out of habit, tinged with a sore weariness, and motioned with bandaged hands for them to take a seat. "Mr. Kreident? Miss Mitchell? I'm José Aragon. Pleased to meet you."

He held up his bandaged arms. "I'd offer you my hand, but I'm under doctor's orders not to do anything but air them out." His wife came over to stand by his side. "What can I do for you?"

Craig withdrew a notepad and snagged the pen from his pocket. "I've been assigned to conduct the investigation into Dr. Michaelson's death. Do you mind answering some questions?"

Aragon's face fell slack. He gestured to the floral-print sofa beside them. "Please, have a seat. I'm glad to answer any questions I can, but I'm not sure I can help you." He shook his head. "Terrible news about Hal. A tremendous man and a great asset to the Lab."

"Could you please tell me where and when you heard about Dr. Michaelson's death?" Craig asked.

Aragon nodded to his wife who hovered behind him. "Rona heard the news yesterday on *Good Morning America.* I was at the Kaiser Medical Center for most of the day with this." He held up his bandages. "I haven't been to work since."

Craig looked at Aragon's bandaged hands more closely. They were covered from the elbow down with thick gauze, stained from within with a brownish-yellow antibacterial ointment. "What happened to your hands, Mr. Aragon?"

Aragon looked dismayed. "I only wish I knew. Two nights ago I woke up feeling like my hands were on fire. I went to the doctor the next morning and learned I had been exposed to some kind of acid. They had to remove a large circle in the middle of my right palm and excised the outer layers of skin from my hands. I'll be scarred, but still able to use my hands once I heal up."

Craig kept the emotion out of his voice as he took a gamble. "Where were you exposed to the hydrofluoric acid?"

"That's the strangest thing. My Directorate covers a lot of territory, tech transfer and defense conversion. My only guess would be our glass-etching facility, but I visited the facility last week, not two days ago. I'd need to check my day planner."

Craig wrote down a note on his pad and glanced at Paige. Her blue eyes were wide, but she said nothing to let on that Aragon had admitted to knowing about the HF.

"When was the last time you saw Dr. Michaelson?"

"Two days ago, just before he died. I took him on a tour to get his opinion on recent changes in the Plutonium Facility. He's using that as part of his showcase of new technology for the International Verification Initiative. We're very proud of that."

"Michaelson worked for you, didn't he?"

Sitting on the armrest of her husband's easy chair, Rona stared down at the floor. Aragon smiled thinly. "Officially, yes—Hal Michaelson was assigned to my Directorate. But in practice, Hal worked for no one but himself. With his successful track record, Hal had *carte blanche* to do just about anything he wished."

"Did you two get along?"

"Professionally, yes—very well. But we never socialized much. The only real contact I had with him was through program management, or we both had ties with the Coalition for Family Values. I head up the visitors program for the Coalition, and Hal's programs always attracted the most attention. They were patterned after himself, I believe—flashy and overbearing."

After Craig finished his litany of questions, he closed his notepad and stood. "Mr. Aragon, I appreciate your time and your candor." He gave Aragon's wife a business card. "If you can think of anything else about the last time you saw Dr. Michaelson, please give me a call."

Aragon glanced at the official FBI card and looked worried. "This seems to be a rather in-depth investigation for a heart attack victim."

"Where did you hear he died from a heart attack?" Craig asked.

Aragon blinked his dark, doe-like eyes. "From the news. Was it something else?"

"We'd rather not say at the moment," Craig said. "I'll be back in touch if I need anything else."

Paige stood by his side, brushing down her bright red skirt. "Thank you for your time. We can find our own way out."

Craig shut the door behind them and motioned for Paige not to speak until they were inside her MG. Once they hummed along with the sound of a lawnmower engine, Paige blurted, *"He's* got HF burns, too? Is that some coincidence or what?"

Craig tapped a finger on the dashboard, thinking out loud as the wind whipped past his ears, stirring the gray-streaked hair at his temples. "Yeah, it's some coincidence. As he said, some places in his directorate stockpile the stuff."

Craig glanced at Paige, and she gave him a worried look. Strands of blond hair escaped from her French braid and flew wildly in the wind. "I can track down the doctor Aragon saw through our Benefits Office. Would that help?"

Craig nodded. "We'll have to subpoena the medical records. Even the FBI can't just walk in and get whatever files we want. First, though, when can we get that CAIN access list?"

Paige turned toward the Lab site and accelerated down East Avenue. "I'll check on it again—this is the government, so you can count on efficiency!" She laughed. "Safeguards and Security promised to have it for me by this afternoon."

Inside the T Program trailer complex again, Craig
learned that the FBI forensics team had returned to the
VR chamber, led by his backup agents, Goldfarb and
Jackson.

Since he and Paige had left an hour before, the T Program offices had become a lunatic asylum of activity.
Most of the young workers wore T-shirts and blue jeans,
clustered in groups of two or three at computer workstations. Inside the white-walled VR chamber he spotted two people in suits—FBI agents, of course, but they
worked while sidestepping Coke-drinking, Dorito-
munching techs hammering away at terminals, enhancing diagnostics in the chamber walls.

"What the hell is going on here?" Craig demanded.
He spotted a flash of red hair and a freckled face among
the people tearing apart the VR chamber. "Hey,
Lesserec!"

The flushed computer scientist jittered out of the
chamber while slurping soda in a can. He scowled when
he saw Craig. "I know what you're going to say, Mr.
FBI, but we've been granted leave to get back to work.
So don't go jumping down my throat. We've got serious
time constraints here."

Before Craig could express his disbelief, Lesserec
pulled a folded sheet of paper from his jeans pocket and
shoved it under Craig's nose. "Here, call this number
and argue with her. Don't bug me about it."

Craig snatched the paper from Lesserec. The number
was a direct line to his FBI supervisor, June Atwood. He
turned without saying a word and marched to the phone
in Lesserec's cubicle. Punching in the digits he listened
to two rings before June Atwood answered.

"This is Craig. What in the living hell is going on down here? Am I on an investigation, or did I just get invited to somebody's Christmas party?" He didn't wait for her to reply. "I've got a room full of computer nerds walking all over a crime scene. No telling what they're screwing up."

June sounded nonplussed. Her voice remained smooth and cool. "Craig, calm down."

"First, I'm put on admin leave for the NanoWare case, and now this investigation is being royally botched. Is somebody trying to make me look bad?"

"Craig, listen a minute. Ben Goldfarb tried to get hold of you. The forensics team found no trace of HF in the chamber, or in the entire building for that matter. Right after that, I received a very belligerent call from the Director, insisting that we open up the VR lab or we would hear from the President himself."

"What's the Livermore Lab Director doing calling you? Doesn't anybody care about this investigation—"

"Not the Livermore director—*our* FBI director back in Washington. The White House, the Department of Energy, and the State Department are screaming at the Justice Department because we're holding up the most important new project the President has in his Administration. Our national prestige is on the line."

Craig opened his mouth, but decided not to say anything. He glanced around and saw Paige standing next to Lesserec; her arms were folded and she looked grim, but Lesserec grinned a goofy smile at him. Craig growled and turned away.

"This is not kid's stuff, Craig," June continued. "The President sees his International Verification Initiative as *the* defining program of the decade, the transition from the Cold War into a nuclear safe world—and, no doubt, his ticket to next year's election. It's on par with the Manhattan Project, the Apollo program—"

"A man was murdered, June."

"Your investigation can continue."

"But they've already screwed up so much evidence—"

"The President does not want this demonstration delayed. Is that clear? The Nevada Test Site is already prepping a nuke from the stockpile for the actual demonstration, as well as mounting a high-explosives test for a trial run. Meanwhile, you find out what you can. Deal with it. DOE and Livermore have given me their word they'll cooperate as long as their scientists can have access to the VR chamber."

Craig snorted. "Just like they gave their word in the fifties that radiation from atomic blasts were harmless."

June spoke slowly. "Craig, you *do not* have a choice in this matter. Do you understand? Would you rather I turned the whole matter over to Goldfarb? Think about what your answer is going to be, because if it's anything other than yes, I will order your immediate dismissal."

Craig listened to himself breathing. "I understand," he said, and hung up the phone.

Turning, he headed straight for the VR chamber to collar Goldfarb and Jackson. Lesserec snagged his arm. "Get the story straight, Mr. FBI?"

Craig squashed the urge to deck the freckle-faced hacker. Instead he kept his voice level. "Feel free to go about your business, Mr. Lesserec."

Craig stepped into the VR chamber, fuming, and Paige followed him. "Nice control, Craig. Remind me to invite you next time I break up with a boyfriend."

Goldfarb and Jackson stood as he entered the white room, wiping their hands. "Hey, boss. Results are in—

no trace of HF anywhere in this building. Clean as a whistle."

Craig sighed. "So where could the HF have come from?"

Paige answered before the other two agents could say anything. "I checked that, remember? Unfortunately, hydrofluoric acid is used in small quantities in plenty of our analytical labs. Our Plutonium Facility, the glass-etching labs, and some of the fabrication facilities keep particularly large amounts. Even on the outside, though, you can buy HF from a chemical supply company for about fifty dollars a liter, so anybody could have gotten some."

Craig thought for a moment. "Plutonium building—why does that sound familiar?"

"That Lesserec kid said they were installing sensors for this VR test there," offered Goldfarb.

Craig nodded. "And José Aragon took Michaelson to the plutonium building the day he died. I wonder, did Aragon accidentally spill some acid on himself while dosing Michaelson?"

Paige brushed wisps of stray hair with her hands. "But why would Aragon have done that? Don't you need a motive?"

Craig looked into her blue, blue eyes. "That's the next step."

Friday

Laser Implosion Fusion Facility
Lawrence Livermore National
Laboratory

While Paige continued making phone calls to track down the computer records of CAIN booth use, Craig unfolded a Livermore site map tucked into the back of a battered LLNL telephone book. He had to get away from this madhouse of T Program scientists to think. With his fingernail he traced his way over to the moth-balled Laser Implosion Fusion Facility, which Hal Michaelson had spent so many years developing.

Outside, Craig shoved his sunglasses firmly against his nose. He dropped his heavy leather briefcase into the battered basket of a clunky Lab bicycle and swung onto the worn black seat. The rusty springs squeaked, and the kickstand drooped back toward the pavement as he began pedaling. He hadn't ridden a bicycle since his teenage years—luckily for him, rumor claimed it was impossible to forget how to ride a bike.

Craig had his doubts, though, as he wobbled along, steering the fat tires onto the bicycle path and picking up speed. In his dark suit and flapping tie he must have presented a bizarre picture as he pedaled over to the towering research center, but none of the Lab employees paid him any attention. It wasn't so much his riding the bicycle that made him stand out, it was his formal attire. He hadn't seen more than one other person in a suit during his entire time inside the chain-link fence.

The abandoned Laser Implosion Fusion Facility stood four stories tall, unmistakable in the middle of its own cleared parking area. In its heyday, the place had been a bustling complex, but now it was an eyesore: a concrete cube one hundred feet wide, braced by support pillars and blue-painted steel girders. According to the reports Craig had read, the structural supports extended another four stories beneath the ground to provide stability in the event of an earthquake.

The LIFF's huge bay door looked like a football field of segmented metal strips rolled partway up. He supposed that was the simplest way to allow air circulation inside the building the size of an airplane hangar. Inside, orangish lights had little success against the shadows in contrast to the brilliant California sunshine outside.

Craig leaned his bike against one of the carefully tended sumac trees that gave the Livermore Lab a campus-like appearance. He stood with hands on his hips, catching his breath on the asphalt apron in front of the partially open hangar door. Trailers and permanent office buildings were distributed around the LIFF building, leftovers from the height of the fusion power project, no longer necessary and now serving as temporary quarters for other programs.

He craned his neck and looked up at mammoth-sized, useless building, and a phrase tickled through his mind: *Your tax dollars at work.* The Laser Implosion Fusion Facility had been one of the largest boondoggles in the history of the Lawrence Livermore Lab. Teams of top researchers had spent ten years of their lives developing the project, bringing it to the final phase, then only to have it canceled at the last possible moment, purely for politics. LIFF was an embarrassment on the political level, a tragedy on the scientific level.

Craig pondered the correspondence files of Michaelson's old memos relating to José Aragon, describing the long-standing feud between the two men. The memos gave just an inkling of the force of Michaelson's personality. His words slashed like razor blades across the page, eviscerating Aragon, questioning his competence, his scientific understanding—even his parentage. Even recent memos from Michaelson, such as the one curtly posting Gary Lesserec's position, held the same biting edge.

Craig wondered if Lesserec had known that Michaelson was preparing to fire him. Did that mean that Lesserec himself might be a suspect as well?

Craig had scanned a photocopy of the old fax Michaelson had sent from his on-site inspection tour in Eastern Europe upon learning that LIFF funding had been cut. Michaelson had pleaded and cajoled and intimidated an entire list of congressmen and senators, wielding endorsements and support from other scientists. He had hopped a flight back to the United States weeks before his Moscow assignment ended, leaving the inspection team in the hands of his deputy, Diana Unteling.

Craig kept staring at the behemoth building, and the empty facility seemed to yawn in front of him. It had all been for nothing. After ten years and a billion dollars, the LIFF had been shut down before it could even be turned on. The debacle had cost the Lab Director his job and several congressmen their careers.

Such a failure would have destroyed most people utterly, Craig thought, but Michaelson, with his pit-bull persistence and refusal to accept the inevitable, had risen like a phoenix from the ashes with T Program, his wild and unorthodox proposal to use virtual reality sensors for remote but on-site inspections anywhere in the world, at anytime.

Meanwhile, the LIFF sat like an enormous mausoleum too immense to be ignored.

Craig ducked his head and stepped inside the gigantic echoing space. He snapped off his sunglasses and tucked them in his suit pocket while waiting for his eyes to adjust.

The place smelled like old oil and cool dusty air. He heard the rattling hum of generators and a sound of someone driving a forklift at the other side of the bay, moving pallets of supplies. Here, though, he seemed to be alone.

Catwalks laced the ceiling four stories overhead, but a spherical, stainless-steel vacuum vessel—large enough to hold a house—occupied the bulk of the interior. He had seen schematics of the test chamber, so he recognized the hundreds of coolant conduits, the long tubes of laser amplifiers, diagnostic ports tapped at random places inside the welded metal plates that formed the walls.

Once the initial sight of the awesome high-tech apparatus wore off, Craig noticed other things that seemed out of place. The concrete floor of the giant facility was too dirty and cluttered for scientists to be able to walk around and take measurements. Instead, much of the empty space was stacked high with crates of decommissioned machinery; identifying labels had been stenciled on the sides of the wooden slats, and shipping tags dangled from staples on the planks. Pallets filled with cases of photocopier paper stood taller than Craig's head. Under the weak yellow-orange light, most of the LIFF apparatus appeared smudged and covered with dust.

As he stared at the enormous, somehow disturbing, machinery, Craig thought about how José Aragon had supposedly brought the entire project to ruin and how a vengeful Hal Michaelson had attempted to get even with him. Yet somehow, through a labyrinth of reasoning that only government officials could fathom, Michaelson and everyone else associated with the LIFF had been severely chastised, while Aragon blithely found himself promoted.

He shook his head. The dispute over the LIFF, as described in Michaelson's sequence of inflammatory memos, had not managed to convey the sense of majesty and high stakes Craig felt upon standing inside the actual facility. The place reeked of high hopes and lost dreams.

Inside the echoing LIFF hangar, Craig wondered if this could be sufficient cause for a murder.

Friday

**Security Office
Lawrence Livermore National
Laboratory**

Paige Mitchell drove past the guard shack poised at the Lab's south gate, then hung a hard right in her MG. The old security headquarters stood just outside the sprawling complex, still in use but waiting to be torn down.

After parking in one of the Government Vehicle Only spots out front, she entered the World War II–vintage wooden building, which had originally been built as barracks long ago when the site had been a Navy base. It did not surprise Paige to see business-suited defense contractors standing in a long line beside construction workers, gangly teenagers employed part-time, and a pair of nattily dressed new graduates recruited to work at the Lab, all processing forms for temporary clearances. Paige stepped around the line and rapped her knuckles on a door to the left of the counter. The door opened after she knocked twice more.

"Hi, Jeannie," Paige said.

"Paige, thank goodness it's you!" The short, frumpy woman looked up at her, then turned to motion her into the back room. "I was ready to strangle the next reporter who barged in on us."

"Pretty busy, I take it?"

Jeannie smiled wanly. "I remember how bad it was a few years ago when the public learned about the enhanced neutron weapon we were working on. Now everyone's sniffing a scandal over what happened to Dr. Michaelson yesterday. Is that why you need those CAIN booth records?"

"Yeah. I've been baby-sitting the FBI agent conducting the investigation. He's a bull in a china shop. Nearly ripped the head off one of the T Program scientists this morning."

"Maybe you should have let him. Michaelson trained all his people to be as arrogant as he was." She chuckled. "You didn't expect me to have those records pulled already, did you? You just called this morning."

Paige shook her head. It would certainly have been nice, but she knew how complicated it could be to access records from storage, especially from the Lab's new "state-of-the-art" tracking software.

"I'd like to get an estimate on when you'll have them, though. Things are happening pretty fast, and it would be nice to have an answer for the FBI agent when he asks."

"Just a minute," Jeannie said, moving slowly over to her desk and terminal. The long string of pearls dangling below the wattles of her neck seemed to drag her shoulders down. She could barely find a workspace in and around all the potted plants gracing her desk. "Let me check the status of the job order. Somebody's probably on break."

Hollywood had convinced the public that security people would be hard to get along with, but Paige enjoyed working with the security department. They were ultimately responsible for literally millions of classified documents stored at Livermore, some of which could cause "grave damage" to national security. The security people scoped for leaks, espionage, or attempts by Third World countries to steal nuclear weapons designs. But that didn't mean security personnel couldn't be professional and courteous when she submitted a legitimate request.

Jeannie stood up from her terminal, reappearing from behind a tall spider plant. African violets and begonias seemed to thrive in the warm exhaust from the computer fan. "Bad news," she said. "They're still having problems with the new database over in the green area. You might want to check back on Monday. Yours will be the first printout, once we get back on line."

"Thanks, Jeannie." Paige wasn't happy, and she knew Craig would complain, but arguing would only do harm. And she knew that no one would even dream of working through the weekend.

Other people came in full of bluster, demanding action Right Now—and they invariably had to wait the longest. Paige accomplished much of her business through an exchange of brownie points, remembering birthdays, buying doughnuts to show her appreciation. When she asked for favors in return, she usually got them. Jeannie just might pull off a miracle, and she certainly wouldn't drag her feet. Once she got the CAIN list, Paige would go to the nursery and buy Jeannie a nice little plant to add to her collection.

She left the rickety security barracks and drove back inside the fence, returning to the T Program area. Lab management claimed to be doing everything possible to help with the investigation, but she supposed that didn't extend far enough down the food chain to bypass normal bureaucratic delays.

Stepping through the CAIN booth into the T Program trailers, Paige saw that the door to the white-walled VR chamber was closed. Several people congregated around Michaelson's office door at the back. She wondered how long they normally remained at work on a Friday afternoon.

Making her way around the computer equipment and the cluttered tables, she stepped up to the two FBI agents she had met earlier with Craig. They nodded and moved aside, granting her access to Michaelson's office.

A short, thin man not much older than herself sat on the edge of Michaelson's desk. Dressed in slacks and a knit shirt, he held a sheaf of paper that was crammed full of inventory numbers and arcane titles. She recognized him from the Classification Office, but he had tucked his badge into his shirt pocket, and she could not see his name.

Looking hot and uncomfortable, Craig Kreident rocked back in a chair and listened with a vacant expression. But he looked at Paige and smiled with something akin to relief.

The man from the Classification Office said, "I told you, this is a straightforward process. I've gone through Dr. Michaelson's entire repository and there are nearly fifty classified memos missing, all of them transmitted from DOE Headquarters. And that's only the documented list. Who knows how many Secret Work Papers are gone?" He looked accusingly at Tansy Beaumont, who looked back sourly at him with her wrinkled face as if she had just swallowed a dill pickle whole.

Craig's gray eyes seemed to focus away from the wall and back on the document control officer. "That's pretty unusual, isn't it? So many missing papers, and all of them originating from the same place?"

Tansy Beaumont shrugged. "Not if Dr. Michaelson kept them all in the same folder. He took classified work home a lot of the time. He wasn't supposed to, but nobody dared tell him what to do. Not more than once, anyway."

The document control officer looked shocked, as if gnarled old Tansy had just told him she wasn't wearing any underwear.

"So, any idea what's in those memos?" Craig asked, changing the subject. "Tansy, did you type any of them?"

She blinked her dark eyes. "No, sir! I had enough to do around here just keeping the forms filled out and doing travel papers and telling everybody on the phone that Dr. Michaelson didn't want to talk to them. He always wrote his own memos, never let me see them. Probably never even ran a spell-checker."

Craig sighed. "Since they were transmitted to DOE Headquarters, could it have something to do with espionage and nuclear secrets? Sounds important to me."

Paige interrupted. "Craig, let me straighten you out—off the record, of course, because it would get them all up in arms to hear this. But the people back at DOE are basically a bunch of beancounters—half of them spend their days writing endless and opaque procedures we all have to follow, and the other half conduct audits so they can ding us about the stuff we aren't doing well enough.

It's mostly self-generated reporting. None of the critical research is done back there, and our status reports are usually watered down by the time they get through that bureaucracy."

"Hah!" Tansy Beaumont said with a laugh. "Dr. Michaelson never even submitted status reports!"

Paige kept her attention on Craig. "What I mean is that messages from DOE Headquarters are things like program plans and budgets. More often than not, they're probably handwritten faxes, outlining funding strategy."

Craig frowned, chewing over the information. "Then why on Earth are they classified?"

Paige smiled wearily. "So the press—or even worse, God forbid, Congress!—won't get hold of it. You'd be surprised at what headquarters classifies."

The document control officer looked decidedly uncomfortable.

"So what does that really mean about the missing memos?" Craig asked, turning to the fidgety man.

"I suppose it could mean that Michaelson might have tossed everything he got from DOE into the burn bag without even reading it." He made an expression of disgust. "Possibly without even documenting them as destroyed."

"That's the type of guy he was," Tansy said, putting in her two-cents' worth.

"But we don't know that for sure," Craig persisted.

The thin man looked sour, but conceded. "That's right."

Craig thought for a moment. "Who else would have had access to these memos?"

"Nobody. And except for the Associate Director, no one else at LLNL has a need-to-know once DOE HQ documents are received."

Paige spoke up suddenly. "José Aragon is Michaelson's Associate Director."

"Was." Tansy looked around. "Dr. Michaelson's upper management right now is God and nobody else." She shrugged her bony shoulders. " 'Course, that's pretty much the way he worked when he was alive, too."

The two FBI agents on either side of Paige exchanged glances. Craig straightened. "Would Michaelson have realized these classified memos were numbered and inventoried?"

The document control officer gave a weary grin. "We've been on Michaelson's case since day one. Why do you think this entire program is in an exclusion area? Not because their virtual reality work is any more classified than other programs. No, Michaelson racked up so many security violations he would have been tossed out *years* ago—if he'd been an ordinary employee, that is. They put him here, behind a second fence, so he didn't have to be so careful."

Craig tapped his fingers on Michaelson's desktop. "So, did he know the memos were inventoried or not?"

Tansy answered. "I doubt if he cared much either way." She extended her finger toward Craig like a grandmother lecturing. "I suppose you could believe they were stolen if you want, but my guess is that Dr. Michaelson just took them home to work on them, and got killed before he could bring them back. Why don't you go out to the ranch and take a look around his desk there?"

Craig pushed up from his seat and shook the document control officer's hand. "I appreciate your time. Could I get a copy of those missing document titles?"

"No problem. I'll burn a copy right now and fax it back to the STU phone . . . here?" He raised his eyebrows questioningly at Tansy.

"I'll give you the number," she answered and led him out of Michaelson's office.

Craig looked at Paige. "What's a STU?"

"Secure telephone unit. A phone for classified conversations and faxes."

Craig laughed. "With all these acronyms, this case is getting more complicated than one of my patent law classes at Stanford!" He motioned to the two FBI agents. "Paige, have you met Special Agents Jackson and Goldfarb?"

She nodded to them. "Yes, we met in the VR chamber, after you and I returned from Mr. Aragon's."

Craig shook his head and flopped back down into the chair. "That's right, I must be going crazy. In only two days, this is the goofiest investigation I've ever conducted. It's like pulling teeth trying to get information from people, and we're all supposed to be on the same team—PSOs 'sanitizing' the site of a mysterious death for classified material before anybody got a look, Lesserec and his weird priorities, and now Michaelson and his missing documents. I came here to investigate a murder and uncovered *Animal House* instead."

He ran a hand through his thinning hair. "Did you get that computer listing of who used the CAIN booth?"

Paige felt her cheeks grow warm. "I'm working on it, but the database is down. We'll have it by Monday."

"It takes three days just to get a computer listing?" Craig said in disbelief, shaking his head.

"And these guys pulled off the Manhattan Project?" muttered Jackson. Goldfarb snickered.

"All right, let me think." Craig lifted his head and rubbed at his eyes.

Paige felt sorry for the man. He'd been going at full speed all yesterday and today. Maybe she could haul him out somewhere, get him to exercise, or maybe just kick back and relax.

"All right, Jackson—did you and Goldfarb go through Michaelson's house?"

"We went over and knocked this morning, but nobody was home. The guy lived alone, I take it," said Jackson.

"Okay." Craig looked as though he had made up his mind. "With these missing documents we can probably get a search warrant PDQ. Paige, do you know where Michaelson lived? Once we get that list of document titles, we can take a look around. Tansy told me she's got a spare key."

"Guy must have really trusted his secretary," Goldfarb muttered.

"Administrative assistant," both Craig and Paige said in unison, then they laughed.

"If we find those missing classified memos, we might find a link to all this," Craig said.

Friday

Michaelson's Ranch
Tracy, California

The high brown grass surrounding Hal Michaelson's ranch house near the rural town of Tracy made the dead scientist's residence look like a home on the range. But the dead grass was not wheat; and Michaelson's ranch sat not in a remote area, but near where the I-580 freeway spewed commuters over the rolling Altamont hills toward San Francisco. The Friday afternoon going-home traffic made a constant, droning white noise in the air, even more than a mile from the interstate.

Craig stepped out from Paige's MG, stretched his legs, and held a hand up to shade his sunglasses. The sun slanted low over the golden hills, making the air too yellow, too bright.

Paint peeled from Michaelson's white two-story ranch house. A long dirt drive ran to a circle in front of the house; an old porch held a half-dozen chairs, and off to the left stood a large, rundown storage barn exactly where Craig expected to see one. Creosote-covered utility poles carried a thick above-ground powerline to the house and the barn.

This was not the sort of place he expected an important Lawrence Livermore scientist to choose, Craig thought—but then Hal Michaelson had been eccentric in everything else.

Paige slammed her car door, making the only sound over the whisper of the nearby freeway. Craig expected to see a couple of big black dogs stirring to life on the porch, sauntering over to bark at visitors; but the ranch remained quiet. Since he lived alone, Michaelson probably hadn't had time to bother with pets.

Craig took off his suit jacket and folded it over the passenger seat in Paige's green MG. He sniffed the air. "No cattle or horses around. I wonder what Michaelson kept in there." He rolled up his shirt sleeves as he started toward the old barn. Paige followed.

Craig knocked a long metal hook out of an eye that served as the only lock on the barn door. He grunted as he shoved sideways, sliding the square plank door along a rusty track. As the afternoon light poured into the shadows, he whistled. "What in the world is all this junk?"

Open wooden crates stood in stacks against the far barn wall filled with white, pink, and green styrofoam peanuts. Big white blocks of packing material lay discarded in the grimy corners.

In the middle of the barn, a square concrete pad extended fifty feet on a side, on which rested an army of scattered old computers like a bizarre high-tech chess game. Two towering machines stood sentinel in the middle of the whole mess, thick phallic symbols six feet high. Red padded seats encircled each tower like a slanted bench.

With Paige beside him, Craig stepped into the barn. She found a light switch near the rickety door and flicked it on, flooding the shadowy interior with light from a set of naked bulbs wired to the rafters above.

The barn smelled musty, as if it had not been aired out in a month. Standing among the dusty monitors and clunky keyboards on the concrete pad, Craig placed a hand on one of the towering machines and rubbed at a tarnished and fading placard: CRAY: Serial 001.

"These are Cray-1s," said Craig. "He's got the original Cray 1 supercomputer in here, serial one." Glancing around, he made out the hulk of another squat computer with the words CDC CYBER 6600. He spotted a CYBER 7600 and an IBM 360 occupying their own territory on the concrete slab. "Jeez, do you think he's got an old Texas Instruments hand calculator around here, too? The kind that weighed a few pounds, cost a hundred bucks, and could add, subtract, multiply, and divide? Maybe he's got a slide rule, or an abacus!"

Paige joined him on the concrete pad and surveyed the junk around her. "What was Michaelson doing with this stuff?"

"Who knows?" Craig said, lifting up a plastic cover and smelling the unique odor of old electronics. "They've got computers a million times faster than these back at the Lab. Is there a market for antique computers? I doubt it. Maybe he was just collecting them."

"Other people collect stamps," Paige observed.

Craig poked around the rest of the barn, but soon decided that Michaelson was probably nothing more than a high-tech pack rat. Wiping a dusty hand on his suit pants, he said, "Let's check out the house. No telling what he's got squirreled away in there."

Craig dug in his pocket for the key to Michaelson's

house Tansy had given him. He rang the doorbell, just
for the sake of procedure, knowing no one would answer. After a few seconds, touching his crisp new search
warrant for reassurance, he slid the key into the lock.

Pushing the door open, Craig and Paige stepped into
a richly decorated hallway. The walls were filled with
framed photographs, some of them black-and-white
glossies, some in color. Every one of them showed
Michaelson standing and grinning with at least one
other person. Craig recognized the President, a former
governor of California, several senators, the House majority leader, venerable old scientists, Edward Teller,
Lowell Wood, Clifford Rhoades. . . .

Craig finally stopped. "Michaelson was well connected."

"A lot of friends—and a lot of people who couldn't
stand him," Paige said.

They walked past the wall of photographs to a meticulously decorated living room. It reminded Craig of
his grandmother's formal parlor. He wondered who
Michaelson entertained in there.

The kitchen gave him an entirely different impression
altogether: dirty dishes, aluminum TV trays, and ripped-
open empty frozen-dinner boxes cluttered the sink.
Green Perrier bottles, stacked three and four levels high,
lined the tile counter. The smell of old food made the air
thick and sour.

Paige wrinkled her nose. "What a mess."

"Think of it as a . . . uh, as a treasure hunt," Craig
said. "Try not to disturb too much, but we've got to look
for those memos. I'll look around upstairs if you want
to check out the study down here."

"Just don't expect me to do the dishes," she said.

"Ah, that would be destroying evidence."

Craig walked briskly through the upstairs of the house, giving a cursory examination to the master bedroom, a guest room, and a bathroom. He found nothing. Just off the hall he saw a narrow set of wooden stairs that led up to an old door. He creaked up the stairs, feeling as if he were in an old horror movie.

But when he pushed open the dark-brown door, giving a shove with his hip to squeak it out of the old jamb, he found a perfectly normal attic through a cloud of dust. He sneezed. Craig doubted Michaelson would have found it easy to fit his large frame into the cramped, low-ceilinged attic.

He went back to the guest room and started going through the drawers of a small desk and nightstand.

Paige called upstairs. "Find anything?"

"Not yet. What about you?"

"Nothing. The guy doesn't even have any cookbooks. For a scientist, he doesn't own any electric gadgets either. No TV, no radio or computer. Besides the coffeemaker—a vital item, I suppose—the only thing he's got down there is an answering machine."

Craig looked up. "Any messages on the machine?"

"Eight. Even dead, Dr. Michaelson's a busy guy."

Craig nudged shut the dresser drawer and stood up. "I'm coming. Let's check it out."

Downstairs, Craig pressed the solid-state device. A filtered voice immediately drifted up from the small speaker, "Hey, Doc Michaelson—we've filled your freezer with another month's supply of Gourmet De'lite dinners. The Perrier water is under the sink. We've billed your account. Thanks."

"Gee, we could stay here for a nice dinner, I suppose," Paige suggested. Craig ignored her and moved closer to the machine.

After the fourth message came a woman's voice, tired and disappointed. "Hal, this is Diana. Pick up if you're there." A pause. "Where *are* you? I got into Livermore last night and you're not home. I thought you were catching the red-eye. Give me a call when you get in. I'm staying at the Pleasanton Sheraton. I must have missed you on the plane."

Paige raised her eyebrows. "A girlfriend, you think?"

"Could be," Craig said.

The next message, recorded some time later, was the same woman's voice, more distraught this time. "Dammit, it's ten o'clock in the morning and you *still* haven't gotten in—or you're not returning my calls. What the hell's going on?" She continued to talk, and Craig listened with deepening interest.

"You might think this is all a big joke and you'll be able to breeze past this senate confirmation, but you're not bulletproof. Get that through your thick, arrogant skull. If they ever find out about us, it's going to be one hell of a ride for you."

She paused, and Craig stared at Paige. The woman, Diana, sounded as if she had been drinking. "People have had their careers ruined for far less than fucking administration officials. Talk to me—or do I have to threaten you?" Then she hung up.

"A woman scorned, you suppose?" Craig suggested.

Paige's blue eyes went wide. "Somebody else who doesn't have Michaelson on their Favorite People in the World list."

Saturday

**Recreation Facility
Lawrence Livermore National
Laboratory**

Craig felt uncomfortable standing in his new swimming trunks as he looked out across the blue expanse of the Livermore Lab's Olympic-sized swimming pool. Black lines rippled under the water, marking lanes of traffic for those wishing to swim.

Children splashed their parents in the shallow end, while show-offs attempted fancy dives in the deep water. This was not at all the way he had expected to spend his Saturday morning.

Paige Mitchell tread water in front of Craig, smiling up at him as water drops glistened on her face. She stroked backward, swimming out of his way. The curves enclosed within her sleek black one-piece distracted him from thoughts of the water. "Come on, Craig— what are you waiting for?"

She had invited him to come to Livermore on a Saturday, even though she didn't normally work weekends. Craig, on the other hand, lived inside a case once he took it on, filling his mind with the convolutions and the information, poking and prodding the whole thing until

it fit together. Discouraged that the weekend had interrupted his investigation, he had found Paige's offer too
good to be true.

"Bring a suit," she had told him—and in his mind
he'd pictured his usual dark suit and tie. She had
laughed when she corrected him, saying, "No, your
bathing suit! You don't think I'm going into the Lab to
work do you? It's my swimming day."

And so, since it was the only chance for him to talk
over the case with someone who knew as many details
as he did, he'd taken her up on the offer.

But now, as the water stretched out in front of him, he
had to dive in or continue to look silly. Squeezing his
eyes shut, he abandoned elegance and leaped into the
air, grabbing his knees in the classic cannonball maneu-
ver he remembered from junior high.

He splashed down into what seemed like the Arctic
Ocean. He came up gasping and sputtering, flinging
chlorinated water from his eyes and blinking in amazement at Paige, who swam back toward him, giggling.

"It's cold!" he said.

"Not *cold,*" Paige said, "just unheated. There's a difference."

Craig shivered and stroked across the pool, generat-
ing body heat before his skin could grow numb. "I'd
sure like to know the difference before my brain freezes
over."

"You're a wimp," Paige said. She swam briskly toward the other side of the pool.

He followed her, feeling his body adjust to the temperature as he kept moving. Under the warm noon
sunshine he found after a few moments that it wasn't

so unpleasant after all. Craig didn't want to admit that fact, though.

"Is this torture part of your training for the Security Department?" Craig said, coming alongside her and looking her in the eyes. She had tied back her sandy hair with a rubber band, and the wetness had streaked it a darker brown. She continued to swim with an easy gliding motion across the water.

"Security?" Paige answered, raising her eyebrows. "I don't work for them."

Craig looked puzzled. "I thought you were my security escort."

She shook her head, splashing water. "Not me! I work for the Protocol Office. I'm Lab liaison. I spent four years here as a technical editor, then moved to the Visitor's Center, got into Public Relations. Over the course of my assignments I picked up all kinds of background on how Lawrence Livermore works, so I'm in charge of escorting VIPs around the site."

"VIPs like me, you mean?"

"Fishing for a compliment?"

Craig stroked to keep up with her. "Actually, I was swimming for one."

"Well, if you want to earn points with me," Paige said, "you can at least close your mouth when you stare at my swimsuit, kay-O? Don't you have a girlfriend or something, since you're a big impressive FBI agent and all?"

Her bluntness took Craig aback, and he let her swim to the tile wall before he stroked to catch up with her. "Sorry, Paige, it's just that . . ." Then he raised his right hand out of the water. "Oh forget it, no excuses. Guilty as charged.

"And to answer your question, no, I don't have a girl-friend. Had one for a couple of years. She was named Trish, went to Stanford Medical School. I thought everything was just fine between us, but then she got her degree, got an offer out at Johns Hopkins, and suddenly went through a pre-midlife crisis." He rattled off the facts like Jack Webb summarizing a Dragnet case. "Changed her name to *Patrice* and moved to the East Coast, where I hear she's now bringing in about a hundred thousand a year." He sighed. "Which comes out to about two dollars an hour, judging from the amount of time she spends at the hospital."

At the shallow end of the pool a swimming lesson had started. A group of young children splashed and squealed, while their instructor seemed in love with his high-pitched whistle.

Hanging onto the smooth wall of the pool, Craig caught himself and swallowed. "I generally make it a policy not to talk about old girlfriends, especially not with another lady present."

Paige eyed him, and her deep blue eyes seemed like polished sapphires in contrast to the color of the swimming pool. "Is that an FBI rule, part of your training?"

Craig shook his head. "No, just common sense."

The line of conversation made him uncomfortable, though, and he tried to steer toward a safer subject. "So . . . I've been thinking about the case." His clumsy diversion was so blatant that Paige blinked at him in disbelief.

"I went to see Aragon at his home again last night," Craig pushed on. "He's still on a lot of pain killers, but he made the connection right away in his mind when I told him that Michaelson had died from a fatal dose of

HF—the same acid that had been spilled all over his own hands.

"You should have seen how defensive he became. I get the impression Aragon is usually a mellow sort of guy, always wants to be friends with everyone, disregards problems and conflicts, but as soon as he put together in his mind that he might be a murder suspect, he started pointing those bandaged fingers as fast as he could."

Paige frowned. Together they slowly swam toward the shallow end of the pool. "Who did he blame?"

"Well, Aragon says Gary Lesserec should be our prime suspect. Michaelson died in the VR chamber, after all, and Lesserec's the one who spends most of his time there."

Paige reached shallow enough water to stand up. She waded over to the steps. "Not too convincing," she said.

Craig followed her. "Well, he pointed out something I didn't know before, though. Apparently Michaelson stole a bunch of Lesserec's ideas—took them as his own when he pitched his International Verification Initiative. Lesserec claims he just wants to work on the project, that Michaelson could have the glory and the controversy. But Aragon doesn't think Lesserec was satisfied with that after all."

"And there's that memo in Michaelson's desk, posting Lesserec's position," Paige reminded him. "I wonder if Leserec even knew about it?"

She climbed out of the pool and stood glistening and dripping in the sunshine. Craig stared at how the droplets played on the ripples of her back. Paige turned and furrowed her brow. "Makes sense to consider him a suspect."

"I have to agree," Craig said. "But then, I can't stand Gary Lesserec, and I would take a greater pleasure in finding him guilty than somebody else."

"Not a very professional attitude," Paige said.

"Tell me about it. So, Lesserec had access to the VR chamber, and we know Aragon was somehow in contact with hydrofluoric acid—but Lesserec was also doing prep work in the Plutonium Facility. And someone named Diana is leaving threatening messages on Michaelson's answering machine."

"The plot thickens," Paige said.

"And time grows short," Craig answered. "I want to check out those places around the site Michaelson visited before he died. Can I get in to them today?"

Craig stood shivering beside her as Paige handed him a towel. In the other corner of the shallow end, the group of kids held their noses and practiced putting their faces in the water. The instructor blew his whistle again for the mere effect.

"I don't know. Let's discuss it over lunch." She turned and smiled at him. "Got an FBI expense account?"

Sunday

Building 332—Plutonium Facility

"Very stylish," Craig said as Paige emerged from the women's dressing room in the Plutonium Facility. "Good to see you in your Sunday best, since you're working overtime."

She wore a bright orange lab coat identical to the one he himself had plucked out of the visitor's bin inside the men's change room. They both had pulled plastic booties over their street shoes, with elastic bands tight against their ankles.

Paige rubbed her knuckles over the worn cotton fabric of the lab smock and smiled at him. "Yeah, I feel like I'm in that old rock group Devo. It's quite the rage."

Craig still wore his tie, but he'd left his suit jacket hanging in one of the empty lockers. He smoothed the orange lab coat, self-conscious about his appearance.

"Okay, let's get you badged in," Paige said, leading him to the fortress-like portal that allowed access into the Radioactive Materials Area, or RMA.

The place reminded Craig of the old Checkpoint Charlie at the Berlin Wall. A PSO waited near a metal detector, another sat inside a bullet-proof glassed-in booth. A radiation counter stood on the other side to make sure no one smuggled fissionable materials out, although Craig couldn't imagine anyone stupid enough to stick a lump of raw plutonium in a back pocket.

"We've got to give you a special dosimeter for this building, a Nuclear Accident Dosimeter," Paige said as the guard by the metal detector drew two black plastic rectangles from a box.

"What for?" Craig asked.

Paige shrugged. "If we have an uncontrolled criticality here, they can take your glowing body and determine which direction the radiation came from," she said with a wicked smile. "It's all routine of course."

Craig swallowed. "Thanks a lot."

She had showed him a safety videotape for visitors to the building, a dizzying list of the various sirens and klaxons and bleeps that signified fire alarms or radiation hazards or security breaches. Craig had already forgotten what some of the noises meant; he just knew he would run like hell along with the others to the emergency crash-out doors if anything happened.

"Well, you wanted to come in here," Paige said. "It's not normally on the flashy tour we give visiting dignitaries, although we've got the Coalition for Family Values bringing a group in next Friday. That, and the upcoming visit by the foreign nationals has got everybody working overtime to clean up the whole building. Otherwise, you would have have had to wait until Monday."

"I think it's important that I see firsthand the place where Michaelson might have been exposed to the HF. I want to see if we can retrace his steps."

"Right this way," Paige said. "Just don't expect any beautiful scenery."

Craig passed over his guest badge and his FBI ID card to the PSO sitting in the glassed-in security booth. The guard didn't seem impressed by Craig's FBI status.

The Plutonium Facility reminded Craig of an old industrial building from the fifties, with its white-painted cinder-block walls, worn linoleum floors, and naked conduits in a tangle of pipes and wires along the ceiling.

Paige spent an hour taking him to the large lab rooms filled with banks of glove boxes: metal enclosures fronted with Plexiglas panels, allowing workers to stand on the outside, thrusting their hands into thick mounted gloves for handling radioactive materials.

She showed him the room where classified parts were stored, sample mock-up pits of nuclear weapons, Nuclear Explosive-Like Assemblies, or NELAs. She led him into experimental chambers where experimenters tested techniques of isotope separation and new fabrication methods for the highly expensive and highly toxic plutonium metal.

Upon leaving each laboratory area, he and Paige stepped up to an alpha counter machine, a device that looked like an automatic shoe-shining apparatus. One foot at a time, Craig placed his booties against an angled flat grill. A silvery foil detector scanned the bottom of his foot to check if he had inadvertently stepped into a spilled radioactive substance. He placed his hands flat against an upper grill and waited for a tense second until the automatic scanner declared him free of contamination.

Paige said, "If somebody were to walk off with a chunk of material inside their lab coat, all the radiation alarms would sound off."

Craig saw everything and heard the words Paige said, but his attention wandered to the technicians in the

building. Orange-smocked employees working in their
own areas talked loudly to each other over the hum of
background noise, oblivious to the radiation hazard they
lived with every day, grumbling about having to work
on a Sunday.

"They don't seem too concerned about where they're
working," Craig said, nodding to two large men wheeling a metal cart down the hall.

"We have so many checkpoints and safeguards in
place that sometimes they complain about not being
able to get their work done," Paige said. "Operations
here are no more hazardous than on an automobile assembly line—safer, in fact, according to our accident
statistics.

"Besides, while the amount of radiation in sealed
sources here would give you a dose, it wouldn't make
you glow in the dark." She added quickly, "Radiation
hazards are serious, yeah, but they're about a thousand
times less deadly than popular opinion would have them
be. It's not something we should run and hide under the
bed from. We're careful."

Craig nodded distantly. "I'll take your word for it."

As he and Paige walked down the corridor, Craig
stopped a passing technician on impulse. "Excuse me,"
he said.

The beefy man turned and set his square jaw. The
chemical scent of strong aftershave wafted around him.
His green lab badge identified him as Ronald Cobb. The
man narrowed his eyes. "Yeah, what?"

"Were you working last Wednesday afternoon?"

The man looked at him as if trying to figure out a
missing piece of information. "I didn't leave early, if

that's what you're asking. I put in ten hours of overtime already. Who are you?"

Paige stepped in, though she looked at Craig with a puzzled expression. "This is Special Agent Kreident from the FBI. I'm with the Protocol Office. We'd appreciate it if you'd answer his questions."

Craig continued in a reassuring voice. "I was just wondering if you remembered seeing some visitors. One would have been Associate Director José Aragon and the other Dr. Hal Michaelson."

Ronald frowned. "You mean the guy who died? Tall man, right? Built like an ox?" Ronald chewed his lip as he tried to remember. "And he had a little sissy mustache, right? Pencil thin, like he drew it on with mascara? Reminded me of . . . what's his name? Cary Grant."

Craig restrained a smile. "Yes, that's Dr. Michaelson."

"Yeah, I saw him in here," Ronald said. "He was with some uptight dude, leisure-suit type, slicked back hair."

"Do you remember anything about their tour here?" Craig asked, trying to hide his excitement. "What rooms they went into?"

Ronald shrugged, then flashed a suspicious glance at Paige. "That guy showing him around didn't seem to know a thing about this building. They went into every one of the rooms and he was yakking a mile a minute. Then they got into a big argument in the hall."

"Do you remember where, or what it was about?"

Ronald looked sour. "We got work to do here, Mister. I can't go keeping an eye on all the tourists wandering through, especially now that we have to make the plutonium building look pretty for the public. How many other people have to work today? Don't you think we should be getting more than time and a half for working on weekends?" Ronald grumbled to himself. "Look, I'm busy. Got any more questions, or can I go now?"

Craig shook Ronald's hand. "Thanks. You've told me what I wanted to know." He made a show of taking out his notebook and squinting at Ronald Cobb's badge. "Thank you for your cooperation," he said as he jotted the man's name down. Ronald practically beamed with self-importance as he went about his work.

"What was that all about?" Paige asked as they went to the airlock leading into another section of the RMA.

Craig sighed. "Just what I was afraid of. You've met Aragon. You think he could sneak in here and get some HF from one of these people? He'd stick out like a neon light." He paused as he pondered. "I still want to run a full inventory of all the hydrofluoric acid in this building, though. Find out if anything's missing."

Paige looked at him skeptically. "You saw the glove boxes, Craig. Over half of them have small bottles of chemicals in there and HF is a common item. It would only have taken a teaspoon to give Michaelson a fatal dose."

"I know it's probably a wild goose chase, but I still want to know where it was distributed, who had access to it, and how much, if any, is missing."

"I guess that's a start," Paige said, sounding pessimistic.

Craig smiled at her as they walked through the airlock door. "Yeah, it's a start."

Monday

Building 433—T Program

Back in the T Program offices, ready to start a new week, Craig had moved into Gary Lesserec's little-used cubicle to keep his notes and write his reports.

Paige came to him, grinning broadly as she held the drooping paper of a fax. "Finally got it, Craig—first thing of the morning. It's the list of all the people who used this CAIN booth in the days preceding and following Michaelson's death."

Craig sat up from jotting notes on a yellow legal pad. "About time," he said. "We were supposed to have that last Friday."

"I know," Paige said with a sheepish expression, "but we're lucky Jeannie came in today. She has one of the most sophisticated computer tracking systems on site, so naturally it didn't work right and broke down. If we had to look through punch cards, I probably would have found it within an hour."

He shook his head and took the fax from her. She pulled up a chair next to him in Lesserec's cubicle, removed a felt-tip pen, and made check marks beside some of the names.

"These are the PSOs who came in to do random inspections at odd hours," she said.

Craig squinted down and picked up a different colored pen, ticking off the names of familiar T Program workers. Gary Lesserec had gone in and out many times. Michaelson himself had left in mid-afternoon, presumably to go on his tour of the Plutonium Facility with José Aragon and then off to his meeting at the Director's Office. He hadn't returned here until after five when, according to the records, virtually everyone had checked out for the evening.

Gary Lesserec had been one of the last to leave before Michaelson returned. They had missed each other by only about five minutes.

"Nothing's really obvious," Craig said, scanning the list of names again.

Paige sat waiting for him, fidgeting in her chair. She remained quiet for no longer than two seconds. "Look at the next sheet. It's the people who came in the following day. One name in particular is interesting, I think."

Craig looked it over, spotted the times of entry and exit—and immediately fixed upon one that didn't belong: *Diana Unteling* at eleven forty-five P.M. He recognized the name, but couldn't place it. "Who's this?" he said. "Another one of the PSOs?"

"No," Paige said, drawing out the answer and trying to cover her smile. "It's very interesting, in fact."

Then suddenly Craig remembered where he had seen her name. Diana Unteling had been Michaelson's deputy on the on-site inspection team in the former Soviet Union years before. Michaelson had left her in charge when he had flown back to rescue the Laser Implosion Fusion Facility.

"I thought she was at DOE Headquarters in Washington," Craig said. "Was she back at Livermore on business?"

"According to Tansy's schedules, Unteling and Michaelson had no meetings set up. So why was she out here that late at night? After you had ordered it sealed? The place was empty, but she stayed about an hour. What was she doing all that time?"

Craig made his mouth into a straight firm line, staring down at the fax paper. He suddenly sat bolt upright.

"Diana," he said then he changed the tone of his voice. " 'Hal this is Diana, where the hell are you?' "

"Now you're getting it!" Paige said. "You think Diana Unteling from DOE Headquarters is the voice on the tape? This is bad news, or good news, because it's another whole line of reasoning we haven't looked into yet."

Craig stood up from the chair, leaving his clutter on Gary Lesserec's desktop. "Let's find out if Ms. Unteling is back at DOE Headquarters or still out here. If I have to, I'll travel to Washington, D.C., tomorrow so I can talk to her face to face. I want to watch her expression before she has time to make up an excuse."

"Do you think the FBI will fly you there?" Paige asked. "Won't they just bring in one of their own agents in D.C.?"

Craig took a deep breath, remembering June Atwood threatening to pull him off the investigation. "It usually works that way, but right now my boss owes me a few big favors."

Monday

Building 32—Plutonium Facility

Carefully, very carefully, Duane Hopkins measured out a sample of hydrofluoric acid inside his glove-box container.

Ronald or some of his buddies were full of bluster and bravado, not caring about the dangers to which they exposed themselves in their work. But Duane had a healthy respect for the terrible things he worked with. He knew the bad things radiation and poisonous chemicals could do to people. Stevie was living proof.

On his clipboard he made a careful note of the amount of acid he kept in his glove box, then added a little bit just to make sure no one thought he had lost any. Duane didn't want to get into trouble.

Ronald had said an FBI man had been in on Sunday asking questions, and immediately the Plutonium Facility manager had ordered a full and complete inventory of all the controlled chemicals in all the glove boxes in Building 332.

Duane didn't know what had prompted this extreme investigation, but he secretly hoped that something bad had happened, something bad enough to cause a full-scale crackdown. Maybe that would force the Lab to get rid of the dangerous substances like the ones that had made Stevie so sick. Duane didn't know if it was radiation or poisonous chemicals that had given Stevie his cerebral palsy—maybe poisonous radioactive chemicals?—but people needed to be aware of the hazards. An FBI investigation might bring about a complete shakeup.

He had tried to telephone Mr. Lesserec over at the Virtual Reality program, but the man had not returned his calls. He wondered what this was all about.

Duane didn't want to see his job disturbed, but maybe this would be worth it.

In the change room during the early afternoon break, Duane meticulously unbuttoned the front of his smock and changed into his street clothes, tucking in his green flannel shirt and sliding the jingling car keys in his pants.

With his voice raised against the loud background noise, Ronald barged into the change room with his cronies, laughing about some crude joke; but Ronald stopped upon seeing Duane in his street clothes.

"Hey, Beavis! Where you think you're going?"

Duane turned away and continued to get dressed, closing his locker door. "I have to go home. I'm taking the rest of the day off."

Ronald scowled and took two steps toward him. "You didn't ask me, Beavis. I didn't say you could go home. You've got work to do, and some of my stuff, too."

"I can't, Ronald," Duane said. "Stevie's got a doctor's appointment. He's really sick. I have to take him in."

One member of Ronald's gang snorted. "The retard's

probably getting a brain transplant." The others laughed.

"Yeah, Beavis here is donating his own brain. They need a microscope to find it, though." Ronald guffawed.

Duane didn't answer, but hurried out of the locker room. He didn't know what else he could do to get even with Ronald, to get the bully off his back. It seemed everything he thought of went without notice, or he chickened out before carrying out his plans, knowing Ronald would catch him and beat him to a pulp.

Maybe Duane could report him to that FBI man. Ronald had done so many things blatantly wrong that he must have been part of whatever the agent was investigating. Or maybe that nice man Gary Lesserec would help; Lesserec had said that he'd owe Duane one for that material he had provided.

But as Duane hurried out of the secure facility, past the checkpoints and the fence to his battered old Ford station wagon in the parking lot, he knew that all such thoughts were just fantasies.

He would never have the courage to stand up to Ronald Cobb, and nobody else would help him. He was doomed to be stepped on for the rest of his working life.

Tuesday

**Forrestal Building, DOE
Headquarters
Washington, D.C.**

Craig Kreident paused at the top of the Metro escalator
to get his bearings. This had already been one hell of a
long trip, and he'd just arrived. His suit was damp and
wrinkled from his own perspiration, and the humidity in
the Washington area hit him like a sledgehammer after
California's dry heat.

He had not cared for changing planes in Chicago, fidgeting for an hour in the circus of O'Hare; but this flight
took him into National Airport, which allowed him to
bypass the crazy D.C. traffic and ride the Metro instead.
His boss, June Atwood, had highly recommended that
route.

After living in the Bay Area most of his life, Craig
knew what to expect from California drivers: as long as
he moved with the traffic, it didn't matter if he was
going seventy-five or standing still. People drove com-
petently. They followed the rules.

But Washington, D.C., was home to not only the
worst drivers in the nation, but also to ambassadors in
big limousines whose drivers had more diplomatic im-

munity than they had functional traffic experience. The whole city area resembled a bumper car ride that Craig had no stomach for, rental car or not.

Adjusting his sunglasses, he tried to flow with the crowd of pedestrians as he hurried along the wide sidewalks to the Department of Energy's Forrestal Building. Here in the capital, at least, his suit and tie did not stand out. It seemed even the joggers wore ties. But when he asked for directions, twice, the people looked at him as if he had offended them.

The Forrestal Building was supported by massive pillars and extended over a plaza. Bored guards—yes, he saw they were actually called "guards" here, imagine that!—sat at stations inside the lobby. Craig snapped his sunglasses shut and slid them into his pocket. He groped for his Bureau ID as he approached the desk.

A weary-looking woman didn't say a word as she took his ID and checked a computer list. Chewing on a mentholated cough drop, she pushed a form at Craig and motioned for him to sign the document. When he finished, she flipped a Visitor's badge across the counter, then turned away, all without speaking. She dug in her purse for another cough drop.

Craig clipped the large DOE HQ badge onto his suit lapel, then tapped the plastic so that it dangled properly. He looked around. The civil servant attitude struck him like a blizzard, a cold brushoff. People slowly agreed to help only after being asked, and then they offered assistance only under great duress. In his mind he contrasted it with the bouncy "please let me help you" demeanor back at Livermore. He thought of how enthusiastic Paige Mitchell had been.

He snagged a guard standing just inside the secure

part of the building. He held out his badge and brought out his Bureau ID, just in case he needed heavier ammunition. "Excuse me, I'm looking for Ms. Diana Unteling, Deputy Assistant Secretary for International Affairs."

The guard scanned a thick list protected by a plastic cover. "Yeah. Fourth floor, room 4023. Got an appointment?"

Craig decided this was no time to debate details. "Yes," he said firmly.

The guard squinted at Craig's badge, and as if the words FBI suddenly clicked with him, he nodded to the left. "Those elevators will take you directly there, sir."

"Thanks."

Craig found the suite of seventies-vintage administrative offices without any further trouble. The glass door opened to a young black woman sitting behind a metal low-bid desk. She was dressed to kill in more finery than California women wore when they went to a formal party. Three office doors stood closed behind the woman, bearing engraved name plaques. The only access to Diana Unteling would be through this moat dragon.

The secretary looked up. "Yes?"

Thinking to fit right in with the Washington milieu, Craig decided to dispense with the Nice Guy act. He spoke brusquely and got straight to the point as he flashed his badge and ID. "I'm Special Agent Kreident from the Federal Bureau of Investigation, here to see Ms. Unteling."

The woman looked confused. "Mrs. Unteling has already had her security interview for her Assistant Secretary appointment."

"This isn't a background check."

She made a show of looking down at the appointment calendar on her government-issue desk. "I don't believe you have an appointment, Mr. Kreident."

"I don't," Craig said. "But I need to see her, anyway."

"May I tell her what this is about?"

"No."

Her ebony eyes widened. Her eye shadow looked as if it had been applied with a spoon. A large one.

"Just a moment, sir." She pushed up from her chair, which rolled across a hard plastic floor mat, and walked on two-inch high heels to the door on the far right. Rapping softly, she entered. Craig mulled over what the moat dragon had said. An Assistant Secretary position? That must be what Unteling had been pestering Michaelson about on his answering machine.

The secretary reappeared and held the door. "Mrs. Unteling will see you now, sir." Craig placed a smile—not much of one, just enough—on his face and took a deep breath. He held his briefcase like a shield in front of him as he entered the room.

Unteling's office smacked of her former California background: a nicely matted watercolor series of golden brown hills, vineyards, and sandy beaches, and a stark Ansel Adams photograph of El Capitan in Yosemite.

A trim, no-nonsense woman with graying blond hair rose from behind her desk—a polished wooden desk, he noticed. She extended a hand. The gold in her wedding band was thick; the too-large diamond sparkled. "Mr. Kreident, is it? Agent Kreident?"

"That's right. I appreciate your time. Sorry to barge in on you unannounced."

Sitting back in her chair without offering Craig a seat,

she dispensed with any pleasantries. "What can I do for you, Mr. Kreident? You have caught me at a particularly busy time."

Craig pulled up a chair, easing close to her desk. "I'd like to ask you a few questions about Dr. Hal Michaelson."

Her face was stony, and it may have whitened, but it could also have been his imagination. "I heard that he died. Terrible thing to happen. He was one of our top people at Livermore. Why are you questioning me?"

"Just routine questions, Ma'am." He remembered how much Paige had hated being called Ma'am. "Dr. Michaelson died on federal property, and until we can get a firm cause of his death, I'm interviewing all of his past associates. His close associates." He paused, but again saw no reaction. "Did you know Dr. Michaelson very well?"

"I worked for him when I lived in Livermore. I was also part of his on-site inspection group that went to the former Soviet Union to oversee the dismantling of their nuclear weapons complex. But that was many years ago."

"Have you maintained your contact with him since that time?"

Her dark eyebrows arched slightly. "In what way? I'm from Livermore, as you probably know. He was a family friend, but living on different coasts makes it hard to get together too often. I'm afraid he didn't put much stock in my husband's work on the Coalition for Family Values."

"When was the last time you saw Dr. Michaelson?"

"I can't recall. Last year, maybe."

"How about the last time you spoke with him?"

She twisted in her chair and tapped a long fingernail on her wooden desktop. "What are you getting at, Mr. Kreident? How often do you recall speaking with a friend?"

"Ms. Unteling—"

"*Mrs.* Unteling, please. I'm a happily married woman."

Craig lifted his eyebrows. *I'm sure your husband would like to know that—especially after hearing the messages you left on Michaelson's answering machine.* "I went through Dr. Michaelson's office with a classification specialist. They were able to open his safe and inventory his classified documents, but several were missing."

She stiffened. "Why are you telling me this, Mr. Kreident? Do you have any idea how many classified papers are created every year at Livermore?"

"This is a special case, I think. You see"—he steepled his fingers and leaned closer to her; she backed away—"every one of the missing documents originated from your office, Mrs. Unteling. There were sixty memos, all transmitted over the past year and a half." He watched her closely.

"Once the documents are out of our hands, they are no longer our responsibility," she said.

"Then what about the subject matter? If I provide you with a numerical list of specific classified memos, could you tell me what they contained?"

She shook her head. "Impossible. I'm afraid, Mr. Kreident, you don't have the proper need-to-know. You would have to get a specific search warrant for those specific memos, and in order to do that I think you would have to make an extremely compelling argument to prove they are in some way connected with Hal's death. And that's not just a DOE regulation—that's the law."

He tried a throwaway comment, anything to make her yield. He shut his notebook and stashed it in his briefcase again. "Dr. Michaelson personally signed for those documents; they all came from your office. Now he's dead, and those memos are missing for a while. I thought you might want to talk about it." He had a sudden flash of insight. "In light of your recent nomination for Assistant Secretary, I mean."

Diana Unteling's face grew even colder, like a glacier calving icebergs. "Mr. Kreident, my office had the responsibility for coordinating those classified memos with Lawrence Livermore. Every document was logged out of this office and transmitted over secure communication channels in strict accordance with DOE security regulations.

"It is not your place or duty to question that procedure. If you have any questions about the disposition of classified material at Livermore, then I strongly suggest that you direct your queries *there,* and not here, since that appears to be where the breach of security occurred, if in fact there was any breach."

Craig studied the unflinching woman. Nothing seemed to crack her exterior. He smiled instead. "Oh, you misunderstand me, Ma'am. I said the memos were missing from Michaelson's document repository. I didn't say we haven't found them." He breathed slowly as he kept his voice calm, taking a big gamble. "I just wanted to look you in the eye and ask *you* what was in them. But you're quite right. You don't have to tell me."

Craig clicked his briefcase shut and placed it on his lap. "Thank you for your time, Mrs. Unteling." He stood and held out a hand; she ignored it.

From the door Craig said, "I'll leave my card in case you decide to get hold of me." He placed one of his FBI cards on the wooden desk and patted it. "Don't hesitate to call."

Pressing her lips together, Unteling didn't say a word. Craig could almost feel her gaze boring into his back as he departed. He still couldn't tie down all the details, but he felt as if he had jabbed a hornet's nest with a stick.

Wednesday

**Building 433—T Program
Lawrence Livermore National
Laboratory**

Paige spotted it first, noticing the obvious and making Craig want to kick himself for not seeing it.

When he came into the T Program trailer complex late Wednesday morning, Craig still felt breary-eyed from his late flight back from Washington, D.C. But he had taken the time to shave and change into a clean suit, white shirt, and dark red tie. But he felt rundown and fuzzy.

Paige met him in the T Program trailer, wearing a large but conspiratorial grin on her face. She had clipped back her honey-colored hair with a pair of black barrettes, and she wore a loose peach-colored silk blouse over trim black slacks. She looked comfortable, easing up on her rigid dress as she spent more time working with Craig as a friend rather than as an official protocol escort. Her smile at him was brighter than the sheen of her silk blouse.

"So did you learn anything in Washington, D.C.?" she asked, obviously hiding something.

"Unteling denies everything, of course, but I think I rattled her. Something's not right, and we just need to pinpoint what it is. She's sweating."

Paige leaned closer to him. "I've found something else that's not quite right," she said, lowering her voice. She sat down on one of the chairs in Gary Lesserec's cubicle.

Outside in the computer area Lesserec leaned over two other programmers who hammered busily at keyboards. Lesserec looked like a junior Napoleon trying to rein in his troops. He flashed a glance at Craig, frowned with distaste, then bent back to the workstations. He ignored Craig entirely, which was just fine with him.

"What is it?" Craig asked, also keeping his voice low.

Paige indicated the paraphernalia in Lesserec's cubicle. "Take a look. It's right in front of your eyes."

Craig had seen it all a dozen times before, but he glanced again, trying to determine what Paige had noticed. The big-screen workstation, the bumper sticker about Porsches, the plastic Snoopy doll, the empty Diet Coke cans scattered everywhere, the photograph of Lesserec and his "too sexy for a nerd" girlfriend standing at Lake Tahoe, the debris of diskettes, software manuals, and old sticky-notes. He stared and stared, unwilling to admit he couldn't see anything new.

Paige didn't wait for him to ask. "Come on, let's go for a bike ride." She whispered. "Someplace we can talk."

Craig nodded. They passed back through the CAIN booth to the outside of the trailer complex and found two Lab bicycles perched against a bike rack. He blinked in the sun until he settled his sunglasses in place. Craig adjusted the black bike seat as Paige swung herself into place. She started pedaling, making him work to catch up with her.

She found a bike path lined with eucalyptus trees, and they rode past the Restricted Area fence. Without talking, they kept going around the perimeter of the site where the research buildings were scattered farther apart, leaving only pumping stations and generator buildings run by Plant Engineering.

"All right, Ms. Detective, open up. What is it?" Craig said, looking across at her. His sunglasses kept slipping down his nose, and he lifted one hand from the handlebars to straighten them.

"You know that bumper sticker about Porsches?" Paige said. "Well, I checked—Lesserec really owns one. Brand new. Sixty-five thousand dollars." She waited for that to sink in, then continued. "You know the photo Lesserec keeps on his desk, him and his girlfriend by their condo at Lake Tahoe?"

"Yes." Craig nodded again, beginning to see.

"Lesserec bought the condo in the last nine months. He really owns it. He's also got a very nice house up in Blackhawk, one of the exclusive, upscale subdivisions in Danville, just about the most expensive area to live in this whole valley." She paused meaningfully. "Gary Lesserec should not be able to afford that sort of thing."

"Okay," Craig said cautiously. "Why not? He's the Deputy Program Director for the entire VR Project. Isn't that a prestigious position?"

They passed under some low-hanging, pungent eucalyptus branches. Paige looked back at him. "Craig, I've got a printout of all the Lab salaries in case you need actual proof, but trust me, we're *University of California employees.* Even important people here don't scratch the salaries they could be making as consultants on the outside. The highest paid person in the Livermore Lab doesn't pull in much more than a hundred thousand a year, and I guarantee you Lesserec doesn't make that much. At least he's not supposed to be."

"Well," Craig said pondering as they pedaled past fenced-in softball fields the employees used at lunch, "what about the girlfriend? Could she be rich? Maybe she's the one with money?"

Paige pursed her lips. "I asked about that. It seems Tansy Beaumont has a great deal to say on the subject. Tansy thinks Lesserec's girlfriend has been sponging off him for about two years now. In her own words, 'You can see what he gets out of that girl.'" Paige laughed. "If *she* was rich, why would she be with someone like him? You've got to admit Gary Lesserec is no prize specimen."

Craig cracked a smile. "I'll agree with that."

"According to Tansy," Paige continued, "the girl-friend doesn't even have a job, claims to be 'an aspiring poet,' who sits at home all day and spends Lesserec's money. No, Lesserec's the one with the cash—but where did he get it? That's what I want to know."

"Couldn't he be a consultant or something?" Craig asked. "Don't a lot of people here do that sort of thing on the side?"

Paige agreed. "You're right. But I do have a little pull around here, you know. I called up our Lab Counsel Department and had them run a check. Anybody who does outside work beyond their regular employment has to file a form every year stating their consulting activities. That's to prevent conflict of interest. Guess what I found?"

Craig answered. "No paperwork on file for Lesserec."

"Bingo," Paige said.

"So, he's not openly declared that he's engaging in consulting activities. His girlfriend doesn't have any money. His Lab salary is decent, but not enough for the kind of life-style he's living. These are the classic signs of espionage involvement."

Paige looked at him with her blue, blue eyes. "Just like that Ames spy case with the CIA. Everybody saw the signs and nobody paid attention. I'm just amazed nobody's caught it before this. We're all supposed to be watching out for exactly those things. I've given the security lecture myself to some of our new employees."

"It was a good idea to discuss this out here, away from the crowds," Craig said. "Let's keep quiet about it while we make some discreet inquiries. The best thing we can do is get hold of Lesserec's phone records, both for home and at the office. I'll have to call the Bureau and get the appropriate subpoenas issued, but that shouldn't be a problem. They're hot to solve Michaelson's murder."

Paige kept pedaling as they turned the corner onto another path heading back toward T Program.

"I can get his Lab phone records for you," Paige volunteered. "They're open access. I just need to contact the Lab telephone systems."

"Good," Craig said. "And thanks for keeping your eyes peeled while I was gone."

She smiled at him, and as he looked back at her his foot slipped from the pedal of the bike. He wobbled before he could catch his balance.

"Just happy to help," Paige said. "My civic duty."

"The more we find out, the more complicated it gets," Craig said, knocking the kickstand down on his bike as they parked outside the T Program trailers again. The sun was warm, and the exercise had felt good to him.

"I wish we'd stop digging up more questions though," he said. "I want to start finding some answers soon."

Thursday

**Building 433—T Program
Lawrence Livermore National
Laboratory**

The next day Craig and Paige sat in the back of the T
Program conference room as if they belonged there;
they were the only two to show up on time for the briefing they had accidentally heard about, thanks to Tansy
Beaumont.

The other team members came bustling in at least
five minutes late. Craig watched the motley group of
young geniuses hurry in. Some of the programmers carried personal mugs of coffee, but most held the ubiquitous cans of Diet Coke, as if signifying membership in
a club. Craig marveled at their casual clothes, their dis-
regard for basic personal hygiene. He couldn't imagine
how people could consider themselves professionals,
yet dress so sloppily.

Paige, on the other hand, sat next to him wearing a
bright teal dress with a subtle floral pattern marked out
in lighter blue. Her scent carried just a hint of perfume,
enough to make Craig notice.

The people lounging in the room chatted in low

voices, fidgeting with the obvious distaste that so many of the scientists seemed to have for meetings.

Breathless, Gary Lesserec plowed through the door, his red hair unkempt. He headed straight for the overhead projector resting at the head of the long table, dodging chairs and glancing at his watch. He slapped a manila folder filled with plastic transparencies on the table, looked up at the gathered coworkers, and froze for just an instant when he saw Craig.

Then Lesserec ignored him entirely and addressed his team. "I'll keep this short," he said. "I promise. We've got to get back to work, but I figured it's best if we all know where we stand. I'm going to give you a summary of everything to expect for tomorrow's high-explosive demonstration out at the Nevada Test Site."

"Awww, high explosives," a thin black woman said with a frown. "Why don't we just use a nuke ourselves to test things out?"

Lesserec sighed. "Believe me, we would if we could, Danielle, but the testing moratorium has screwed up all the timing at NTS. The President has only cleared one device out of the stockpile, and we've got to save that one for the big bells and whistles when the foreigners are watching."

Lesserec shot a cold glance at Craig and cleared his throat. "I take it I don't need to introduce our uninvited visitors. I suggest we continue to give Mr. FBI our full cooperation"—Lesserec's tone said exactly the opposite—"so he can be on his way and off bothering somebody else as soon as possible.

"Meanwhile," Lesserec turned back to the projector and flipped on the bright bulb, "our counterparts out at Frenchman Flat in Nevada have set up a nice little practice bang for us. Five hundred tons of high explosive laced with our special detectors and high-speed fiberoptic data-transmission cables. *Kaboom!* to the sixth power.

"One lucky volunteer is going to get to sit inside the VR chamber hooked up and watching the explosion in real time. But don't worry," Lesserec said, pushing down with his hand as if to quell imaginary grumbling, though no one in T Program had said a word. "It's recorded, of course, so you'll all get to watch it, one by one, after the test. It won't make any difference."

Lesserec slapped a transparent viewgraph on the glass of the overhead projector. Photos of the barren desert flat out in Nevada where nuclear tests had been conducted blurred across the white screen as Lesserec cranked the focus knob.

He put up a diagram explaining the type of explosive and the configuration for the test blast, but Craig paid little attention. Instead, he studied the laser-printed list clipped to a yellow legal pad on which he jotted detailed notes. The Bureau had obtained the telephone numbers dialed and the duration of calls made from Gary Lesserec's home line. Paige had given him a printout of calls made from the office phone in Lesserec's cubicle on site.

Craig had already spent hours skimming the numbers, the calls, the names, eliminating the obvious ones. Lesserec's parents in Ohio, frequent calls from the office to Lesserec's home, presumably to talk to his "aspiring poet" girlfriend.

Most curious, though, were a dozen or so phone calls to electronic gaming and toy companies. Some calls had occurred during working hours, but others—after detailed digging by Craig, as well as agents Goldfarb and

Jackson back at the main Oakland office—had been made late at night to the homes of chief executives in various entertainment companies.

Craig had circled several of the most suspicious calls with a pink highlighter. Now, in the conference room, he tapped his pen against the phone numbers, thinking, staring at them, running possibilities over in his mind.

Paige glanced at him, then looked up as Lesserec continued to talk about actual preparations for the down-hole detonation, the first underground nuclear explosion in years: the test that dozens of foreign nationals would observe, putting their virtual hands on the outside casing of an American device. They would watch with enhanced computer speed the slow-motion detonation of the equivalent of a twenty kiloton nuclear bomb.

From the evidence of the phone numbers, and the obvious fact of living beyond his established means, Craig decided that Lesserec was almost certainly involved in illegal activities. But he had been following the wrong train of thought when he considered that the red-haired kid might be selling secret research data to the Middle East or China.

No, industrial espionage could be even more insidious. Lesserec was a bright, highly motivated researcher. His talent was undeniable, but so was his naiveté.

Hal Michaelson had seemed a lot more savvy. Had the T Program leader found out what Lesserec was doing, then asked too many questions? Had Lesserec killed him as part of a cover-up?

At the front of the room, Lesserec continued his talk, filled with "umms," strained jokes, and the disorganized shuffling of viewgraphs. Craig looked up to see a diagram of the T Program VR chamber.

"For the actual event, first we'll go through our boring benchmark demonstration, having the foreign observers visit and walk around the LLNL Plutonium Facility so they can get the right look and feel for the VR systems."

Lesserec's muddy green eyes sparkled as he grinned, making freckles flow across his chubby cheeks like scum on a pond. "Then we'll take our guests down-hole and blow their socks off."

"Excuse me," Craig said, raising his hand.

Lesserec stopped in mid-sentence and looked at Craig. "Yes, Mr. FBI?" The kid's sarcasm was maddening, but Craig was too professional to let his annoyance show.

"Are these foreign representatives qualified in any particular way to observe the explosion? I mean, do they need training to use the VR chamber?"

Lesserec rolled his eyes. "You seem to be unclear on the concept, Mr. Kreident. You just sit there and watch, like in a movie theater. The VR technology does all the work. Our 3-D sensors plunge you into the environment. The suspended microspheres and our special effects technology inside the chamber make it all seem real, but you don't have to *do* anything, just occupy space."

"Thank you, Mr. Lesserec," Craig said. "That's just what I thought. Since you've been unable to find the simulation Dr. Michaelson was running on the evening of his death, I'm still interested in learning about this technology and how it could be connected. So I have a suggestion: why don't you let me be the observer tomorrow? I'll be your guinea pig in the VR chamber for the demonstration."

A group of the T Program members began grumbling loudly. "Wait a minute, I wanted to be first!"

"We should draw names."

"That's not fair. He hasn't worked at all on it."

"I've been giving up my weekends for this thing."

Lesserec looked offended at Craig for a moment, then suddenly he smiled. "Shut up!" he yelled at the others in the room. "Why would you want to be a guinea pig, Mr. FBI?"

Craig shrugged, spreading his hands innocently on top of the yellow legal pad on his briefcase. "Think about it, and you'll see it makes sense. All the rest of you are intimately familiar with the VR technology. You know what to expect, and you're going to watch the demonstration with an ultra-critical eye. Myself, though, I'll be like one of those foreign visitors. I'm willing to let you—what was your phrase?—knock my socks off."

"Craig, do you know what you're doing?" Paige said quietly, but he squeezed her forearm for reassurance.

"As you say," Craig continued, "you're recording the whole simulation. Everybody's going to get their chance to experience it. So what difference does it make? You couldn't find a better test case than me."

Lesserec remained silent, looking at the others who were obviously not happy. But Craig ignored them, fixing his attention on Gary Lesserec alone. He thought he saw an inner smile behind the redhead's carefully controlled expression.

"All right," Lesserec said. "Does anyone here have serious *technical* objections to Mr. FBI being our guinea pig? Or are they all just childish complaints?"

Nobody answered. "Okay," Lesserec said. "Walter and Danielle, after this meeting gets out, take Mr. Kreident into the chamber and give him a user-friendly tour of everything he's going to need to know."

As eyes fastened on him, Craig pondered whether he should feel elated with his victory, or trepidation about what he had gotten himself into.

After Gary Lesserec finished returning a few of the calls that had piled up during the meeting, he returned to his small cubicle. He wondered when he could appropriately shift everything into Michaelson's empty office, since it appeared he would be Acting Group Leader for quite a while. Michaelson's office was a lot larger than his own dumpy little desk and cloth-partition walls, and his new position demanded more prestige.

With a splatting sound, Lesserec dropped his folder full of plastic viewgraphs onto the narrow workspace. Then he noticed Craig Kreident's dark blue suit jacket draped over the chair; the FBI man's briefcase and notes took up half the space in the cubicle.

Annoyance and simmering anger bubbled within him. Even now, with all the work left to be done, the FBI agent had taken two of his best programmers to show him how the VR chamber worked, as if he owned the place. Luckily, the engineers had installed the rest of the new beta-test NanoWare chips yesterday.

Of all the workspaces available for Kreident to set up camp, the FBI man spent most of his time in Lesserec's cubicle, as if it were his own. He wondered if it was some kind of childish power play, Kreident showing off that he could walk wherever he wanted, horn in on whichever office or space he chose, like a bully on a playground.

Consciously, and with a smirk on his face, Lesserec

used his left arm to sweep Kreident's briefcase and notepad onto the floor.

"Oops!" Lesserec said with mock dismay. He enjoyed the feeling for a moment, but then thought better of it. He didn't need to act as childish as the FBI man did. He bent over to pick up the briefcase and the notepad. He stuck it in an out-of-the-way corner by the other computer user's manuals.

A white paper on top caught his attention as he saw a list of telephone numbers—a printout from the phone company, and another one from the LLNL telephone system. He noticed his own name at the top . . . and felt a cold like liquid nitrogen seep through his body.

"What the hell?" he said and picked up the numbers, scanning them. It seemed to be his complete telephone records for the last month or so. Several numbers had been highlighted, and although Lesserec didn't have a photographic memory for specific phone numbers, he knew exactly which ones Craig Kreident had identified.

"Holy shit!" he said, swallowing hard. Then he carefully replaced the briefcase and notepad exactly where Kreident had left them, hoping the FBI man would not notice his belongings had been disturbed.

Lesserec backed out of his cubicle and decided to use one of the other phones. He scratched his head, feeling sweat prickle through his reddish hair. His mind whirled.

He was trapped and could not decide how best to handle the situation, how to exercise sufficient damage control.

He was afraid he would have to take some drastic measures, change a few plans.

Thursday

Building 443—T Program
Lawrence Livermore National
Laboratory

Special Agent Ben Goldfarb wished for a cigarette for the first time in fifteen years. He'd stopped smoking the day he'd gotten married and hadn't had the urge since—well, not often anyway—even through all the stakeouts, the finely focused investigations, and criminal interviews.

But today, baby-sitting the egocentric scientists in this neurotic government lab, he felt that if he didn't have a smoke within the next few minutes, he just might rip the head off that jerk Lesserec.

Clad in a Superboy T-shirt, blue jeans, and Velcro tennis shoes, Lesserec joked with the other programmers, treating multimillion-dollar equipment as toys instead of cutting-edge technology. The Bureau would kill for access to half of these computers, and these Lawrence Livermore kids treated them like fast-food wrappers.

Goldfarb crossed his arms and held back a scowl; his dark suit was hot, but Bureau rules against "down dressing" during an investigation ran all the way back to J. Edgar Hoover. Agents were professionals, after all.

He felt a nudge at his shoulder. He turned to see Special Agent Jackson waving a sheaf of computer paper.

"Hey man. Craig needs to see us. Says he's got a hot project. Just like on TV."

"He probably wants some fresh doughnuts or something," Goldfarb muttered, then threw a glance back toward the Virtual Reality chamber. Freckle-blotched Lesserec rocked back in his chair, staring at his computer screen and picking his nose. "But I suppose even that sounds exciting right now."

When they reached Michaelson's abandoned office, Craig Kreident hung up the phone, looking grim. He looked at the two special agents. "Looks like we've got a rabbit on the run. Diana Unteling's secretary said she just left for Dulles Airport. She's flying to Livermore. Her flight arrives at San Francisco this afternoon."

Craig's gray eyes narrowed. "You can swing by the Oakland office to get the file I set up on her. It has a recent DOE photo. Get out there and tail her, but be discreet. I don't want you to do anything yet—just find out where she's going and get back to me."

"Anything special we're watching for?" Goldfarb asked. He realized he no longer wanted a cigarette.

Craig ticked off points in rapid-fire sequence. "She's involved in this, and she lies. She said she hasn't spoken to Michaelson in some time, but we've got her voice on an answering machine tape made the day he died. She came out here and broke into T Program after the murder, even though I had this building sealed. Supposedly"—he made a grumbling sound—"all of those missing classified memos originated in her office, but she claims not to remember anything about them. Smells a little rancid to me. This might be our break."

"Right," said Goldfarb, already heading for the trailer's CAIN booth exit with Jackson in tow. He ducked as a wad of paper sailed across his path and neatly hit a trash can set up on the far side of the work area. He shuddered, thinking that the nation's defense rested on the shoulders of these goofballs.

Surrounded by the bustle in San Francisco International, Goldfarb drew back as the first passenger walked briskly through the gate from the direct flight from Dulles Airport in Washington, D.C. The stern-faced woman's short gray-blond hair flopped up and down as she moved rapidly into the press of people, ignoring all the others waiting to greet friends or relatives. She moved at her own speed, a few notches ahead of the rest of the crowd.

Goldfarb squinted at her: dark eyebrows, ice-blue eyes, five feet five, and slender build. Diana Unteling looked exactly like the picture in her dossier. Of course she would have sat in First Class, and she had barged up the ramp before any other passenger. She carried a gray-tweed hangup bag and moved aside for no one.

"Well, that was easy," Goldfarb muttered to himself.

He folded his newspaper and fell in behind her, keeping a distance of twenty feet between them. He walked along with eyes narrowed but a blank expression on his face, as if he were a businessman going to an out-of-town meeting. He wouldn't need to hurry until Unteling was about to leave the terminal. Jackson would be waiting with the car out by the curb.

Unteling plowed through a crowd of Japanese tourists like an icebreaker ship at the beginning of spring. Goldfarb took the long way around the crowd, reaching the terminal doors ahead of Unteling. Apparently, she had no baggage to pick up.

Jackson spotted him and maneuvered their nondescript blue Ford Taurus around the other waiting vehicles. Goldfarb climbed into the passenger side as Diana Unteling flagged down a man lounging outside a long black limousine. "That's our baby," he said.

Goldfarb and Jackson sat parked with the engine running, watching her dicker with the limo driver for a minute. The driver opened the back door to help his passenger inside, then jogged around to the front and got in.

"She might as well have used a neon sign with that limo," said Jackson, whistling. The Taurus merged into the airport traffic, keeping a good distance behind. "Finally got a tail I don't have to work at."

Goldfarb relaxed back into his seat and tapped his fingers on the door armrest. "We've got a good idea where she's going, anyway." Cars whizzed by as they drove along, pacing the limo. The traffic snaked down Highway 101, then turned east for the Hayward–San Mateo Bridge.

Goldfarb shook his head. "She must be nuts thinking she can keep a low profile anymore. With her political appointment and Michaelson's death, she's lucky *60 Minutes* isn't tailing her."

Jackson glanced at the other cars on the freeway and lowered his voice to a conspiratorial whisper. "Maybe they are."

Jackson eased onto the long span of the San Mateo Bridge. The sky overhead reflected a porcelain blue off the flat slate of the Bay shallows. A seagull flew overhead, oblivious to the thousands of cars below.

The two agents fell silent, listening to the rhythmic

thump-thump-thump of the bridge sections beneath the wheels. When they reached the opposite shore on the Livermore side of the San Francisco Bay, they followed the limo north to Interstate 880 before turning onto I-580 toward Livermore. Goldfarb reached for the car phone. "I'll check in with Craig and let him know his pigeon is on the way."

But when they reached the freeway exits for the city of Livermore, the limo kept driving, continuing east over the grassy Altamont hills that divided the Livermore Valley from the larger Central Valley and the rural city of Tracy.

"Where is she going?" Jackson said. "You'd better call Craig again."

Goldfarb nodded. "She's going to Michaelson's ranch."

Jackson dropped even farther behind, keeping the limo just in sight so as to not arouse suspicion.

The interstate wound eastward up into the golden brown hills. They passed hundreds of white and silver windmills, with blades turning lazily in the breeze. The freeway scrolled through the low mountains, then descended on the other side into a flat ocean of farmland.

Goldfarb tapped the car phone on his leg. "Come on," he muttered.

"There, she's turning off," said Jackson.

"Keep back—I don't see any other cars getting off. We know where she's going."

Jackson slowed to increase the separation distance. A car behind him honked at the sudden change in speed, then roared by on the left. The driver flipped them off. "Same to you buddy," muttered Jackson.

The limo drove to the top of the off ramp, then turned right, heading deeper into the hills and the farm roads.

Goldfarb punched numbers into the car phone. He waited; then said, "Craig, yeah, listen. We've got Unteling in sight. She bypassed Livermore and seems to be making a beeline for Michaelson's ranch. Thought you might want to come out for a visit."

Goldfarb listened for a moment, then said, "We'll wait for you and hang back. Just hurry up—if she's dumb enough to return to Michaelson's, no telling what she has in mind." He pushed the button to terminate the call.

Thursday

Michaelson's Ranch
Tracy, California

As Paige parked her MG on the road outside Michaelson's ranch house, Craig checked the bullets in his revolver. He placed the weapon beneath his dark suit jacket in its shoulder holster before looking up to see astonishment cross her face.

"Don't leave the car. Jackson will be here with you. He's our backup in case anything goes wrong."

"Is there going to be shooting?" asked Paige.

A sudden memory flashed through Craig's mind: Miles Skraling, the NanoWare exec, locked behind a door and the sound of a single *pop!* gunshot. "There's no telling what Unteling is going to do. No telling what she's already done, but we're going to find out." He forced a smile. "Don't worry, it's standard procedure. Just like your radiation dosimeters."

He turned to Goldfarb as he climbed out of the cramped MG. "Ready?"

Goldfarb holstered his own weapon and pocketed a flip phone to keep in communication with Jackson. "Let's go, boss."

They set off on foot down the dirt drive toward

Michaelson's ranch. As they rounded the corner, the farmhouse and barn came into sight, sitting in a wide open area. The tall dry grass rustled with the sound of witches' brooms.

The long black limousine sat outside Michaelson's house. The driver sucked on a cigarette as he lounged against the car, flipping through the glossy pages of a magazine. He looked bored, expecting no one to come up the long driveway.

Craig waved Goldfarb back to put some distance between them, spreading out to make themselves a harder target to hit. Deep down he didn't really think it would come to shooting, but he knew the instant he let down his guard, things would go to hell.

The limo driver flicked his cigarette away, then hurried to stomp it out before the dry grass could catch fire. He still hadn't noticed the two FBI agents. The driver bent to rummage inside the limo. Craig felt his pulse quicken. Was he reaching for a weapon?

Craig touched his fingertips to the outside of his shoulder holster, tensing as the driver straightened. Craig suddenly heard the booming bass of a car stereo. He relaxed.

The limo driver spotted them, jerked backward with surprise, then grinned in embarrassment. He strode around the front of the limo and called out. "You guys lost?"

They were still a good twenty yards away. Craig flipped out his badge. "FBI."

The driver's eyes widened. "Hey, man, is this a bust or what? I *thought* that lady was too uptight!"

Craig nodded to the peeling white ranch house. "What's going on in there?"

The driver backed up. He wet his lips and looked nervously at Goldfarb, who was still circling around. "Hey, I just gave her a ride from the airport—she paid half in advance, cash. I'm getting a bonus just for waiting here while she's inside."

Craig tucked his ID back into his pocket, keeping his hands free, his arms loose. "Did she say what she needed to do?"

The driver fidgeted in uneasiness. "She's collecting some stuff to bring back with her. Said she had to get some old records."

"I'll cover the back," Goldfarb said in a low voice, rustling through the grass alongside the house.

Craig turned back to the driver. "Isn't it unusual to drive fifty miles from the airport to a ranch house, then wait around to take them back?"

The driver looked incredulous. "Unusual? Man, what planet are you from? This is the San Francisco area!"

Craig shook his head with a weak smile. "Never mind," he muttered. "Just pull the limo to the end of the driveway. The farther the better."

Craig turned for the front door of the house, leaving the bewildered driver behind. As he approached the old home, he drew his weapon from his shoulder holsters. Better safe than sorry. The last thing he wanted to do was to spook Diana Unteling, but he didn't know how she would react if she had killed Michaelson, and was now destroying evidence.

Holding his revolver upright, Craig stepped on the creaking porch. Unteling had left the door ajar, and he expected it to squeak as he pushed, but the hinges remained mercifully silent.

Inside the front hall, he paused a moment before continuing. Nothing. He moved inside, past Michaelson's brag wall of framed photographs with famous people and into the kitchen. As far as he could tell, nothing had been altered from when he and Paige had been there—the dishes were still dirty, trash cans still full, scattered crumbs still on the cutting board.

Craig felt his heart rate increase. There were too many similarities between this and the NanoWare case. *But this time, would the bullet have my name on it?*

The ceiling above him groaned. He stopped. Was she in the master bedroom?

Entering from the back door, Goldfarb silently joined him at the base of the stairs. Craig nodded for Goldfarb to lag behind, then started up. He took the stairs slowly, one step at a time.

The sound of a book hitting the floor made him freeze. He heard muttering coming from the bedroom. Rounding the corner in the hall, he saw Diana Unteling kneeling at an oak nightstand beside Michaelson's bed, where she had popped the bottom out of the lower drawer. The bed and floor around her were strewn with stacks of papers, each bearing a thick red border and the letters SRD, Secret Restricted Data, stamped at the bottom and the top.

He saw no sign of a gun. Craig lowered his weapon and stepped into the room. "Hello again, Mrs. Unteling."

Unteling spun around on the floor, scrambling to her knees. Her short blond hair flopped back, and her ice-blue eyes glinted in the dim light filtering through the drawn shades. Her face filled with fright, then darkened with anger as she recognized Craig. "You—what are you doing here!"

Craig looked at the papers she had assembled. "I'd ask you the same thing, Mrs. Unteling."

"That's none of your damned business."

"Dr. Michaelson's house is under federal jurisdiction until the investigation is complete. My search warrant is still valid." Craig heard Goldfarb step up the stairs, but the other FBI agent stayed out of sight, behind him.

"Damn your investigation! I have a perfect right to get my possessions back from here." She bent and hurriedly started brushing the stacks of classified material into piles. She looked up as he watched. "What are you going to do, shoot me? These are mine, you know."

"Last time I looked," said Craig softly, "classified documents belong to the government, not to individuals."

Her gaze bore into him like twin ice picks; she clutched her hand into a fist, so tightly it seemed as if she would break a fingernail.

"What's in the memos, Mrs. Unteling?" he asked. He tried a long shot. "What's going to happen when your husband finds out about you and Michaelson?"

As Craig stared back, a crack appeared in her glacial features, until slowly her hardened expression melted, and her face grew slack.

She looked around the room. Pictures, snapshots and open photo albums were scattered on the bed, parts of the "classified documents." But he could see that most of the photos showed her and Michaelson: standing in front of a *dacha,* toasting each other while dressed in elegant dinner clothes, dressed in parkas with a world of white around them. Cute pictures, love letters, all incorporated into red-bordered documents. Classified information. What sort of game had they been playing?

Unteling plopped down on the big bed with her eyes closed. She slowly shook her head. "Another week or so and we could have taken care of all this. But Hal wouldn't return my calls. The bastard! Now look at the mess he got me into."

Goldfarb stepped into the room and looked around, his dark eyes wide at the sight of the classified documents. Craig holstered his weapon and motioned with his head for Goldfarb to call for Jackson. As Goldfarb quietly spoke into his flip phone, Craig talked to Unteling.

"Looks to me like you did a pretty good job of getting yourself into a mess." She said nothing, and neither did he, prompting her with his continued silence.

"I loved him," she said dully, finally. "I really loved him." She shook her head. "Most people hated the son of a bitch, let his Neanderthal ego grate on their nerves. But no one could go up against him one on one. He was just too damn smart. And that's what drew me to him."

"Then why did you kill him?" said Craig.

She laughed a short high giggle. "Kill him? Sometimes I wish I had. It would have made life a lot easier back then, back when I was his executive assistant at Livermore, and my husband's Coalition was taking off. Some of Hal's outrageous demands didn't endear anyone to him.

"But you know what? He got things accomplished that way. He made things *happen,* when other people failed. Hal Michaelson didn't care who you were or what position you had—if you got in his way, he would bull right through you. When he left Livermore for Russia, I jumped at the chance to go along, to be at the center of history in the making.

"Besides, I had to get away from my husband for a while. Fred wanted me to give up my whole career so I could help him with his work—with a capital *W*. Everybody loved Fred, but he was just so . . . so *vanilla*. Calm and comfortable, without a spark of passion in his whole body. He didn't have a clue."

Craig picked up a stack of photos showing Hal Michaelson and Diana Unteling. The photos were not those of friends; there was something much deeper present, a longing of unspoken intimacy. "That's when you started your affair."

"If you thought Hal was relentless during a Congressional testimony, it was nothing compared to his stamina in bed. The guy didn't know how to do anything slow. It wasn't his nature."

Craig tossed the photos on the nightstand and picked up two of the classified documents Unteling had found. Each message had a cover sheet, but the interior document was a personal letter, one from Michaelson to Unteling; another from Unteling to Michaelson.

Goldfarb waited at the back of the room, listening to the testimony. Diana Unteling watched Craig flip through the classified memos. She laughed; but it was a tired laugh, worn out, defeated.

"That was our game, the only absolutely certain way that we could communicate with no one else catching on. We were each Classifiers. We could stamp whatever we wanted on the documents."

"Pretty elaborate precautions just to hide an affair," said Craig.

"Just an affair?" Unteling looked at him bitterly. "Mr. Kreident, I am the wife of the nation's number-one protector of morality. My husband's Coalition for Family

Values went national, and he decided to move the whole organization to Washington, D.C. Can you imagine what a field day the press would have if they found out I was cuckolding my dear husband? That would have done far more harm to his coalition than any assault by a hate organization.

"Fred worked on this for years, and my entire family life was wrapped up in promoting it. My son went into a seminary, even after I encouraged him to study engineering, his first love. Millions of people's lives have been turned around because of Fred's outreach program. Just *think* what could have happened if word had gotten out—that the coalition director's wife was fucking Hal Michaelson."

She paused. "I was offered a job back at DOE headquarters after the on-site inspection work, and exchanging classified memos with Hal seemed to be the only way to keep the affair quiet."

Diana Unteling looked up sharply when Craig didn't say anything. "I don't expect you to condone what I've done, Mr. Kreident, but the very least you can do is keep it out of the papers."

"I'm not a press agent, Mrs. Unteling," Craig said. "I don't write news releases. Maybe you can tell me why you were present in Dr. Michaelson's lab the night after his body was found. We have both the CAIN booth records and the threatening message you left on his answering machine."

She looked defeated. "I was looking for these memos! I thought I could destroy them before they were discovered. I didn't think at first that he might have kept classified material at home. When I found them missing from his repository, I thought you had already confiscated them.

"But when you came to talk to me, I knew you were lying. You didn't have them. You didn't have any idea what the memos contained, or your attitude would have been entirely different. Then I thought I knew where Hal might have kept them, and it would be only a matter of time before you did go through his house with a fine-tooth comb." She shrugged. "I needed to find them first."

She stood, ignoring the documents now and brushing aside any pretense of innocence. "But no, the killer wasn't me, Mr. Kreident. I wanted Hal to live . . . even if only so I could cut off his balls."

Craig told Goldfarb to start gathering the classified documents and photos together. "I'll need to get a statement from you, Mrs. Unteling. And fingerprints as well."

Unteling set her mouth, but her shoulders sagged. "My fingerprints are already on file with my security clearance, Mr. Kreident. But I suppose this statement will affect my confirmation hearing."

"We'll have to give the Senate committee everything in your records. Now, if you'll come with me, I need to take you to our Oakland office."

As they left the old farmhouse, Jackson stepped from the blue Ford Taurus, having driven up after Goldfarb's call. They held the back door open for her. As she ducked to get in the car, she stared at Craig, then disappeared inside. Jackson slammed the door behind her.

. . . .

Thursday

Valley Memorial Hospital
Livermore, California

Late in the evening, as the doctors and nurses and orderlies rushed around him, Duane Hopkins felt small and invisible. He wasn't part of their concern, but he didn't need to be.

Stevie was the one they should be paying attention to.

He had not seen his son since they had whisked him back into the examination rooms. Duane sat quietly in the blue plastic chair of the emergency room waiting area, looking at his knees. Empty sounds buzzed in his head. He wished one of the doctors would tell him something about his boy, but he didn't want to be a bother.

The old Zenith TV in the corner of the waiting room droned at low volume, broadcasting the Home Shopping Channel. The picture showed products while the announcers discussed their amazing virtues. Duane Hopkins would never be able to afford such things, but he enjoyed watching, anyway . . . at any time other than now.

A quiet moan of concern and fear built in Duane's throat. The clerks at the admitting desk seemed incredibly busy, though this late in the evening nothing else seemed to be happening in the emergency room. No one else sat in the hard plastic chairs, waiting with him. Waiting.

Stevie's day nurse and the woman from the Coalition for Family Values had been so concerned about the boy's unrelenting cough that they had finally convinced Duane to take him to see a doctor on Monday. The physician had diagnosed Stevie's problem as pneumonia and had given Duane some antibiotics and a strong decongestant, but Stevie seemed too weak to fight off the cough. Duane had given him the medicine and waited, expecting it to cure Stevie like magic. But it hadn't—Stevie just got worse. The boy made bubbling, gurgling sounds as he breathed.

Finally, now on Thursday night, Duane had been getting ready to go to bed when he heard Stevie choking, making loud panicked noises in his room. Duane had rushed in to find the boy blue in the face, convulsing and unable to breathe.

Duane had smacked him on the back, shaken his scarecrow body, until the boy coughed free a throatful of phlegm. Duane had bundled Stevie up in his worn maroon bathrobe and carried him out to the car. In terror, he cradled the boy's jerky assortment of mismatched and uncooperative arms and legs, buckling him into the seat belt.

During the drive Stevie's eyes had looked bleary and distant, not bright and filled with the unconditional love Duane was accustomed to seeing there. This was pain and unreasoning fright, as well as a question in his eyes, wondering why his father couldn't make things right as he had always done before.

"I'm sorry, Stevie," Duane had whispered and rushed to the hospital emergency room as fast as he could.

The doctor's expression was grim, his voice clucking with disapproval. He wore gold wire-rimmed glasses and had a shiny pink-bald pate surrounded by a rim of mussed light brown hair. "Your boy's lungs are filled with fluid, Mr. Hopkins. How could you have waited so long to bring him in here? This is serious."

The doctor called a nurse, and the two of them had hustled Stevie toward the swinging doors, taking the boy away from him. Duane stood up to accompany them, but the doctor motioned him back into the waiting room.

"You just give the admitting clerk all the information she needs. We'll take care of things here." Without another word, the gruff doctor rushed Stevie back behind gray doors that swung back and forth on their hinges.

Duane caught a glimpse of Stevie's head bouncing to one side, his eyes rolling toward the ceiling as if he was trying to get a glimpse of his father before these strange people took him away.

Seated on an uncomfortable stool at the front desk, Duane answered endless questions from the admitting clerk. He was distracted, confused as to why they would want so much information when all they needed to do was take care of Stevie.

Duane looked at the forms in front of him. He had no idea where the boy's mother was. He couldn't remember her social security number. Rhonda hadn't sent so much as a Christmas card in seven years. He didn't remember his insurance card number, either, though luckily he had it tucked among all sorts of other debris in his wallet, next to his membership card in the National Geographic Society and another card for the Coalition for Family Values.

He sat watching the Home Shopping Channel, and he waited. He felt very alone. He didn't know what he would do if anything happened to Stevie. The boy was his entire life. His heart was inextricably connected with his son.

Stevie could not live without him: Duane protected him, cared for him, loved him when no one else in the world even noticed his existence. Stevie, on the other hand, gave Duane something to live *for,* someone to love when Rhonda had left him and when the bullies at the Plutonium Facility made his job a daily hell.

Red-eyed, he continued to watch the assortment of jewelry and kitchen appliances. An hour passed, and still he heard nothing from the doctor, though occasionally he saw a flurry of activity in the back examination rooms.

Duane stood up, felt his knees crack, and he shuffled over toward the admitting clerk's desk. He moved tentatively, but before the woman noticed him, she stood up with a manila folder and strode purposefully back behind the counters with the file tucked between her elbow and her side.

Duane hesitated, then realized that he didn't have the nerve to pester the doctors. They would come out when they had some information for him. He tried calling Gary Lesserec, who had wanted all that information about Stevie and his condition, so maybe he could help. But no one was home. Reluctantly, Duane went back to his chair.

After a few minutes he looked at his watch again. He

pulled out his wallet, removing the card from the Coalition for Family Values. He was distraught. He needed to talk to someone, but he had no friends, no one he could open up his heart to.

The Coalition people had always been helpful and understanding. He rubbed the card between his thumb and forefinger to straighten the damp wrinkles pressed into it during its years of being buried in his wallet. He went to the pay phone by the wall of the waiting room and dialed the number. He squinted at the small printed words: *Any time of the day or night, we're there for you with our hopes and prayers.*

He thought he recognized the voice of the woman on the phone, and he wondered how many people worked for the Livermore office of the Coalition.

The group had expanded greatly over the last five years, joining other local organizations and becoming a nationally recognized religious community-service organization; but it was always the same people who brought meals and printed literature to Duane's home. He kept the pamphlets, though he never found time to read them. He didn't go to church either, because it was too difficult to keep Stevie quiet for an hour, so Duane did his duty by watching televised services on Sunday mornings.

As soon as he identified himself to the woman on the phone, her manner changed abruptly. Duane wondered for a dizzying instant if they'd somehow had a premonition about Stevie's poor health, but then the coalition woman spoke rapidly.

"Mr. Hopkins! We've been trying to call you this evening. I don't know how it managed to slip our minds because we know you work at the Lawrence Livermore Lab, in the Plutonium Building? Well, we wanted to let you know that we're bringing a tour through in the morning just as we did with the Virtual Reality chamber. You recall that?"

Duane wanted to interrupt, wanted to say something, but her words came so quickly they washed over him like an ocean wave. "We wondered if we might stop and say hello, see you hard at work. The children will be very interested in watching just what goes on at our local scientific lab. We wondered if—"

Finally, with a broken sob, Duane cut her off. "I'm at the hospital," he said. "Stevie's sick. He's in the emergency room. I don't know what's going to happen."

The raw plea in his voice kept the woman silent for a full five seconds. "Oh, Mr. Hopkins, I'm so sorry," she finally said. "When did you take him to the hospital? Is there anything we can do?"

When she asked the question, Duane suddenly realized that he didn't know *what* he wanted. He wanted someone to make Stevie better, to take care of his problems, but he knew that would never happen.

"I don't—" and then his throat caught, constricting a sob. Just telling someone about Stevie's condition suddenly made it more real to him, more terrifying—and he knew he couldn't face it alone.

"There, there, Mr. Hopkins," the woman said. "I'll have someone come right over to pray with you. We'll *all* pray for you. You've got the best doctors in the area, and Stevie's fate is in God's hands now.

"Oh, and we'll send a message directly to our director, Mr. Unteling. You know he's originally from Livermore, and he always takes a special interest in problems from his hometown. We'll do what we can, I promise.

We'll have someone over at Valley Memorial to be with you soon. Everything will turn out right, if that's the way God intends."

"Thanks," Duane said as he hung up.

The doctor came out half an hour later, five minutes after a quiet young man from the Coalition for Family Values showed up. The doctor's face wore a shadowed scowl. He marched directly over to Duane like a quarterback heading for the goal posts.

"It's not good, Mr. Hopkins," the doctor said without preamble, without an attempt at a kind bedside manner. His pink bald head glistened with perspiration, and he squinted through his gold wire-rimmed glasses.

"Your boy is very weak and not responding well. We've already drained his lungs, but I'm afraid there's been a lot of damage. We have him on a respirator right now. It's as if he's not even fighting, though. He's very frightened."

Duane had an image in his mind of what exactly had been going on behind those gray swinging doors: Stevie hooked up to beeping machines and gasping tubes . . . the doctors plunging long needles like silver spears between the ridges of Stevie's ribs, drawing out pinkish yellow fluid from his lung tissue.

"I'm scared, too," Duane said in a small voice.

The doctor's expression softened just a little. "Why don't you go in and sit with him? Maybe that'll help."

"I'll wait for you," said the quiet young man from the Coalition for Family Values.

Duane hurried in the wake of the emergency room doctor as they passed through the swinging doors. The doors made a hollow, final *thump* behind them.

Hours later, the life-support machines made squealing, alarming sounds that seemed to scare the spirit out of Stevie's frail body. Duane shouted for the doctors, for the nurses, but they did not arrive until it was already too late.

He held Stevie's scrawny, bony body as it shuddered in its last convulsions, jerking in time with Duane's own sobs.

Stevie died at 2:48 A.M.

Thursday

Lyons Brewery
Dublin, California

As Paige spun the corner into the strip mall parking lot during the Thursday late-dinner rush, Craig gripped the door of the forest-green MG. He made no comment about her driving, since he had no particular desire to walk home.

He scoped the shopping center, spotting a waffle place and a Japanese restaurant, but Paige drove past them to the back of the mall. "Where are we going?" he finally asked, afraid of her answer.

"One of my favorite places," she answered, then came to a sudden stop in front of a small storefront with a large, colorful scrolled sign over the door: Lyons Brewery.

Though it was a Thursday night and just past the supper hour, dozens of cars already filled the spaces. The thumping strains of loud jazz music reverberated through the walls.

He squinted at the sign. "Paige, I've got a lot of work to do tonight. I thought we were going to talk about the case, not go out on a date."

She raised her eyebrows, but he couldn't tell if she

was amused or angry. "A date? Don't get ahead of yourself, buddy. Come on, this'll be a great place to talk."

He followed her through the glass door. A posterboard sign taped above the handle pleaded "Save the Ales!"

Paige had changed into a pair of jeans that complimented her figure and a mint-green blouse that rippled slowly as she walked. Inside, the band had already started a new song, played through amplifiers that must have been designed for a large stadium rather than a small bar.

"I won't be able to hear what you're saying!" he said, leaning closer and raising his voice.

"Neither will anybody else."

He looked smug. "Then this *is* a date."

She led him to one of the tables, sturdy monstrosities made of dark wood and marred from years of hard use. The place had been outfitted like an old British pub, with colorful foreign flags draped in streamers across the ceiling.

The bar itself was long and crowded, as two bartenders hustled to fill a constant babble of orders. The wall bristled with a dizzying array of tap spigots from dozens of microbreweries. Hanging above the bar, a green slateboard listed four columns of beers Craig had never heard of.

"What kind do you like?" Paige asked.

Craig felt at a loss. "Heineken," he said after a moment's hesitation.

Paige looked at him in distaste. "Oh, please!" Craig looked up and noticed a ceiling draped with Yuppie neckties that had been tied into nooses, strangling bottles of popular beers—Coors, Budweiser, Corona,

Heineken. "Try something special, Craig. They've got everything here."

"Okay," he said, overloaded with choices chalked on the green slateboard. "How about something dark? Do they have any dark beers?"

Paige laughed. "Let me get you one. Go sit down at a table." She approached the bar like a combat commander trying to take a hill.

Moments later she returned with two pints, a rich amber beer for herself and a thick black substance that looked as if it had been brewed in the tar pits. He blinked in amazement as she handed it to him. He raised his voice, looking down at the beer. "Did you bring me a spoon?"

She laughed. "St. Stans Dark Altbier. Guaranteed to be the *chewiest* beer you'll ever have in your life."

He took a sip and grimaced because that was what she seemed to expect him to do. But as he rolled the rich, chocolatey-tasting beer around in his mouth, Craig realized how delicious it was. "What are you having?" he asked.

She took a sip and closed her eyes before answering. "Best beer in the world. Red Nectar Ale." He hadn't heard of it, but he nodded in agreement.

She sat down across from him, propped her elbows on the scarred wooden table, and leaned closer. "Let's brainstorm, Kay-O?" Her change of subject jarred him. "That's what we came here for. This isn't a date, after all."

"Right," he said, unconvinced.

"What about Diana Unteling?" she asked, plowing ahead. "Sounds like she's got plenty of skeletons in her closet."

Craig took a small sip of his beer. "You're really getting into this, Miss Detective."

Paige ignored him and persisted. "Do you really believe she killed Michaelson?"

"She could have gotten the HF from any chemical supply place," Craig pointed out. "She didn't need access to the plutonium building."

"That's beside the point," Paige said.

Craig nodded slowly. "I know. All right, I keep coming back to Gary Lesserec and those telephone calls of his. If he's working overtime for Nintendo or something, it's none of my business; it's not a part of this investigation. What has it got to do with murder? There has to be some kind of connection. I don't believe in coincidences."

Paige took a long, long drink of her beer, and Craig sipped his again, rolling it around in his mouth. "Think about what Lesserec does. What he does *best.*"

"Virtual reality stuff," Craig said.

"And if you were him, think how tempting it would be to sell what you know, the systems you've developed, the classified information for a real VR system, more real *than* real. Toy and game companies would be in line ten deep to get their hands on your patents. Just imagine, say, Disneyland mass-producing virtual reality chambers like the one in T Program."

Craig took a big swallow of his thick beer just as the band ceased playing. The silence rang in his ears. He thought of amusement parks, arcades with chambers equivalent to the one Michaelson and Lesserec had developed. Three-dimensional, *tactile* virtual reality chambers that required no suits, no goggles, just people standing in a room and experiencing the ultimate adventure. Like the Holodeck on *Star Trek*.

"But the Livermore VR chamber might have killed a man," Craig said. "What if it's too real?"

Paige stared at him, and he felt swallowed up in those incredibly blue eyes. "You sure you want to be the guinea pig in the explosives demonstration tomorrow?" she asked. "I'm worried about you."

"I'm worried, too," he said. "I'm not stupid. But I think that's the only way we're going to catch Lesserec in his games. It's a risk I have to take."

Paige set her empty pint glass down on the table. "Drink up, Craig. I need another one."

He took a too-large swallow, feeling the dark beer burn as it went down. He looked up and stared at the beer bottles swinging on their necktie nooses.

Craig suddenly knew, without a doubt, that he was going to have a hangover when he arrived for the big demonstration in the morning.

Friday

Building 433—T Program
Virtual Reality Chamber

"It's the same philosophy that made NASA so successful during the Apollo days," said Gary Lesserec, looking down at Craig like a mad doctor about to perform brain surgery on an unanesthetized patient.

Tightening a buckle, he made sure Craig was securely strapped to his motion simulator seat in the VR chamber. "NASA practiced everything so much, ran over so many contingencies, that *nothing* came as a surprise." He snorted. "Too bad the space program lost their good luck. Seems they got politics now."

Craig nodded, but paid little attention, facing away from the redhead. The red-padded chair in the VR chamber stood among a row of others, but Craig would be the only one in here during the high-explosive dress rehearsal. Now that he was buckled in, the only way to get away from Lesserec's bad breath would be to unstrap himself and leave.

Paige Mitchell stood at the doorway with her arms folded. She watched like a den mother, but she said nothing to Craig.

Lesserec said, "Ready to ride the first nuclear test in nearly a decade?"

Craig turned in his padded seat and looked quizzical. "I thought this was a high-explosive test."

"Right—that's what I meant," said Lesserec, almost too quickly. He patted Craig on the shoulder. "Five hundred *tons* of HE, or a kiloton of nuclear yield equivalent." Lesserec gave a supercilious grin. "The factor of two difference is due to the percentage of explosive energy that goes into blast and shock versus the radiation yield for a real nuke."

He made a dismissive gesture. "You wouldn't understand the difference, but you don't need to. This dress rehearsal will simulate nearly every aspect of the real thing. That's why it's so critical that everything goes right. We're recording it all. In fact this is going to be our *real* test. The demonstration for the foreign nationals is just show-and-tell."

Craig looked around, flicking his gaze around the dull, featureless chamber. "So what am I supposed to see? Won't this explosion be over pretty fast?"

Lesserec grinned, freckles and all. "Quicker than you can blink—but that's the secret of using VR during the explosion. For the real test we've got the hole out at the Nevada Test Site just bristling with sensors and humongous data-storage devices. We've got new 'enhancing' chips in the image processors. Our computers will slow the explosion down by nearly a million times so you'll 'see' the explosion in slow motion. You'll experience the whole thing on a slow enough time scale that it'll be just like having God's eye view." He sighed. "I envy you the experience, Mr. FBI."

Craig thought for a moment. "I thought you were going to show this to everyone else, anyway?"

Lesserec looked shocked that Craig would even ask the question. "Of course I am. But you get to experience it *first*. We'll be processing nearly a thousand times more data than any other simulation we've done, so we're only allowing one person in here at a time. Otherwise, even our supercomputers might not be able to keep up with all the changing viewing angles, aspect ratios and such."

Paige called from the doorway. "Good luck, Craig. I'll be monitoring you outside with the techs."

Lesserec looked at his wristwatch. "Gotta go. Just be patient. Only about five more minutes to the Big Bang."

The heavy vault door swung shut; a soft glow oozed out of the walls in a bath of illumination.

Craig grunted as he turned back to the front of the VR chamber. At first the chamber walls had seemed solid, dimpled with round indentations. Now that he had a chance to sit back and wait before the test, he saw that the indentations were actually laser projection lenses, flush with the chamber wall. A breeze from the air-recirculating systems tickled his cheeks. His suit jacket seemed too warm.

Lesserec's nasal voice came from speakers in the ceiling. "I just checked. They're about ready out at the test site. Powering up our simulation here. I'll take you on down the hole, let you sight-see before we begin."

Before Craig had a chance to answer, the walls around him transformed to rough gray-tan dirt. He found himself in a vertical cave, thirty feet in diameter. Cables and fiberoptic links ran like tentacles down the tunnel wall; small black boxes hung on the cables every five feet or so. Some sort of sensors, he supposed.

The room started descending, and Craig felt a cool, damp breeze waft up from below; a musty smell permeated his senses. *My God,* he thought, reeling. *I can't tell the difference between this simulation and really being in a bore shaft!* Craig felt a deepening, grudging respect for the redheaded computer whiz.

Craig looked up and saw distant blackness. Squinting at what must have been an enhanced computer graphic, he thought he could make out a cap to the tunnel; but from what Lesserec had told him earlier, the top was a great distance above him. Some fifty feet below sat a brightly lit canister, which Craig knew should hold the high explosives, though it looked too small to contain tons worth.

The cables from above came together at four junction boxes to the left of the explosive canister. Thickly wound rope and a myriad of diagnostic cables lay on the bottom of the pit like serpents, spreading out from the device. As his image drew closer to the ground, Craig saw four tunnels that led away from the sealed container of explosives.

"Hello? Can anybody hear me?" he called. "Where do these tunnels go?"

Lesserec's disembodied voice came from somewhere above and behind the tunnel wall. "They lead to additional sensors and test beds to run shock-wave studies. Some of the tunnels are a quarter mile long so measurements can be made of the radiation yield before the sensors are destroyed."

Craig's image settled to the ground with a silent *bump.* Down one of the tunnels he saw massive steel doors that looked to be a foot thick. *Blast doors,* he thought. Those must be the explosively driven doors Lesserec had told his group about yesterday. But why so much for the practice run with regular high explosives? These details seemed just like the setup for a real down-hole nuclear test.

Craig felt stunned. With a virtual hand, he reached behind him to touch the hard, packed-dirt walls. He felt the cool earth, the rough texture. "This is incredible. It's so realistic," he said aloud.

Lesserec's voice sounded smug. "We can even display a real-time computer calculation of what *should* happen during the explosion so the weapon designers have a one-to-one mapping of what is taking place."

From the invisible speakers came the sound of papers rustling and hushed voices speaking, keyboards being rattled. Lesserec's voice came again. "Mr. Kreident, we've been informed the Nevada Test Site is ready. Countdown for the test has been started. Everyone has gone to their workstations. You'll experience a short period of darkness while we get in sync with the NTS sensors."

Craig's image craned his neck and took in the huge artificial cavern, the tunnels leading off into the distance behind the blast doors, and the monstrous bore hole extending straight up to the desert surface far overhead.

"How real is this simulation going to be, Mr. Lesserec?" Craig asked. *Hell of a time to think of a question like that,* he chided himself.

"Just close your eyes if you get frightened," said Lesserec. "Remember, you're in a VR chamber, not down a hole. It's not real. I'm going to link you up with the test in a few seconds. You'll lose contact with me, but we can still monitor you."

The light suddenly blinked, and Craig felt a momentary sense of disorientation. Oily blackness swallowed him, oppressive and thick. He *knew* he stood nearly a mile beneath the Earth, in the presence of five hundred tons of high explosive that was set to go off any minute now.

Faint lights came up again, enhanced by the VR sensors, and he could look at the canister of high explosives. It was going to explode in his face, and the computers would slow it down enough that he could enjoy every little phase of the detonation.

He should be able to see the detonation wave of the chemical explosion reach the metal casing, buckle it outward. He could stand there and watch as the blast wave rumbled down the tunnel.

Five hundred tons of high explosives. Again, he had trouble believing that so much chemical explosive could be packed into a volume that small. Craig stared at the canister. Five hundred tons.

It *was* hard to believe.

Craig frowned. "Hey, Lesserec, your distance scale must have changed as well!" he shouted at the dirt walls. "No way that casing holds five hundred tons." He glanced around the artificial cavern. The rocky cave gave him no sense of proportion. The cavern could have been a mile across or ten feet . . . nothing gave him any sense of scale. But yet . . .

He glanced up at the tunnel above him. What was it Lesserec had said?—that the tunnel was thirty feet in diameter? And if that was the case, then that weapon casing couldn't be more than a few *feet* across.

Even filled with lead it would weigh two tons, max—hundreds of times less than what Lesserec had said it would weigh. What the hell was going on? Another one of Lesserec's cute tricks?

"Lesserec?" called Craig. "Paige—what's going on here? This isn't a high-explosive test." No answer. "Can you hear me?"

Still nothing.

Craig muttered to himself. "All right, what's up?" He started to get angry; there was no response from Lesserec, nor any indication that anyone could hear him.

Craig fumbled at the straps on his seat. He unbuckled and stood. "Lesserec, I want to know what you're trying to pull. This is supposed to be a high-explosive test, and none of your hand-waving is going to convince me this can holds anywhere near five hundred tons of TNT." He rapped on the metal casing with his knuckles.

Craig heard only the soft, resonant hum of electrical sensors and diagnostic equipment around the cavern. He took a tentative step away from the invisible row of chairs in the VR chamber and walked out into the cavern.

The floor felt rocky beneath the soles of his leather shoes, just as it looked. Squatting, Craig touched the ground; he pulled his hand away from the damp, packed dirt, rubbing his fingers together. It even *felt* real. He brushed his hand on his slacks.

He walked to the fat metal casing in the middle of the chamber. Light from down the tunnel lit his way. Thick strands of black cable ran in twisted pairs away from the device. It looked like a wide cigar with strings running out the end.

As he grew closer, Craig spotted a three-bladed magenta-on-yellow symbol painted on the side of the dull metal casing: the international radiation symbol. And then it hit him.

A nuclear weapon—a *real* warhead.

This wasn't any test explosion—this was the real thing! It seemed as if the room had suddenly been thrust in a freezer; a trickle of sweat ran down his back and he shivered. His feet felt bolted to the floor, unable to move.

"Hey! Get me out of here!" he shouted, looking for the door to the chamber, but saw only the tunnels and the dirt wall.

"My God," he whispered. He looked around the cavern in panic. Why would they substitute a real nuke in place of a high-explosive test? Was someone trying to sabotage the International Verification Initiative? Was this the real reason Michaelson had died—did he discover something insidious about having a virtual reality watchdog on disarmament teams?

Or was it that Michaelson had discovered Lesserec exploiting this technology for his own private use? Perhaps the HF was just a ruse, something to throw them off the track? He wondered if he was in danger from the blast, if he would die the same way as Michaelson? More real than real.

Craig looked up at the tall borehole, impossibly far away. He knew the actual VR chamber wall should be only a few feet away, but the chamber tricked him, disorienting him. "Lesserec—let me out of here! Stop this, now!"

Craig didn't wait for an answer. He strode over to the wall behind him, fully expecting to find the chamber door—

He bumped into a rocky wall. He rubbed his cheek, surprised to find blood on his hand. Real blood. "Lesserec!"

Clicking sounds came from the device in the center of the cavern. Time had slowed down. The light seemed different.

Craig wet his lips, swallowed in a dry throat from the events that cascaded around him. He remembered the briefings Paige had quickly covered on nuclear weapons when he had first showed up at Lawrence Livermore; the device must be going through some sort of arming procedure.

Craig whirled. *The chairs!* If nothing else, he could strap himself back into the VR chair and ride out this nightmare. Maybe that was how Michaelson had really died—maybe he had been disoriented, trapped in this chamber from hell, and Lesserec had sprayed him with acid, afterwards.

Craig rubbed his sweaty hands aginst his pants, then quickly brought them close to his eyes. *Do I have HF on me now?* In this simulation where everything seemed real, how would he ever know?

The VR chairs—

He looked wildly around . . . but they had disappeared, nowhere to be seen. "Damn it, Lesserec—get me out of here!"

Craig crouched low and swept his hands back and forth across the floor; the row of chairs *had* to be here . . . somewhere.

A humming sound grew in intensity from the device. Craig straightened, sweat rolling from his face. His entire body felt drenched. "Oh, shit."

He started running for the tunnel to his right, toward

the thick steel blast door. But just as he turned, the entire room pulsed a brilliant white—

Incandescent purple splotches mixed with red, green, and yellow. Craig was immersed in a white-noise roar of unbelievable intensity. He felt as if every single nerve in his body had been stimulated all at once. He screamed as his body tumbled down the tunnel with the inexorable shock wave, slowed down so he could experience every nuance, every nanosecond of flight.

The cave walls closed down on him, turning liquid-metal purple, reflecting the light from the underground nuclear explosion back onto him. He heard a hissing as yellow and red particles popped off the surface of the liquid, boiling into a swirling plasma—

Streams of vaporized ejecta roared past, right behind a wave front of impossibly blue-white light. His body moved with the particles, down the constricting tunnel as it stripped away the integrity of his image.

Electromagnetic waves set up resonances. His entire body became an amplifier of ever-increasing frequencies of light—

As his image roared down the tunnel, he tried to scream, but nothing came from his throat. Ahead, the battleship-thick blast doors seemed to crawl together, automatically closing off his path. The wavefront of light and a precursor of material shot past . . . and he thought he was going to make it past the closing barrier, to safety.

But the foot-thick steel doors inched shut just as he arrived.

Craig screamed as he impacted the thick, high-density shield, and felt himself spraying off into a million different directions.

The heat of a thousand suns struck him from behind.

Friday

Building 433—T Program
Virtual Reality Chamber

The huge explosion took place deep in the Nevada desert, five hundred miles from Livermore. But the spectators within the T Program laboratories witnessed it through status lines that scrolled across the workstation screens. PROCESSING.

The sealed door of the VR chamber looked like a bank vault slammed shut, holding Craig inside. Paige watched the silent door and wondered what Craig was seeing even now.

The explosion itself had lasted only a second, but the enhancements from the VR software manipulated terabytes of transmitted data and slowed the explosion down so that the human mind could grasp and experience every instant, stretching time so that an observer could truly witness hands-on, holding a nuclear explosion in his lap.

Paige heard the sudden sharp rumble of sound inside the chambers. An outcry of what might have been Craig's voice, muffled and insulated through the thick walls of the chamber—and then silence.

They waited.

The computer monitors showed that the simulation had continued running. Gary Lesserec moved about like a demon, checking screen after screen with a broad grin on his face, showing his teeth like a manic Jimmy Olsen. His pale skin was flushed, his reddish hair mussed and damp with sweat.

"How long do we sit here?" Paige asked.

Lesserec whirled as if he had been yelled at. "It should be about done by now. I don't know why he hasn't come out."

Ben Goldfarb stood alarmed, yanking down on his conservative FBI tie. "Let's get him out of there now. We don't know what we're dealing with here."

"*You* don't know," Lesserec snapped back. "I know damn well what I'm doing. Let a professional handle this."

Goldfarb spoke with an Antarctic chill. "I am a professional, Mr. Lesserec, and I know when things aren't going the way they're supposed to." He grabbed Lesserec by the collar of his X Men T-shirt; with his other hand he pulled on the young man's badge chain. "Use your magic code and get Craig out of there. Pronto."

"I'd do what he says if I were you," said Jackson, quietly.

"All right, all right," Lesserec answered with an expression of disgust as he slapped at Goldfarb's hand, but the special agent would not let go.

Paige stood by the badge reader at the access panel and pounded on the door of the VR chamber. "Craig, can you hear me? Are you all right?" Hearing no answer, she turned to shout, "Lesserec, get your damn badge over here!"

Lesserec lurched to the device, assisted by Goldfarb's anxiety. When Goldfarb released his grip on the T-shirt, Lesserec smoothed the cotton fabric, then slid his laminated badge into the magnetic strip reader. After he punched in his access code, the locks disengaged with a heavy mechanical *thump,* and the insulated pneumatic seals unseated themselves. Goldfarb and Paige dug their fingers into the crack and pulled the heavy door open.

Inside, the room was lit only by dim, flickering sparks projected in holograms—the aftermath of the fading explosion out at the Nevada Test Site.

Craig Kreident lay on the floor in a veritable lake of his own sweat. He had toppled out of the automated chair and sprawled with an expression of extreme stress on his face. His eyes were squeezed shut, surrounded by wrinkles like tight slits. His mouth had been pulled back in a grimace. His skin seemed dry and desiccated, as if he had been mummified.

Paige rushed over. "Craig!" she said, dropping to her knees in front of him. She grasped his soaked shirt and pulled on his shoulders to raise him to a sitting position. He breathed shallowly, but at least he breathed.

"Let's get him out of here. Help me," she said.

Around them, the grayness and flickering static of the Virtual Reality chamber muted all sounds. Goldfarb and Jackson helped her lift Craig, shaking him until he groaned. His papery eyelids flickered open.

Paige shuddered when she saw the expression behind them, as if the holocaust were still playing inside his mind.

"I'll get help," said Jackson and took off.

Gary Lesserec's muddy green eyes bugged out at the

sight. He turned and ran back to the computer workstations.

"Hey, help us here!" Goldfarb said. Lesserec made no
response as he disappeared.

"Asshole," Goldfarb muttered and slung Craig's right
arm over his shoulders. Paige grabbed his waist. Craig
groaned and his legs dangled from his body, twitching
as if his nerves kept misfiring.

"Craig, are you all right?" Paige said. "Can you hear
me? Say something."

His breath rattled through his mouth, but Paige could
decipher no words. Goldfarb and Paige moved forward,
hauling Craig along with them. His shoes caught on the
carpeted floor, and his jittery legs staggered forward,
but Paige thought that might be more of a reflex action
than a voluntary effort to assist them.

They walked him out to the main laboratory areas. T
Program people scurried around, amazed at Lesserec's
sudden frenzy, but he wouldn't speak to them at all. He
had gone directly to his own workstation, knocking
Danielle aside.

"Hey, somebody! Get me some water!" Paige yelled
as she and Goldfarb let Craig slump into one of the
swivel workstation chairs. His arms dangled behind
him. Rivulets of sweat trickled from his fingertips to the
floor.

"What did you see, Craig?" she said, whispering in
his ear.

His gray eyes flew open. "I saw!" he said in a croak-
ing whisper. "I—" But he could say nothing else.

Danielle hurried up with a cold can of Diet Coke she
had yanked from the refrigerator. Paige grimaced at it,
then popped the top and pressed the cool aluminum rim

against Craig's parched lips. He sipped some, then coughed, spewing soft drink.

Paige looked wildly around. "Get me some water!"

Tansy Beaumont brought a coffee mug half-filled with water, knelt and handed it to Paige. Craig slurped from the tilted cup. Once his lips were wet, Craig began to gulp and gulp.

He gasped, shook his head, and the fog behind his eyes seemed to clear somewhat. He tried to focus on his surroundings again.

"I saw the explosion," he said. "I held it in my hands but . . . not just high explosives—*a nuclear device!* I saw it down-hole. I touched it and then . . . and then it went off in my face."

An Asian man with lanky black hair and dark-rimmed glasses leaned over Lesserec at his workstation. His voice was loud enough and filled with sufficient alarm that Paige and Goldfarb both looked over at him.

"Gary!" the Asian man said. "What are you deleting? You said we could all watch that simulation."

"Shut up, Walter," Lesserec said and hammered a command into the computer.

Goldfarb left Craig's side and dashed over to Lesserec's chair, clamping his hand on the redhead's left shoulder like a bear trap slamming home. "I think that's enough, Mr. Lesserec."

"Leave me alone," Lesserec said. "We have to shut down the simulation before anyone else sees it. You saw what it did to Mr. FBI."

To emphasize his point, Goldfarb reached with his other hand and physically lifted Lesserec's wrist away from the keyboard.

"I don't think so. I saw something happen to Craig—

but what exactly was it? Just the simulation, or are you running something else here? Playing some sort of game?"

Walter Shing squinted at the workstation, at the line of commands Lesserec had punched in. "Gary, what the hell is this 'auto-enhance' routine? You haven't told us about anything like that. I thought we were working as a team."

"Shut *up,* Walter!" Lesserec said again.

"That wasn't just a test run," Craig said, hissing his words. He pushed the water away and looked around. "No way that was a high-explosive simulation. Lesserec changed it." He shook his head, and droplets of sweat sprayed out like a dog flinging water free from its fur after a bath.

Goldfarb hauled Lesserec back from the workstation, pulling his wheeled swivel chair toward the center of the control area. "Is that what you did to Michaelson? Put hydrofluoric acid in the chamber, ran one of your 'enhanced simulations' for him so that he died without even knowing what he was getting into?"

"No way!" Lesserec said with an expression of scorn.

"We've got the files here. I'm impounding all of your workstations. I don't care if it's National Security Information. The Bureau has authority. A crime was committed here. A man died—and all of T Program's work is currently frozen."

The rest of the T Program members, already in an uproar, pressed closer to Lesserec and Goldfarb like an angry mob.

"You can't do that," Danielle cried. "We've got the President coming and the foreign nationals in two weeks."

"What about our demonstration?" Walter Shing added. "We've worked so hard."

Lesserec slumped back in his chair, pouting. Spots of red appeared on his skin, showing how much anger he was holding inside. "Screw the fucking demonstration!" Lesserec said. *"This* was the demonstration."

Everyone turned expressions of confusion or amazement at him. Lesserec looked as if he wanted to spit.

"Yeah, Kreident saw an enhanced version of the explosion. He couldn't tell the difference between a pile of high explosives and a nuclear device going off underground. That was my *point*—and if I didn't show it now, we'd make total fools of ourselves with the President and the foreign nationals. Better we have a postponement than an international embarrassment in a couple of weeks."

"Gary, what are you talking about?" Walter Shing said. "We've worked day and night on this."

"And I was trying to get us all some benefit from it. National Security! Shit, Michaelson had his head up his butt all along, as usual. Virtual Inspectors. International Verification Initiative. What a crock!

"Michaelson just bulldozes ahead when he gets an idea in his mind and he loses his ability to perform rational thought. Did he stop to think what good one of these Virtual Inspectors is? If anyone with a little knowhow like me can doctor the results and make an observer see anything I want, what good would the verification be then?"

As Paige and Goldfarb looked at him, perplexed, Lesserec made a noise of disgust. "The first thing foreign nationals will do is figure out how to bypass the system, show a nice filmloop to our long-distance inspectors. They'll fool us into happily observing some peaceful washing-machine assembly line. But it'll all be an illusion. They'll really be building warheads—and we won't even know it.

"On the other hand, you can bet the United States is gonna hire me first thing," he gestured with his hand, "or any one of you, to bypass the system we've created ourselves. Virtual Inspectors won't work."

Goldfarb moved toward him, fists clenched, but Lesserec stood firmly on his soapbox now.

"But what we're missing," he continued, "is the *real* application for VR technology. It could be worth tens of billions of dollars to the American entertainment industry. Think of it. The Nintendo Corporation and Sony, all the Japanese conglomerates will vanish like a puff of smoke because we're decades ahead of them in virtual technology. Think of amusement parks, movies that you can experience as well as watch!"

He took a deep breath. "And there's medical possibilities, too. Physical therapy, treatments for handicapped people, letting them go places they've never dreamed of! You should have seen the tour group we had here last week, very sick kids who had never been to Yosemite, never even been swimming. I've got one test case, a little boy with cerebral palsy, who was practically in heaven because I took him to the top of Half Dome. His father provided me with the kid's entire medical history—think of how this virtual technology could help people like him!

"Yet, because we developed the techniques here at the Lawrence Livermore National Laboratory, people like Michaelson can only think about the defense applications. They want to use this incredible technology I developed in order to be better *spies?* How ridiculous!"

Craig croaked from across the room. "So you killed Michaelson because that would let you run T Program down the toilet, and secretly sell the applications to toy companies."

"What?" Lesserec said, flushing a deeper red and starting to stand up. "Give me a break!" But Goldfarb pushed on his shoulder, shoving him back down in the chair.

"Yes," Paige said. "You got hydrofluoric acid from the Plutonium Facility during one of your sensor installations and sprayed it on Michaelson when he came in to try out your new simulation."

Lesserec rolled his muddy green eyes. "Oh, for Pete's sake! Of course I didn't kill him. I never *heard* of hydrofluoric acid before Michaelson got killed. Yes, I ran one of my enhanced simulations for him on the night he died. Tested the new beta chips. It was a prehistoric landscape, nothing harmful in the least. I wanted to show him just what I could do, and how far behind he had fallen in his own game.

"I'm the one who came up with all this stuff, you know—and Michaelson always took the credit for it. I needed to let him know who the real brains was. I hoped we could work out some kind of deal to let me sell spin-offs on the side."

"Cute," Goldfarb said.

"Well, why the hell not?" Lesserec bellowed, twisting around in his chair. "This is supposedly Secret National Security Information—and here we are bringing in a team of high-level observers from every country in the world, even our enemies. We're handing it to them on a silver platter."

He snorted. "Sure, we can do that—but the moment we try to sell it to an *American* company, the moment we try to exploit it for the good of *this* country instead of someone else's, then everybody has a fit. Then it's espionage. Then it's illegal. We have one set of grossly screwed up priorities if you ask me."

"Oh, we'll be asking you," Goldfarb said. "We'll be asking you a lot of things." His voice changed, became flatter, harder. "By the authority vested in me by the Federal Bureau of Investigation, I'm placing you under arrest."

"But I didn't kill Michaelson," Lesserec protested. "I didn't do it!"

"You've done enough," Goldfarb said. "That's a start."

Friday

Building 433—T Program

Craig struggled to his feet as Goldfarb read Lesserec his Miranda rights. Paige helped him up, and he grasped her shoulder weakly. His arms trembled.

It felt as if someone had reached inside his spine and yanked out his entire network of nerves like a gardener uprooting a persistent weed. His skin still sizzled from the imagined shockwave of the detonation engulfing him.

What had Hal Michaelson experienced that had obliterated him? And where had the hydrofluoric acid come from?

Colored spots swam in front of Craig's eyes, and he lost his balance, reeling against Paige for support. He felt completely drained. He wouldn't be surprised if he had sweated five pounds of his body weight in the few minutes he was in the chamber. He swallowed some more water from Tansy's coffee mug, and then turned dizzily.

"The rest room," he said. "I . . . I need to wash up, get some life back into me."

"Craig, I think we should just take you to the hospital. I'll call the Lab Emergency Response and—"

"No." Craig cut her off. "Just give me a minute to rest. Let me splash some water on my face, and then we'll talk about it, okay?"

"Kay-O." Reluctantly she guided him one tentative step at a time down the corridor to the men's room.

"Do you need any help?" Paige asked.

Craig forced a wan smile. "If you're trying to give me a thrill, I'm not really up to it right now."

She let out an amused sigh. "Haven't you already seen how much damage an overactive imagination can cause, Craig?" She pushed open the bathroom door for him.

He swayed, then staggered over to the white porcelain sinks. He slapped at the cold water tap until a rushing stream splashed out. He leaned over the basin, smelling the coolness, feeling the prickles of sweat like bee-stings in his burned nerve endings.

Craig dunked his still-shaking hands under the stream of water, and the cold shock jarred him closer to full awareness. *Man, oh man,* he thought. Did Lesserec really think people would pay for an experience like that? With a long sigh, he cupped his hands and bent over the sink, splashing the water on his cheeks, removing the salty rivulets of perspiration.

He rubbed at his burning eyes. Then he reached over with his left hand to hit the soap dispenser, pumping the round metal plunger to squirt pink liquid soap into the palm of his hand. He rubbed his hands together and bent over the running water again, splashing the soapy water on his face, scrubbing the weariness away. It made him feel tingly and clean as echoes of the simulated nuclear detonation thundered in his head.

He found it difficult to think. His mind had experienced a sensory overload, and his mental snowplow had not yet cleared the main routes.

Craig stared at his hands, felt his face, and sluggishly turned to look at the soap dispenser again. *Something . . . something . . .*

He reached over with his left hand slowly and pushed up on the soap dispenser's metal plunger. The round end pressed down in the center of his palm—a circle squirting liquid soap.

José Aragon had a small circular acid burn directly in the middle of his palm.

Like an automaton, watching his every motion with growing uneasiness, Craig brought his hand over to the running water again, rubbed his hands to lather the soap, and bent to splash his face.

Hal Michaelson's hands and face had been covered with the deadly HF.

On uncooperative legs Craig wheeled away from the sink, forgetting entirely about the water. The faucet kept splashing as he staggered out of the bathroom. He yanked the door open and stood with his face and hands still dripping cold water. He startled Paige, who had been waiting for him just outside.

"Craig, let me help you. What's wrong?"

"Get Aragon on the phone," he gasped. "I want to ask him one question. I think I've figured this out."

"Don't move so fast, Craig. You're going to collapse. I know what you've been through."

"Just get him on the phone!" Craig said, then clapped a wet hand to his forehead. He steadied himself against the wall, and Paige eased him over to a chair.

"All right, I'll call him."

Just thinking about the mystery made Craig come to

his senses more than the cold water had. His heart raced as the pieces of the puzzle clicked together.

Paige handed him a telephone. "I've got Aragon's wife. She's bringing him to the phone."

"Good," Craig said and took the receiver. "Hello," he waited but heard nothing until a moment later.

José Aragon's watery, slightly nasal voice came over the phone. "Yes? Aragon speaking."

"Craig Kreident, FBI," he said. "I have one question for you, Mr. Aragon. When you and Dr. Michaelson were in the Plutonium Facility, did you go into the rest room?"

"What?" Aragon asked.

"Did you use the rest room? Did you wash your hands in the Plutonium Facility?"

"Yes, uh, I think so. Dr. Michaelson and I were having a discussion when we went to the rest room. A rather heated discussion," he added reluctantly. "Hal was tired. He'd flown in from Washington that morning."

"Did he splash water on his face? Did he use the soap dispenser? Did you use the soap dispenser?"

Aragon seemed baffled. "What is the point of this line of questioning, Mr. Kreident?"

"I don't have to explain my reasons to you," Craig snapped in exasperation. "Just answer me."

"Yes, we washed up," Aragon said, sounding miffed. "Hal practically took a shower, if I remember right. I just washed my hands quickly, I think. Do you need to know if I took a piss also?"

"Which rest room did you use, Mr. Aragon? It's important."

"There is only one in the Radioactive Materials Area."

Craig didn't bother thanking him as he hung up the phone. It was clear now.

Michaelson, weary from his red-eye flight, arguing with Aragon, had stepped into the rest room, turned the cold water on, soaped up his hands, splashed his face. Aragon, trying to make excuses, trying to calm Michaelson down, distractedly tapping the soap dispenser, daintily rinsing his hands.

But neither of them had realized that the soap dispenser contained hydrofluoric acid—a small amount, but sufficient. Michaelson had unwittingly gotten it all over his hands and face. Aragon had received only a small exposure, but enough to burn a hole in his hands and force him to have the skin excised. The acid penetrated slowly to the nerves, then the bone. The victim wouldn't even feel it until much later.

But who had placed the acid in the dispenser? Aragon could have planted it, hoping to lure Michaelson . . . after all, it took only a five-percent bodily exposure for a fatal dose.

But Craig couldn't believe even Aragon would be so appallingly stupid to get the acid on his own hand if he knew it was there. Aragon had been in the Plutonium Facility, but how had he known when Michaelson would come through, if ever? It didn't make sense.

Unless it had been Lesserec, who was overseeing the sensors being installed in the Plutonium Facility for the International Verification Initiative. *He* would have known when Michaelson was going through the facility.

"Come on, Paige," said Craig. "You've got to get me back into the Plutonium Facility."

"Plutonium Facility? No way, I'm getting you some medical attention. You need to rest."

"Resting is for wimps," he said. "We'll do that later. I've figured out how Michaelson was killed. I know where. But I still don't know who did it or why."

"But the Plutonium Facility?" she said. "That's an Exclusion Area. How did—?"

"We have to go to the rest room," he said with a weak smile. "That's where it all starts. Goldfarb, are you coming along?" Craig turned, watching the other agent handcuff Gary Lesserec.

"I've got to take custody of Mr. Entertainment here," Goldfarb said. "Do you need me? I could let Jackson escort him."

"No, we can figure this out ourselves," Craig said. "It's just a little wrap-up. I want to check out a hunch I have where Lesserec might have planted the HF. No wonder we didn't find any in the VR chamber."

"I didn't plant any HF!" Lesserec squealed.

Craig ignored him entirely. Paige looked at Craig, frowning, but he put his hands on his hips. "Well, if you want me to rest, the sooner you get me to the Plutonium Facility, the sooner I can finish this up. Then we'll go relax somewhere. I'll buy *you* a beer this time."

She forced a smile. "It's a deal."

Friday

Building 332—Plutonium Facility

By sheer force of habit, Duane Hopkins showed up for work the morning after Stevie died. He didn't know what else to do.

He came in at the ten o'clock break, but he felt like an iron-plated empty shell of a man, hollow and cold inside. Duane made no excuses for being late, didn't even think of any. Nobody asked.

He shuffled into the changing room like a zombie, going through the motions, pulling on his booties, hanging up his street clothes. He selected an orange lab coat and buttoned it with numb fingers.

As he walked past the break room, Ronald and his gorilla friends sat around the table looking bored, waiting for something to do, someone to pick on.

"Hey, Beavis, it's about time you showed up!" Ronald said, rising to his feet. He looked like an orangutan with beady little animal eyes that might have held a strain of intelligence on better days—but not now. Ronald was on the prowl. "What's the matter, couldn't your spaz kid cook breakfast any faster?"

Duane froze but found that the fires of anger turned his tears into steam before they could well up in his eyes. He turned slowly with a rock-hard expression. "You . . . you're going to die too someday, Ronald, and I hope it's soon."

Then, in the silence of Ronald's absolute shock, Duane slipped through the airlock into the main laboratory rooms of the Radioactive Materials Area. He passed through the guard portal and then walked alone down the white linoleum hall into his own glove-box room.

The main materials vault stood open for the morning operations, its five-inch-thick reinforced door propped on its hinges as two technicians conducted an inventory of the fissile material stored inside. Everything was clean and neat, polished up for the tours the facility manager would be giving in preparation for the upcoming visit of the foreign nationals.

In a daze Duane signed out every one of the parts he was working on, putting them on two levels of a rolling metal cart, separated by approved distances to avoid causing a criticality. For a moment he pondered just stacking up the pieces; maybe all the radioactive material together in one place would unleash a burst of radiation, killing everyone in the building. It would wipe out Ronald and all his bullies and everyone else who had picked on him for so many years.

Everyone who had caused Stevie's medical problems.

But that was too uncertain. He didn't know if this was enough plutonium to cause a nuclear explosion . . . or whatever happened when you brought too much of the stuff together. Duane didn't understand it, but he knew enough to be afraid. And besides, he wasn't sure if the radiation burst would reach all the way to Ronald in the lunchroom. If he was going to hurt the bully, Duane wanted to make sure it worked—unlike the first time he had tried.

He hated every one of his coworkers, and with good reason. Even Mr. Lesserec had been his friend just to learn more about Stevie's condition. Only Stevie had given him unconditional love, and now that his boy was dead, Duane didn't know what he was going to do without that love. His life was a shadow, and Stevie had been the only ray of hope.

But that light was snuffed out in a hospital emergency room. Why not let the darkness fall over everything?

Duane wheeled the cart into his glove-box laboratory and let the doors swing shut behind him. They thumped, just like the hospital doors in the emergency room the night before.

He had four quart-sized cans, each containing a single plutonium button. The stainless steel containers shone bright silver under the fluorescent lights. On the sides of the cans, the part numbers had been scrawled with a black magic marker. Out of habit of working safely Duane had spaced the cans properly on opposite corners of the cart, diagonally separated, a pair on top and a criss-crossed pair on bottom.

Duane touched the first stainless steel can with a twinge of superstitious fear, knowing that a dragon's egg slept inside. The can had been sealed on top, tied through with a metal wire and clamped with a soft lead disk, like a fisherman's sinker: a Tamper Indicating Device.

Duane pulled out a pair of wire clippers from his tool

compartment on the side of the nearest glove box and snipped off the disk. He did the same with the Tamper Indicating Devices on the other four cans.

He would do some tampering all right—he'd show that Ronald.

Duane popped open the top and raised the lid slowly, nervously. He thought he could see the evil radioactive rays spewing out of the can, like the air out of a balloon. Trembling, he opened all four cans and then reached in to take out the hot metal lumps, still warm from radioactive decay.

Normally he would have bagged the cans, taken them through the access port at the end of his glove box, then reached through with thick black gloves to manipulate the nuclear pieces. But now he was holding the bare metal with his naked hands—and he didn't care.

The radiation felt purifying. He could sense it burning through him, cleansing the darkness from his life.

He picked up two of the dull metallic hemispheres in each hand, holding them like gems. He knew that plutonium was far more valuable than the most precious jewel on Earth—more than gold. More than silver. Even more than the Hope Diamond. But the special thing about this plutonium was that it surrounded him with a deadly cloud of radiation. Everywhere he walked, he would sear his coworkers, drown them in radiation—even as it killed him, too.

Duane's heart pounded, but his eyes were dry. He felt the skin on his hands crackling. His palms were very hot and burning. How could these plutonium buttons have been so hot and not melted their way through the cans?

He saw the big round clock hanging on the cinderblock

wall. The morning break would be over. Ronald and his friends would be going back to their workstations.

And Duane knew where to find them.

He had to hurry, because the radiation was tearing him apart. Duane wondered if he would go blind first. Even sightless, though, Duane thought he could still find Ronald Cobb just by the smell of his aftershave.

Stevie was already gone, and Duane would be gone soon—but he would be a flaming angel of vengeance, just like those Sunday morning preachers said on the church shows he watched. He would be like a kamikaze.

Stevie had been an innocent child, a loving little boy; but Ronald was not innocent—he deserved this.

Duane straightened and walked slowly. He could feel the poisonous rays creeping up his arms, through his ribcage. He had probably received a fatal dose already, but as long as his legs kept functioning—long enough for him to find Ronald—nothing else mattered.

He heard activity out in the hall, bustling movement, loud voices. And Duane saw his chance. He could encounter as many people as possible, spread the radioactive cloud. He could touch and taint many of those who had hurt him. Then it would all be over.

Carrying his plutonium prizes, Duane strode out of the swinging doors. As he passed the room counters and the alpha radiation monitors, squealing alarms went off, at first startling Duane. But he smiled. That only proved how far the radiation was spreading.

He kept walking, turned the corner, and emerged into the long corridor, holding his plutonium in front of him like a weapon in each hand.

But instead of Ronald and his companions, Duane

came face to face with a large group of young children. Innocent children and their sponsors from the Coalition of Family Values, along with two Lab managers, touring the facility.

The children turned to Duane and stared as he stood with the deadly metal in each hand, frozen.

He screamed in despair.

Friday

Building 332—Plutonium Facility

After emerging from their respective change rooms, Paige and Craig met at the glassed-in security portal for entrance to the Radioactive Materials Area. They passed through the metal detectors, and the PSO handed them each nuclear accident dosimeters to clip onto their own badges.

"Busy day," the guard said. "We just escorted through a dozen kids from the Coalition for Family Values. Now the FBI? Place feels like Grand Central Station."

Craig continued to cling to Paige's arm to keep his balance. He still felt weak and shaky, and his thoughts were muddled; but he needed to see the soap dispenser in the rest room where Hal Michaelson had unknowingly met his death.

"Guess I shouldn't talk about my rough day," the PSO said. "You look like you've been through hell already this morning."

Craig looked up at him with a wan smile. He knew his eyes were red-rimmed and bloodshot. "I think that sums it up fairly well."

They entered the Radioactive Materials Area only seconds before a loud alarm warbled through the intercom. Craig tried to identify it from the confusing series of sounds he remembered from the training videotapes.

The guard sat up startled. "Holy shit, that's a radiation alarm!" Inside the glass cubicle, the second PSO called for backup and other guards stationed in the Plutonium Facility rushed to the location of the disturbance.

"What's happened?" Craig asked.

The first PSO turned to Craig, trying to make light of it. "The Superblock has alarms going off all the time, security alerts usually. Our systems are set so tight that any time two birds sit too close to each other on the razor wire it sets the system off."

"I'm sure it's nothing," said the second guard inside the glassed-in cubicle. "Maybe those kids on the tour group touched something they shouldn't have."

"I don't feel good about this," Craig muttered to Paige, shaking his head again. "I want to go check it out."

"Can't go in there," the first guard said. "The alarms are on. No one gets in or out of the RMA."

"We're already in," Paige said.

Craig fumbled between the buttons of his orange lab coat and pulled out the FBI badge from his suit jacket and flashed the intimidating-looking Bureau seal at the PSOs. "This is my authorization," Craig said and grabbed Paige's arm, pulling her through the swinging double doors.

The FBI identification had no particular authority here at all, but the sight of it befuddled the guard just long enough for them to pass through. Beyond the second set of double doors they ran into the white hallways laced with metal conduits and pipes, fire extinguishers, and metal lockers.

"Do you know where the alarm was tripped?" Craig asked. "Which increment the guard was talking about?"

As Paige shook her head, her blond hair flipped back and forth. "This place isn't that big. If it's a high-level alarm, we should be able to learn what it is. Besides, you wanted to find that one and only rest room, right?"

The set of airlock doors swung open at the far end of the hall. Four people ran toward them; behind them came a stream of fleeing children each wearing a visitor's badge. Many of the children cried, and even the escorts themselves looked panicked. A burly Plutonium Facility worker with a stormy expression on his face scuttled along, looking as if he wanted to ball his hand into a fist and punch through the cinderblock walls. He smelled of potent aftershave. Craig recognized him as Ronald Cobb, the man he had talked to on his last interview in the facility.

"That little turd," Cobb was saying to one of his companions. "I can't believe what a royal screw-up he is. Could you see what he was trying to do to me?"

Ronald looked up and saw Craig. "Hey, it's that FBI guy. Don't go in there, man. There's a crazy dude waving around radioactive material."

Craig and Paige shot a look at each other. "Thanks for the warning," Craig said, then pushed forward, anyway.

They passed through the airlocks into an empty corridor beyond. The alarms continued ringing.

Then, in the far corner slumped next to one of the metal lockers, Craig saw a wispy middle-aged man about forty-five, with limp pale brown hair, thin at the top, and a face that looked like a wad of crumpled tis-

sue paper. His body sagged on its bones just outside of
the swinging greenish doors of a glove-box laboratory.
The man was a mound of despair. Tears streamed down
his cheeks. On the floor beside him lay four dull metal
hemispheres where he had discarded them, each about
two inches across.

"You'd better stay back," said the man. "I didn't want
to hurt anybody . . . who didn't deserve it."

Craig knelt and motioned with a hand for Paige to
step back. "My name's Craig. I don't think I deserve it.
Who are you?"

"Duane . . . Duane Hopkins. I've worked here for
about fifteen years. Bodie . . . a man named Bodie contaminated me ten, twelve years ago, right when I was
married. Stevie was born, and he had cerebral palsy.
Then Ronald kept picking on me, making my life mis-
erable. Now Stevie's dead. I was going to make Ronald
pay."

"You were going to expose him to radiation?" Craig
asked.

"The radiation caused everything," Duane said. "It
caused Stevie to be sick, it made Rhonda leave me. I
tried to get back at Ronald by putting some acid in the
bathroom. I wanted to burn his hands—but nothing ever
happened, so I had to do something bigger. And now
I—" His breath hitched in sobs. "I almost hurt all those
kids. I didn't want that to happen. I just wanted Ronald.
He deserved it, not them."

Craig froze. "You put acid in the soap dispenser?
You're the one?"

Before he could say anything else, the swinging airlock doors at the other end of the hall slammed open;
two Protective Service Officers dressed in dark-blue

uniforms charged through, their guns drawn as if expecting to encounter a terrorist army.

"Nobody moves, nobody gets hurt!" one shouted.

The other PSO glanced from Craig and Paige to Duane Hopkins on the floor, assessing the situation. He saw the plutonium buttons scattered on the linoleum a few feet away from Duane. He pointed his weapon at Duane.

"Get to your feet, sir, and step away from those."

"I'm already dead," Duane said. "I've been holding those things. I've been exposed to all that radiation."

"We need to get him to the hospital," Paige said to the PSO. "He's not armed, and he seems to be having quite a few personal problems."

"Yeah, don't we all," said the PSO, still pointing his gun at Duane. The small man rose slowly to his feet and staggered away from the plutonium on the floor.

"Let's get someone suited up and in here!" the PSO shouted into his walkie-talkie. "Rubber gloves so we can get that stuff locked up. The whole building stays closed down until we get this taken care of."

The two guards escorted Duane out, standing as far away from him as they could, as if afraid that radiation would continue to shower from his body.

Paige and Craig also backed out, following them. "Anything else we need here, Craig?" she asked.

"What I need," Craig said with a weary sigh, "is a long nap for the rest of the afternoon. And then I'll meet you back at that place for a beer, just like I promised."

Friday

**Lyon's Brewery
Dublin, California**

Friday night, and the band played louder than ever.

Craig worked his way through the crowd at the staggered tables and set down two pints of a reddish beer topped with creamy foam. He nudged one across to Paige.

"Red Nectar Ale, right?" he said.

Paige took a long sip and let out a contented sigh. "Best beer ever made." She smiled at him with a little mustache of foam on her lips.

He took a long drink, then shrugged off his suit jacket. He loosened his tie and, after hesitating a moment, pulled it off entirely. He unbuttoned the top button of his white shirt, stuffing the tie into the pocket of his suit jacket.

"Case over," he said to Paige's surprised expression. "I can relax a little now."

"Don't you have to write up a report?" she said.

Craig waved his hand. "That's just busy work."

"You came in here to look into a mysterious death, and you managed to shake up everything. Are you al-

ways like a bull in a china shop when you do your investigations?"

Craig snorted. "It's not my fault everybody we had
under investigation was doing something they weren't
supposed to be doing. The hard part wasn't finding a
guilty person—it was finding the person guilty of the
crime *I* was interested in."

He looked into Paige's blue, blue eyes. "I still can't
believe that of all the people we were questioning, none
of them killed Michaelson. It's unbelievable to think
that a big important man with so many enemies could
have been killed by . . . by *accident*."

Paige shrugged and automatically lowered her voice
as the band stopped playing and fell into a break between songs.

"Remember all those freeway shootings down in LA,
when bored gang members took potshots at cars driving
by on the freeway? Pointless mayhem, senseless violence," she said, then raised a slender finger.

"But suppose, just suppose some kid goes out with a
rifle and shoots into a random car. Say he doesn't like
rich people, so he targets a Mercedes or a Porsche. Pow!
He ends up killing the head of a defense corporation.

"So what happens? Nobody assumes random violence,
even though it is. The kid got lucky and hit somebody important. But the homicide investigator will start out with
the assumption that our defense contractor was assassi-
nated. It throws everybody off on a wild goose chase."

"Good comparison," Craig admitted. "What about
Duane Hopkins. How is he?"

Paige looked down at the table, tracing water stains
on the dark wood. "He obviously didn't know what he
was doing. People like that really bother me."

"What do you mean?" Craig asked.

"Those plutonium buttons he picked up were nickel plated, warm from secondary decay—but they weren't high-level radiation sources at all. He's got a dose, of course. He might have some superficial burning on his hands, and he'll have to be watched for the rest of his life to see if he develops cancer. But he thought he had fireballs in his fists! Sheesh! How can somebody work in the Plutonium Facility for fifteen years and still not have a clue as to what he's working with?"

"What about the alarms?" Craig interrupted. "The radiation detectors were set off."

Paige answered him with an exasperated expression. "Everything is set so sensitive in that room that if you had a luminescent watch it would probably trigger something. As I told you before, we are very, very touchy about radiation exposures. Hopkins is like one of those people terrified that their home electricity comes from a nuclear power plant, afraid of radiation leaking out of the light sockets."

"Radiation is dangerous stuff," Craig said. "You can't treat it lightly."

"And we don't," Paige said, her voice turning brittle. "But ignorance is even more dangerous, and it's probably caused a whole lot more harm."

Craig took another swallow of the beer and felt the coolness slide down his throat. He was still dehydrated from his experience in the VR chamber, but the bitter fruity taste of the Red Nectar Ale was refreshing. If he didn't watch himself, he'd drink it too fast, and it would all go to his head.

Paige ran her finger along the top of the pint mug,

changing subjects. "Do you investigate these sorts of cases often?"

"High-tech crimes," Craig said, nodding. "If I have a specialty, that's it—although in this area, with Silicon Valley and the weapons labs and all the cutting edge industry, it's getting to be more and more common. In fact, it turns out this case ties with another one I made a mess of last week."

"How? Did you find something else?"

Craig shook his head. "Defective computer chips. Ever wonder why Lesserec's simulations were just a little *too* vivid? I had worked on a case where NanoWare Technologies were dumping defective chips. T Program is used as a beta test site for new hardware, and were shipped some of their doctored chips. Lesserec added them all to the VR simulation workstations. He got a little more than he bargained for—and so did I."

Craig took another sip of the beer. "Hey, this stuff is pretty good." After a moment of silence drowned out by the music, he asked. "So what's next for you?"

"This whole thing has caused a public relations debacle like nothing the Livermore Lab has ever seen. Of course, the whole IVI demonstration has been canceled. The foreign nationals are not coming out here, and the President himself is 'reassessing' the entire concept of Virtual Inspectors."

"Is this going to be another shake-up just like the Laser Implosion Fusion Facility? Dr. Michaelson seems to carry that sort of luck along with him."

Paige waved her hand in dismissal. "The LIFF situation involved mismanagement and poor planning," she said. "This one's even worse because actual crimes were involved at every step of the process. But who would have thought that Lesserec's unauthorized handling of the VR chamber would have opened up a new, high-visibility market for the lab?"

Craig nearly choked on his beer. "Lawrence Livermore is going into the entertainment business?"

"No, no," laughed Paige. "Medical applications—psychotherapy, for example! Lesserec had obtained quite a bit of information from Duane Hopkins about his son's medical condition. After seeing the way those handicapped kids reacted, Lesserec wanted to expand the use of the VR chamber to the medical field. So I guess something good did come from that, as warped as Lesserec was."

"You'll be pretty busy then, I take it," Craig said, not knowing quite what he was fishing for.

"And you'll be off on another high-tech case before long, I suppose," Paige said.

"I suppose," Craig answered, then looked down at his pint glass, picking it up and running his fingers nervously along the bottom.

"Tomorrow's Saturday. I'm still going swimming," Paige said. "I wouldn't give that up."

Craig looked up at her. "Should I bring my suit?" He let his smile grow. "As long as it's not a date."

She laughed. "Maybe you won't be quite so formal this time."

"I'll try not to," he said. "But it's difficult for us FBI types, you know."

She raised her glass, and he raised his. They clinked their mugs together. When the band started playing again, they couldn't hear their words. Craig slid his hand across the table and held her hand; they sat looking at each other across the table.

ABOUT THE AUTHORS

Kevin J. Anderson and Doug Beason are true "insiders" in the world of government research laboratories. Kevin has worked for the past twelve years for the Lawrence Livermore National Laboratory. A Lieutenant Colonel in the Air Force, Doug has been the Director of plasma physics research at the Phillips Laboratory and a special assistant to the President's Science Advisor; he is currently on assignment to the National War College in Washington, D.C.

Doug is well experienced with governmental research politics in Washington, D.C., due to his work at the White House. Kevin has visited the Nevada Test Site several times and has witnessed the detailed preparations used to conduct underground nuclear test detonations. Together, these two describe the actual world inside a massive scientific establishment; give real details about the daily life, classification entanglements and security procedures; and provide a hands-on feel to an alien setting that most other people have never experienced.

Virtual Destruction is their sixth collaborative novel. They are currently working on the next Craig Kreident thriller, *Fallout*.